A
Dream
Of
Lights

A
Dream
Of
Lights

Kerry Drewery

HarperCollins *Children's Books*

First published in Great Britain by HarperCollins *Children's Books* in 2013
HarperCollins *Children's Books* is a division of HarperCollins*Publishers* Ltd,
77-85 Fulham Palace Road, Hammersmith, London, W6 8JB.

Visit us on the web at
www.harpercollins.co.uk

1

ISBN: 978-0-00-744659-9

Printed and bound in England by
Clays Ltd, St Ives plc

MIX
Paper from
responsible sources
FSC
www.fsc.org
FSC® C007454

FSC™ is a non-profit international organisation established to promote
the responsible management of the world's forests. Products carrying the
FSC label are independently certified to assure consumers that they come
from forests that are managed to meet the social, economic and
ecological needs of present and future generations,
and other controlled sources.

Find out more about HarperCollins and the environment at
www.harpercollins.co.uk/green

For my children…

Jess – female mannequins *should* be called ladykins

Dan – remembering your wellies, bunny blanket and fireman's hat

and Bowen – no, I won't say anything about kisses and heart shapes and feeling loved

…because sometimes I wish you didn't have to grow up.

Chapter One

It began with something so simple.

A dream.

Of a city like no city I had ever seen before, no city I could possibly have imagined. A city at night-time, down whose streets I floated, mesmerised, as I stared into the white headlights of cars flooding towards me, red trails following behind, more of them than I thought could be possible. Lines and rows and streams, speeding and blurring and hurrying past and around me and away into some distance, some destination, somewhere.

A dream so vivid.

Where I tilted back my head, and my eyes traced the buildings as they stretched for ever up into darkness, with windows lit orange or yellow or white. Another to my side with slatted blinds, half-drawn curtains, or windows bright with flowers in vases or pictures in frames or potted plants resting on sills.

Around me, red jostled with green on street signs showing me where to go, or pink with blue on shopfronts, flashing neon letters or symbols, advertising cinemas or rooms or food.

A dream so real that as I strolled down the narrow streets, I could breathe in the smells of food drifting from restaurants and takeaways, could taste the sweetness on my tongue without knowing what food it might be, and I could run my hands through the steam rising from cookers and ovens and hotplates, condensation like dewdrops on my skin.

I could hear music blaring from bars as I passed, words I didn't understand, rhythms thumping in my chest, and I watched people dancing in clothes of all sorts of colours and styles, and I felt the joy in their smiles.

It was magical.

And then I woke up.

I woke up in the depths of our winter; so dark I could barely see my hands in front of my face, so cold frost was forming in my hair.

I didn't know buildings could be built that high and

not fall over, or so many cars could fit on one road without crashing, or music could sound so alive, or clothes could be that bright, or food could be bought in shops and smell so delicious. It had been so real I expected the dew to be still on my fingers and the taste still on my tongue. But there was nothing.

I was sixteen, had never been allowed a permit from the government to leave our village. Didn't know, had never seen, what lay over the hills and past the fields, or what was at the end of the road that stretched past us, that maybe three cars had driven along since I was old enough to know what a car was.

Maybe beyond us, I thought, *in other villages, people have electricity to light their homes at night and the streets around them. Maybe they have enough fuel to keep the fire lit in winter, to stop the windows freezing up on the inside, and to keep the family warm enough so they don't wake in the morning with lips that are blue and bones that are stiff. Maybe there are places like that somewhere here in North Korea. Maybe our capital, Pyongyang. Maybe that was the city I dreamt about.*

I sighed. *Maybe it's a vision our Dear Leader, Kim Jong Il, has put in my head. Something He wanted me to see.*

On the mat next to me, I heard my father's covers

and blankets move. "Another bad dream, Yoora?" His words disappeared into a yawn.

I rolled over to him. "A strange one," I replied, and I described to him what I'd seen, with the best words I could summon, when so much of what I'd seen I had no words to describe.

"Do you think it could be real?" I whispered.

For a moment he said nothing. I listened to his breathing slow down and a cough catch in his throat, and I watched the tiniest reflection of light in his eyes as he shuffled over towards me. I felt his warm breath gentle on my face. "Yes," he whispered in my ear. "Yes, it's real."

"Where? Further south?"

His hand took mine and rested it on his head, and I felt him nod slowly up and down.

"Our capital? Pyongyang?" I asked, amazement and excitement prickling at me. "Do you think, do you think that maybe, maybe, if we work hard enough, we'd be allowed to go there?"

He paused again, and I felt him roll over towards Mother, then back to me, and I listened to every breath he took as I waited.

And waited.

With seconds stretching like minutes, like hours, between us.

"Father?" I whispered.

"No, Yoora. Forget your dream, forget I said anything."

"What?" I reached my hand back to his face and felt wetness on my fingertips.

"No." He moved my hand, and I heard the rustle of his head moving side to side on the pillow. "Go back to sleep."

"But...?"

"I said no." His voice was firm, and as loud as I thought he would possibly dare without waking Mother.

I stared through the darkness, not understanding what had just happened, searching for that twinkle of light in his eye, angry with him, and frustrated. I wanted to sit up and argue with him, demand he tell me where that place was, if it *was* real.

I reached a hand out to touch him, to make him turn back round to me, but I stopped, thinking of Mother behind him. *Why had he looked to her? Because he didn't want to wake her?*

I pulled the covers up to my chin. *I can wait*, I thought.

And I closed my eyes and brought those images back from my memory, of those people I had seen and food

I had smelt and music I had heard. And I hoped they were real, somewhere here in my country, the best place in the world.

"It was a beautiful place," I whispered across the darkness. "I wish one day we could go there. Together."

There was no reply.

Chapter Two

I woke the next morning, not in wonderment at some sight my imagination had shown me, but in hunger as my stomach rumbled, and in pain as my bones creaked against the cold.

And I remembered the smells of the food.

My body shook as I pulled on my clothes under the blankets, and I padded through from the back room to the other, which served as everything from my grandparents' room at night, to the kitchen, dining and living room during the day. I rubbed my hands down my body to try and warm up.

An image flashed in front of my eyes of tall buildings that looked like homes, comfortable, warm and welcoming.

I stood in front of the fire Father had lit, but although

the troughs and holes and gaps under the floorboards allowed some heat to cross the floor, the air above was cold enough for your breath to form clouds.

I sat down at the table with my parents and grandparents and we gave thanks, as always, to our Dear Leader and His father before him, our Great Leader, for the food He'd provided for our breakfast, our maize porridge. And as we ate, a voice boomed from the speaker in the corner of the room telling us how lucky we were to have the food He provided, how we were so fortunate to live in North Korea, the country that had it so much better than any other in the world.

"Our military strength is the pride of our nation," the voice continued. "Our farmers are proud to give their produce to the government to feed our military and keep them strong to fight off our oppressors."

I glanced up and was shocked to see Father pressing his hands against his ears.

"What are you doing?" I asked him. "You need to listen."

"I have a headache, Yoora," he told me. "It's too loud."

"But that's so you can listen properly. That's why there's no volume control. Or off button, so you don't miss anything."

I heard his sigh, heavy and long, and I heard the words muttered under his breath. "What have we created?" But I didn't understand them. Not then.

I watched him take his hands away, and for a moment, just a moment, he stared straight back at me. What was that I could see behind his eyes? Fear? Worry? A warning for me? Or maybe it was nothing: just my imagination seeing something that wasn't there.

He looked away.

★

It was a Sunday, a day for volunteer work, our patriotic duty, and I stepped from the house into a cold winter morning, a thick mist hiding the fields and dark skeletons of trees trying to reach through.

Stillness and calm stretched over everything. Silence but for my feet on the dirt path, the air through my lungs and the squeak of the bucket swinging in my hand. I passed groups of houses just like ours: two rooms, single-storey, joined together in rows of ten with one roof stretched across their length, each like a giant harmonica, and all in straight, ordered lines.

I continued up the path, and on either side of me, the red and yellow of the small flags that lined our fields appeared from out of the mist. And people appeared too. Men and women, girls and boys, some older than me, some younger, all heading off for their day's duty.

Mine was up on the main road leading out of the village, as it had been for the last two months. I swept the gutters, I cleaned and washed the road, I weeded the borders and dug over the soil. For a mile in one direction and a mile in the other. And on the other side. Then, when I was finished, I started again.

Mine was the cleanest stretch. And often, as I worked, I would imagine the face of our Dear Leader looking down on me, smiling at me, His hands and His Fatherly Love protecting me.

But that day, something had changed. Something intangible, a question not even formed, a shadow in my mind that disappeared when I tried to look at it, because something didn't make sense. I stopped, sat back pigeon-style and closed my eyes.

I could see that food again, in boxes and cartons and wrappers, and I could see people eating it as they walked... and I could see those cars of shiny blue or silver or orange even... *It's real*, I heard Father say again... and I saw those lights again... and those clothes... and people... and smiles... and music... *thud thud thud*.

No, I thought, *that's not music.*

I opened my eyes. Marching towards me was our group leader, his boots like a drum on the surface of the road.

"I'm sorry," I muttered, grabbing my bucket again. But his hand smacked against my face and I was on the floor, my head spinning, the taste of blood in my mouth.

He stared down at me with empty eyes. "Is this how you repay your country for the kindness it's shown you? You think our Dear Leader would be pleased to see you wasting time daydreaming? You're lazy. You won't need a full day's rations if you haven't done a full day's work!"

I scurried to my feet, keeping my head down and plucking frantically at the earth, pulling out weeds and stones, so angry and disappointed with myself.

But still those words of Father's echoed in my head, and I stole a glance up the road and back again. There were no cars. Not one. How *could* that place be real?

★

In the kitchen that evening, after twelve hours of work and while my grandparents rolled out their beds for the night, I took the white cloth from the drawer and bowed low to the only two pictures allowed to hang on the wall in our house – our Dear Leader and our Great Leader. And as I dusted their round, smiling faces with their red cheeks and glinting eyes, I muttered my apologies and asked for their forgiveness.

"Your mother says you were in trouble today."

I turned to see Father standing next to me, his eyes flickering over the bruise on my cheek.

I nodded. "I was daydreaming." I folded the cloth and brushed it across the top of the picture frame.

"What about?" he asked.

I ran the cloth down the edge and along the bottom, but didn't say a word – just shrugged.

"Forget it," he whispered to me. "It won't do any good." And he turned away before I could say a word.

I listened to him putting on his coat, fastening up his shoes and looking for his gloves. I rubbed the cloth across the glass over and over, up and down and round and round in circles.

"I'm going to look for firewood," I heard him tell my mother.

I waited for the door to close. Then I turned round and smiled at her. "I'll go and help him," I said.

★

There was only one place my father could be heading, the only place to find dry wood at this time of year, and so I set off out of the house, round the back and across a field towards a small, dense copse of trees, following a dot of light from his lamp as it swung in and out of view.

The cold air burned in my lungs, and my feet and ankles buckled and turned on the frozen ground as I strode on and on. But as he reached the copse, I was right behind him, and I stretched a hand through the darkness and rested it on his shoulder.

"Father," I said.

He jumped and turned. "Yoora, what are you doing?" The lamplight flickered up on to his face, and for a second I stepped back from this ghostly, other-worldly thing staring at me.

"I... came to help you."

He stared at me, his breathing heavy, his face fixed. "Hold this," he said, passing me the lamp.

I followed close behind him, waving the light over the ground as he picked up twigs and sticks. Waiting for the right moment. He stretched up high, his hand pulling tight on a branch to bring it down, the lamplight flooding his face.

Now, I thought.

"Was it really real, Father, that place in my dream?"

He stopped. His whole body stiffened and his face filled with anger as he stared at me. Then he turned away again, yanking at the branch. "Is that why you followed me down here? To ask me that?"

"No," I lied.

The branch came away in his hands and he strode towards me, towering over me. "I told you to forget it. There's nothing to tell. It was a dream." He turned away.

I shook my head, following him. "That's not right. There's something you're not telling me..."

He spun round, his face in mine, his finger jabbing at me. "I told you, child, to *leave* it." For a second I crumbled, frightened of him. Then I took a breath and I looked up.

"I hate it when you call me child," I spat.

"You behave like one."

"You treat me like one. Why don't you trust me and tell me the truth? Tell me whatever it is you're hiding from me! I'm old enough to know!"

His lips were thin as he stared at me, his chest heaving up and down as he breathed.

"You wouldn't believe me," he hissed.

I didn't move, I didn't argue, I didn't say a word. I just waited, watching as his face relaxed and his shoulders dropped, as his head lowered and his eyes closed.

"All right," he whispered, lifting his head to look at me. "But you have to promise me you won't repeat a word. Not to anyone. And that you'll listen, really listen, to what I have to say."

I nodded. "I promise," I breathed, and my skin prickled and my lungs felt hot and my palms were sweaty with excitement and anticipation.

"Your dream," he whispered with a sigh, "that place you saw in your head, it is real, it does exist."

I stared at him open-mouthed. "It's Pyongyang, isn't it? I think, Father, I think, you know, if I work really hard, that maybe He would let me go there, don't you? If I try really hard? If we all do, He'll let us go together. Today was a mistake, I was wrong, I shouldn't have been daydreaming. But..."

He lifted a finger to my mouth to silence me. "Listen," he said. "If you want me to tell you, then for a minute just listen."

I nodded again.

"It does exist, and it is *just* as you saw it. It has enough food for *everyone*, and medicine if you get ill. It has houses and apartments with bathrooms where you wash and go to the toilet. It has heating where you flick a switch and the room gets warmer." He lowered his voice further. "And it has shops where you can buy things."

I stared at him, and suddenly everything felt very serious.

"Clothes. And music, all different sorts. And they have televisions with programmes and channels you can choose. And books with stories, or about different countries and their leaders, who are voted for."

"We have a leader that we vote for too," I whispered.

He nodded. "But in other countries," he said slowly and carefully, "there is more than one name on the slip. They have a choice." His eyes bored into mine. "One day I'll take you there. I hope you can live there. Have a future there. Be happy... but..." His voice drifted off and I watched as he lifted up the lamp and scanned the darkness around us, as he wiped his hand across his face and took a step towards me.

"Do you understand what I'm saying to you, Yoora?"

I nodded, although I wasn't sure. I thought I did, but I didn't know if I wanted to hear this, didn't understand how anywhere like that could exist. Didn't know whether to believe him. Or to trust him.

He sighed, moving closer to me, looking at me so intently. "What do you think to things here, Yoora? Our country? What do you think to our Dear Leader?"

I felt my body stiffen and my back straighten.

"You think he's fair? Looks after us?"

"Of course," I replied without thinking.

"You think we should feel this hungry? Or this cold?"

"Why are you asking me that? We've got everything we need here. He provides everything. There's nowhere any better than here, He tells us that... He tells us..." My blank eyes stared into Father's and I quoted lines I'd known for ever:

> *"We grow up in the land of freedom*
> *All the little comrades march in rows*
> *Singing in this paradise of peace*
> *Tell me, of what can the world envy us?"*

I focused back on him.

"Freedom?" he asked. "Paradise? You think so? Really, Yoora? After what I've just told you? After seeing that place in your dream?" He shook his head. "Open your eyes, look around you. If this is truly how you imagine freedom and paradise, then you have no imagination."

His voice was alive with passion and anger. "Are you hungry, Yoora? He's not, our *Dear Leader. He* eats Chinese dolphins and French poodles, caviar and sea urchins."

My mouth fell open at the hatred I could hear in his voice. I couldn't speak. I couldn't move. I just stood there, hearing words coming from Father's mouth that I never thought he would say.

I could believe that place was real. I could believe it was in North Korea. I could believe it was somewhere only the most hardworking and loyal citizens were allowed to go. But I could not believe any more than that. Father's words about the city had made me question him, but these... these made me worry about his sanity.

"Are you cold?" Father continued. "He's not. He lives in his palace with fires in every room and people to make them for him. Look how thin you are. Think of what he looks like. Has he ever missed a meal? Eaten only corn for a whole week? Gone to bed hungry? No. Is that how it should be? Is that right? Should he live like that while his people are starving?"

My hands flew over my mouth then over my ears. I strode away and then back. I couldn't believe he dared even *think* the words coming out of his mouth. I didn't want to hear it, didn't want those thoughts and words in my head, corrupting me with reactionary lies, challenging my faith in my country, our Fatherland. What he was saying was a crime against the state, an insult to the authority of the leadership that he could be arrested for. That it was my duty to report him for. That *I* could be arrested for if I didn't.

'I've wanted to share this with you for so long, what I think, really I have. For years your grandfather's been telling your mother that you're old enough to understand and to know not to say anything. But how could I? You had to believe it all, as if it was all true, every word. If you repeated anything I told you at school, we could all have been killed, the whole family, you too.'

I put my hands over my ears again. 'No,' I hissed. 'No, I don't want to hear it. Don't say it. Don't. Don't.'

He pulled my hands away. 'Think of that place from your dream, think how different it was from here. It's real, Yoora, it's real.'

I closed my eyes so I couldn't see him, but still he had hold of my wrists and I couldn't stop his words. So I sang, I recited, over and over –

"Our future and hope depend on you
The People's fate depends on you
Comrade Kim Jong Il!
We are unable to survive without you!"

"Yoora, stop it! Listen to me!" Father hissed.

I kept on chanting, but still I could hear his lies.

"There are places better than this in the world – people aren't starving everywhere, people are happier. Feel that ache of hunger in your stomach, and the cold pulling at your face, and remember the last time you saw Kim Jong Il on television, a big, fat, round man, with clothes that look new, and a warm furry hat on his head."

He put a hand gently over my mouth, and I stopped singing.

"You are my daughter, and I can feel the bones in your arms and legs. I can count your ribs, reach my hands round your waist. But I have no more food to give you. In the mornings while you sleep, I stare at your pale skin and your blue lips, and I rest my hand on your face and feel the cold of it, but I don't have enough fuel to keep you warm. And I can't get you a new coat or an extra blanket, or even a pair of socks with no holes. And it makes me want to cry. And it's all because of that man."

I stared at Father. At his eyes glistening as they filled with tears, at the love I could see in his face as moonlight filtered through the trees and dappled his skin.

So deluded.

"No," I said, taking his hand away from my mouth and wriggling from his grip. "You're wrong. It's because of you. If you worked harder, were a better citizen, then He'd provide us with more food and vouchers to exchange for clothes. It's not His fault the floods came and washed away so many crops." I turned and marched towards home, the lamp swinging in my hand.

"What floods?" Father demanded, following me out of the trees.

"The floods in other parts of the country. And He told us about the American capitalists and the Japanese imperialists, how it's their fault too that we're hungry and cold and tired. All we need to do is what He tells us – eat two meals a day instead of three; work harder, longer hours; be better citizens."

"What do you know about the Americans or Japanese apart from the lies you've been told at school? Do as He says, do as He tells you, believe what He speaks — it's all you've ever lived by. It's not your fault. But I'm trying to tell you it's not right, it's not true."

I stopped again and turned to him. "If that place is real, then how did it get in my head?"

He stared at me for too long. Then, without a word, he shook his head.

"I should report you," I hissed, and I stormed away from him and didn't look back.

Chapter Three

I heard him come into the room that night as I lay under my blankets, but I didn't turn round to say goodnight. My eyes were closed as I listened to him climb into his bed and pull the covers up around him, but sleep was far from me. I was tired and my head ached, but just as Kim Jong Il's voice echoed round our house unbidden, so did my father's in my head. There was no turning it off, no turning it down and no ignoring it.

My body trembled with cold, my stomach grumbled with hunger, and darkness swirled and moved around me, dancing in front of my eyes. And over the background of Father's shocking words, my own came again and again – *How could he even think that of our Dear Leader? How could he question Him?*

And the loudest — *I should report him.*

I remembered, back at school, all the songs and poems, teachings and rhymes I had learnt by heart from nursery through to my last year, things that were unrecognisable to me as anything but truth: unquestionable and sacred.

"*Loyalty and devotion are the supreme qualities of a revolutionary.*"

"*We have nothing to envy in this world.*" But what about Father's loyalty and devotion? And why would *anyone* question what we lived by? Why would anyone not believe?

But Father didn't.

I should report him, I thought again. *He should be taken away for re-education, to learn again how good our Dear Leader is, how to follow Him, to do what is right by Him.*

And I remembered all the stories too, that we had been taught about our Dear Leader; how when He was born a bright star appeared in the sky, and a double rainbow, and a swallow flew down from heaven declaring the birth of a general who would rule all the world; that His mere presence could make flowers bloom and snow melt; that when His rule of our nation began it caused trees to grow and a rare albino sea cucumber to be caught.

How can Father not believe those stories? I thought.

For a second, just a second, my head was clear and I stopped.

I told myself the stories again, but this time I really listened and really heard the words, better than I had ever done before, and whether because of the stories or Father's words or the images from my dream, I allowed the smallest grain of something to settle in my head. Not of doubt, or disbelief. No. It was more like curiosity, or a desire to understand, a continuation of something that had begun a year earlier, when I met Sook.

That, for me and for my family, was the beginning of the end.

Chapter Four

One year earlier

Winters were long and cold, came fast and left slow. Every year school stopped for four months from November until the beginning of spring, yet still our days were filled, with homework – books about the childhood of our Dear Leader to learn by heart, quotas of paper or of metal to collect for recycling – or jobs for my parents, searching for food to bulk out our rations.

There was little time to do anything else, and little else to do.

The year before my dream, which we called Juche 97 – ninety-seven years since the birth of our Great Leader, Kim Il Sung – was the harshest winter even my grandfather could remember. We struggled through every day of it, waiting for spring to come while we watched helplessly as the cold made victims not only of our crops, but also of our neighbours. Too many times we dug into the frozen soil to bury our dead.

It was drawing into December and I stepped from my bed with feeble sunlight straining through the ice on the inside of the windows behind me, the cold clawing at me, icy and damp and unwelcoming. I pulled long socks up my legs, a jumper over my head, watching Father rushing to relight the fire, his body shaking through his layers of clothing.

We were the first up, my mother and grandparents waiting for some warmth to slide across our two rooms before their strained faces emerged from their blankets and duvets. A little while later I stepped from the house into air so cold it hurt your skin like a million needles and made your eyes stream, and I longed for spring and the summer following, the warmth of sunlight on my face, green shoots in the ground promising food, coloured petals opening into a smile.

I walked across the village towards the public toilets in near silence, a metal bucket swinging in one hand, an old spade and a pick in the other, listening to the crunch of stones under my feet, the breeze rustling at bare tree branches and my breath heavy in my ears. No birdsong – it was too cold – and no cars roaring or buses rumbling.

I loved the quiet, the calm and the stillness; no awkwardness to it, just spacious and free; and I loved the countryside, even in winter with its covering of frost over empty fields of mud, rows of houses with wisps of smoke from their chimneys, leading off into the sky and over the tops of trees.

It was rough and it was basic, but it was home and it was beautiful.

It was Monday, my usual day for collecting night soil, a time I liked because I knew no one else would be up yet. But that day, as I turned the corner, someone else was already standing there, his legs stretched over the ditch, his head bent low, his hands scrabbling at chunks of frozen faeces. I stared at him, not believing quite how tall he was, or how filled out his face was, or how developed his muscles looked, how bright his skin. Or, as he glanced up at me and smiled, how friendly, how content and at ease he seemed to be.

Most of us children of whatever age – no, *all* of us – were slender verging on skinny, were short to the point of being stunted, had skin that was dry and hair that was brittle, nails broken, muscles thin.

He stood upright, and I looked away from him quickly, not wanting him to know I was watching.

"Hello," he said, inclining his head.

I gave a courteous smile and a slow nod back, but didn't look up to meet his eyes. I moved to the ditch closest to me, trying to think who he was. I didn't recognise him, didn't know him from school, couldn't place him in the village, what house he lived in or who his parents were. I couldn't understand how he looked so healthy, where he could be getting food from.

He must be an excellent citizen, I thought. *And his family too.*

I rested my bucket nearby, my shovel next to it, and lifted my pick, swinging it in my hands, crashing it down.

"I've never done this before," he said. "We never had to."

I tried not to frown, didn't understand why he wouldn't have had to do this. "It doesn't smell as bad when it's frozen," I offered, "but it takes longer."

We continued in silence, and occasionally I risked a glance upwards, stopping to catch my breath, rubbing my aching back, watching his arms. With those muscles, they should've been so much more capable than mine, but they seemed surprisingly weak. My eyes drifted across the village and I noticed a woman watching me – someone else I didn't recognise. As I struggled to lift the pick above my head and bring it down into the ditches of frozen excrement, her eyes never strayed from me. And it wasn't until I'd finished, when I'd thrown the last lump into the bucket, bringing the level to the top, that she unfolded her arms and walked away.

First this strange boy, I thought, *and now a peculiar woman.*

"Can I walk with you?" the boy asked. "I'm not sure where to go."

I stared at him. A simple request. A few words. But it felt like more. I nodded my reply, though, and we struggled down the path, alongside the fields and away towards the buildings, and I watched his feet walking, his fingers stretching round the handle of the bucket, and I listened to his laboured breathing next to me.

I was an innocent fifteen, had never had a boyfriend, never kissed, never held hands, or even thought that way about anyone. I didn't know about sex, or how babies were made. We had no dating culture, just marriages, arranged usually through parents. Our Dear

Leader gave special instruction that men should marry at thirty, women at twenty-eight, and children should be had only in marriage.

But as I walked with this unknown boy, I felt the possibility of something – something I didn't understand.

"Tell me," he said, his voice warm in the cold air, "why do we have to do this?"

My heart smiled at his naivety. "They use it as fertiliser for the crops," I replied, my own voice quiet and trembling with nerves. "Every family provides a bucketful each week, then it's defrosted and spread on the fields. But we don't have any toilets at home." I shrugged, took a breath, gathered my thoughts and glanced again at his face. "We used to be given a chit in exchange. Then when we handed the chit over, we'd be given food. But that doesn't happen any more."

"Why?"

I paused a moment. I'd never thought why. "I don't think there is much," I replied. "Food, that is." But the second the words were out, I regretted them. What would he think I was saying about our Dear Leader? That He couldn't provide for us, the Father of our Nation? I hadn't intended that meaning, but I didn't know who this person was; he could be a spy, reporting back those not faithful, who would then be arrested and disappear. All for an innocent comment misconstrued.

"Because of the floods and the cold weather," I said. "And the bastard Americans," I added for good measure.

He nodded.

I wanted to ask him where he'd come from. Why he was here. What life was like outside the village. Who his parents were. What they did. If he knew that woman who'd been watching me. But I didn't dare.

I struggled along with my bucket and spade and pick, my fingers stiff from the cold and the metal handle of the bucket burning my skin. Every now and then I sensed the boy's head turn and his eyes rest upon me.

We reached the building without another word and it was strange, not because it felt awkward, but the opposite; because the silence between us didn't feel empty, it felt comfortable and natural, like there was no need to speak.

Our buckets were emptied when we arrived, our chits, despite them being unnecessary, were given and together we wandered out.

"My name's Sook," he said, tilting his head towards me.

"Yoora," I replied.

He smiled, and I watched his eyes flit over me. "You look hungry."

I didn't reply. Weren't we all?

"Here," he said and pulled his hand from deep inside a trouser pocket.

My eyes struggled against the cold, trying to focus, frowning at a bun sitting in his palm. I shook my head. Nobody, *nobody*, gave food away for free. "I can't take that," I said.

"Please," he whispered.

"But... where did you get it? The... the markets are miles away and you'd need a permit to go... and..."

"My mother bakes them. Then sells them."

"But I don't have any money." I knew how valuable it was, was sure she'd miss even one.

"Just take it," he said.

I reached out my hand, my fingers long, stretching, daring, and I didn't care who his mother was or where she got the ingredients from or whether this was going to get me into trouble or not. I just saw food, and I just wanted to eat.

Hunger does strange things to a person, and I had been hungry for a long time.

I held the bun in my fingers, turned away from Sook and lifted it to my mouth and nose, closed my eyes and smelt it, stretched out my tongue and touched the crust, gently. My mouth watered and slowly, slowly I sank my teeth into it.

It was so good.

"I have to go," I heard him say. "My mother will be expecting me."

I turned to him, not chewing, just holding the piece of bun in my mouth, enjoying it for as long as possible.

"I live up there." He pointed to the biggest house in the village, with far more rooms than the two we had. I knew the house: it used to have an orchard in the back before the village kids destroyed it looking for apples, stripping off the fruit and the leaves and the bark and everything. It had been empty since the last family were taken away for treachery. "We moved in yesterday," he said.

He paused a second and I watched him look left and right and back to me. "Meet me sometime," he whispered.

My eyes shot to him.

"After the sun's gone down."

I didn't answer. I couldn't. I simply stared at him, not

believing what he'd said. But I caught movement behind him and I saw her, the woman from earlier. She was marching towards us, her black hair scraped away from her face, her hooded eyes piercing.

I didn't stop to reply, or wait to see who she was, or what she wanted. Instead I muttered an apology, spun round and walked away.

I headed home thinking of my family: my mother and father who would be going to work, both thin and tired, hardworking despite the hunger in their bellies that was never sated. I thought of my grandparents: at home all day, too old, too weak to work, their skin stretched like old leather across their bones, their eyes hollow with sadness and disappointment, my grand-father's stomach growling with hunger like a beast inside slowly dying.

I should share this bun with them, I thought, staring at it in my hand. *But how can I explain where it came from? What will they think?*

I took a guilty bite, and another, and before I even realised, there was too little for me to take home. So I finished it, and it was wonderful: the anticipation as I lifted it to my mouth, my senses screaming as I sank my teeth into it, that wonderful thick feeling as it slid down my throat. I missed proper food so much, couldn't remember what a full stomach felt like, or what it was like to not be hungry.

★

When I neared the house I could hear voices, low and mumbling, lifting and dropping again, and I slowed my pace, trying to make out what they were saying as they spoke over each other. I stepped closer, resting my hand on the door. The wood creaked.

The voices stopped, and I stood for a moment, waiting for someone to speak again. But nothing came. I took a breath, steadied my face and stepped into the house.

The tension was palpable; my mother standing next to a cupboard, pushing the drawer shut as she watched me, my father at the fireplace, my grandparents seated at the table. I felt their eyes, all of them, upon me, all with the question behind them – *What did she hear?* But the guilt I was trying to hide was from eating the bun all by myself, not from overhearing their conversation. Yet I knew for the first time, as I stood watching them, that *something*, some secret, was being shared in my house, only it was not being shared with me.

It scared me.

"I've met somebody new in the village," I said, hoping for the tension to ease. "He lives up in the big house." I looked around, expecting curious glances and inquisitive faces, but instead saw my father fidget, heard my grandfather's intake of breath, saw their eyes shoot to each other, and my mother's almost imperceptible shake of her head.

"Stay away from him," hissed my grandmother, her eyes narrowing at me as if they could see the smile he'd brought to my face earlier. "We don't have any business with them. Remember your place, Yoora."

Uncomfortable, I looked away, and saw my grand-father's eyes drop. "His mother's the new *Inminbanjang*," he whispered.

"What?" I asked, staring at him.

But my mother was marching towards him, wagging her finger in his face. "No," she whispered. "She doesn't need to know. She's only fifteen."

"Know what?" I whispered back.

Over her shoulder my grandfather was shaking his head, and I could hear his mutterings. "Fifteen. She's nearly a woman. She leaves school this year. She's old enough to know the truth, and to be trusted. She *should* know." Calmly he stood up, tucking the chair under the table and striding from the house. Nobody stopped him. Nobody said a word.

But even among all this confusion, the guilt I felt over the bun didn't go away. At least not until that evening, when stomach-ache hit me, my body not used to the richness I'd given it, and I passed my share of thin noodle soup to my grandparents. My guilt then, to some degree, was assuaged.

★

I lay on my bed mat on that long winter night, watching the flames of the fire die, the embers fade and turn to black, and I felt the gradual leaking of cold from around the window frame and under the bottom of the door, felt it like ice forming across my face and cracking my lips, and I thought of Sook. I thought about meeting him, being with him, his face, his smile, his company.

He had given me a spark of light in my life of dark.

Yet his mother was the new *Inminbanjang*, and I *did* know what that meant, even though I had pretended not to, had suspected it as soon as Sook told me where he lived. She was the new head of our local neighbourhood group – a spy for our government.

Every few weeks she would have to report to an agent from the Ministry of Public Security. Inform on people who hadn't worked hard enough, or had said something against our Dear Leader, or failed to wear the badge with His face on over their hearts, or let dust gather on His picture. An endless list.

Other people would work for her too, all reporting back to her, even if only gossip; they had to say something. Some of those reported would be sent to re-education lessons, some to prison, some executed in the fields. I had never known anyone accused to then be found innocent.

It hung over us as we tried to live, shaping everything said and everything done, not because of guilt – we had none, we were good citizens, working hard, doing our duty – but because of the power these people held. Even the most patriotic, the most innocent and best behaved and hardest working could be accused and found guilty of anything, if someone wanted it enough.

"Is anyone incorruptible?" my grandfather used to say to me as a warning. "If they're hungry enough, or sad enough? Or need money to try to buy medicine?"

Or if they want to keep someone away from their son? I wondered.

I didn't think for one moment, though, that the idea of a government spy was the truth my mother was trying to hide from me. There was something more going on in my home that I was not deemed old enough, or sensible enough, or trustworthy enough to be allowed to know.

But as I lay there in the cold, my thoughts again strayed back to Sook, and as my eyes grew heavy with the image of him, a warmth spread through me, sending me to sleep with a smile on my face for the first time I could remember.

Yet not for one moment did I think I was being naive.

Chapter Five

As I walked alongside the fields the next day, my feet stumbling across the frozen earth, heading for the trees on higher ground to look for firewood, I saw a boy moving towards me, his frame slightly bigger than most, his walk slightly faster, his arms swinging, his legs marching.

So obvious he wasn't like the rest of us. Not as hungry, or as weak, or as worn down by tiredness.

My stomach lurched and I could feel the heat rise in my cheeks and my mouth go dry. I looked up to him, and down again, away to the distance, and back to him just as he looked at me. Our paces slowed as we approached, staring at each other. And we stopped.

"Tonight?" I whispered.

"I thought you didn't..."

I shrugged.

"All right." He nodded. "After dark. When everyone's asleep?"

I stared at him, so nervous, so excited.

"Where? On the corner near your house?"

"No," I replied.

He nodded. "No, you're right. At the end of the path then, where it splits in two. Next to the tree?"

I knew where he meant; it was quiet and secluded, away from any houses. I agreed before I could change my mind, and I walked away with a smile in my eyes. I wanted to be with him, spend time with him, find out about him. I knew how dangerous it was, but I didn't listen to that voice in my head questioning why I was doing it, when I'd already turned him down, when it could cause so much trouble if anyone found out, when we could not possibly have any future, the two of us, in this society.

★

My mother asked me if I was ill that evening, my grandmother said I was quiet, my father mentioned that I looked preoccupied. After each I replied I was fine, a bit tired, a little hungry. My grandfather, though, I caught watching me every now and then — across the table as we ate our maize, as I looked back from watching the sun setting through the window, or when I was pulling out the bed mats and unfolding the blankets. But he didn't say a word.

Darkness came early in wintertime, and the nights were long and cold. We would be sleeping by seven thirty, keeping warm under blankets and duvets rather than using firewood and fuel so precious to us.

I waited that first night, and waited, for what felt like hours, lying under my covers, trying to stay awake while tiredness consumed me and sleep pulled at my eyelids. I listened to Father's breathing turn slow, turn heavy, turn to snores, and I whispered Mother's name, watching her shadow in the darkness to see if she turned towards me, or lifted her head, or muttered a reply. But she didn't.

They were asleep. Yet I lay there still, a bit longer, waiting for something, I didn't know what. Maybe for my nerves to subside, or to talk myself out of it, for my indecision to go, or to find the courage to pull away those blankets and step out into the cold.

This wasn't the kind of thing I did. I was a good girl. I worked hard at school and on the fields, I obeyed my parents, I respected them. I had no secrets and told no lies. I was straightforward and honest. My life was uncomplicated.

But this? This *thing* presenting itself to me, this made my chest hot and my breath short and my skin prickle. This made me feel excited, alive.

I stretched my legs out from the warmth of the blankets and into the cold air, and I rolled my body out on to the floor without making a sound. Quickly and quietly I pulled on my clothes, and with my eyes peeled, trying to make sense of the gloom in front of me, I bulked the blankets up on the bed, hoping that if Mother or Father should wake, they'd presume it was me.

*

The wind bit at me as I walked to meet him, the skin on my face tightening and the air freezing inside my lungs. There was no electricity in the village for lights, and that night only a sliver of moon lit the sky, jumping for ever in and out of clouds, plunging me one moment into blackness complete and engulfing, the next allowing me the tiniest piece of glistening light to try and find my way.

And so I moved carefully, shuffling at first, then stepping, then striding; walking by memory with the crunching of gravel or the softness of mud under my feet, the touch to my fingers of a farm building made of wood to my right, a bush with nothing but spiky branches to my left.

I approached with footfalls silent on grass, and my breathing slow and controlled and even. When I could sense he was there I stopped, closed my eyes, hearing the whistle of his breath and the steady scratching of one nervous fingernail on another.

I could turn round and go. Head back home and he would never know, I thought. *He would never say anything and it would be forgotten. My life would carry on steady and simple. And boring.*

I opened my eyes and took those final steps towards him. "Sook," I whispered, and I heard his breathing change and could imagine a smile reaching across his face.

"Yoora," he replied.

For a moment we just stood, and I didn't know what to say or do, and I didn't know what I expected him to say or do either. My clothes were thin and the air was freezing and my knees and legs shook and my teeth chattered, though I was certain it wasn't just because of the cold.

"Here," he whispered, and I felt him wrap a blanket round me.

"W... what about you?" I stammered.

"My clothes are warmer," he replied, and as he stood in front of me, pulling the blanket round my body and up under my chin, I could feel the warmth coming from him, and I could smell him close to me and on the blanket. I looked up at his face as the moon came out from behind a cloud again, catching its light flitting across his skin and showing the outline of his smile. My stomach tipped. I was so close to him, and his hands as they pulled the blanket were nearly touching me.

My life was so routine, so predictable and uneventful and monotonous. Excitement was our Dear Leader's birthday, or the birthday of His father before Him, our Eternal President, Kim Il Sung. When we were allowed a day off school or work to lay a red flower at the feet of their statues and sing their praises.

Dread was a test at school, checking you could recite the details of our Eternal President's life, where He was born, studied, the battles He fought in, the never-ending list of His achievements. And those of our Dear Leader. Knowing the punishment was at least the cane or a punch.

Fear was everybody else. Watching you, forming opinions of you, lying about you with words that could kill.

This? This was something else entirely. This was... exhilarating... thrilling. I felt awake. I felt alive.

"Shall we walk?" he asked, and all I could do was nod my head.

Chapter Six

Together we strolled up the track that led away from the village, my mind racing for things to say as I pulled the blanket tighter around me, felt the roughness of it on my face. I was nervous, a little frightened, and next to me I could feel Sook glancing one way then another, up to the tops of the trees then down to his feet on the ground.

"Are there bugs?" he asked. "Insects and little creatures like that? Or any animals?"

I couldn't help but smile at him. "Of course – it's the countryside."

I heard him suck breath in. "Big ones?"

"What?" I asked. "Like tigers and bears?"

"Yeah."

"Yes," I nodded. "They'll be watching you now, then they'll leap out and grab you and eat you up."

"Really?" His voice trembled.

I paused, letting him believe, just for a moment. "No. Not really. Not here. Further north, yes."

"How do you know that?"

I shrugged. "Everybody knows that. There are some here. Insects of course and a few animals and birds. Owls. Nothing that will hurt you. Lots that you can eat, if you can catch them."

"Snakes?"

I laughed. "No snakes. I promise. You're not from the countryside, are you?"

"No."

I didn't dare ask him any more, it felt rude and intrusive. *He must be from a town. Or a city*, I thought. I already knew the reasons why people were moved – those who had fallen foul of the authorities or committed some crime against the Fatherland, yet nothing bad enough for a prison sentence. That or they had connections that protected them, or they were well thought of. Before.

We stopped walking and turned round, staring down

at the groups of houses and fields that were our village, silver moonlight passing over them as the wind blew at the clouds.

"My father's disabled," he whispered, as if this would answer the questions I didn't dare ask. "We lived in the capital, Pyongyang. He had an accident at work. Lost half his leg. Then we moved."

I nodded. "I see," I replied. But I didn't.

"He doesn't leave the house now. Mother was really angry."

"Why? Was it somebody else's fault?"

"No." He shook his head. "I mean, she was angry that we had to move. But... but... she didn't show it, didn't say anything; she couldn't: she knew we had to do what we were told."

I turned my head to him and stared at his silhouette in the moonlight, surprised how open he was being. "I'm sorry, Sook," I said, and his name felt strange in my mouth, "but I don't think I understand."

He sighed long and heavy and I waited until finally he turned his face to me. "It was Pyongyang," he said.

"I don't... I still don't..."

He leant in closer. "There are no disabled people in Pyongyang. It's not allowed," he whispered.

"Oh," I replied, putting the pieces together in my head. "I didn't know that."

"It's not written anywhere. Nobody says it." He sighed and rubbed his hands over his face. "Business people go there, and tourists, foreigners. It doesn't present a good image, having disabled people or handicapped people in the streets." His voice was so low I could barely make out his words. "Or the old. They move away too. Sent somewhere foreigners aren't allowed to go. Pyongyang is a place for the young and the pretty, for successful people and the trustworthy. People who don't ask questions." And he stared at me, right into me, with such intensity. "I didn't just say that. You wouldn't... you wouldn't...?"

And I knew so well what he was asking for. Reassurance that I wouldn't repeat what he'd said, or report him, because some might think what he'd said was scandalous, punishable, *reactionary*. But to me it wasn't. It made perfect sense. Pyongyang was the face our nation showed to the world, and of course anyone would want that to look as good as possible. Maybe it was surprising to hear that put into words, but not shocking.

But still, I thought to myself, *he must trust me to say it out loud. Or trusts that I wouldn't dare speak out against the son of the* Inminbanjang.

"I... I... won't say anything," I replied.

And there it was. Something we shared. That tied us together. I wished I could tell him something in return, a secret or a suspicion, something dangerous or daring, that meant I had given and trusted, as he had; but I wasn't brave enough, and I didn't have anything to share anyway.

Not then at least.

We walked a little more, that first meeting, and spoke a little more, but we soon headed home, beaten by the cold and my lack of courage. I wanted to be brave and bold, to not care if we were caught or our parents found out, but the consequences frightened me, shouting a warning at me from the back of my mind – *his mother is the* Inminbanjang!

But it was only our first meeting, and I sneaked back into the house while everyone slept on oblivious, and I climbed back into bed, peeling away my layers of clothes under the blankets and looking forward so much to the next time I saw Sook.

★

We met more, and I thought less of being caught and of what might happen. Together, on our evenings, we would stroll up past fields and away from the village, barely able to see each other except for when the moon was out, but it never mattered – we were there for each other's company.

We talked about everything and nothing, shared thoughts and wonderings and sometimes opinions. I asked him if he was proud of his mother when she reported the first reactionary citizen in the village, an old man, recently widowed, who could no longer work and had no family to support him. Someone had overheard him saying that our Dear Leader wasn't providing enough food for His people. He was executed two days later.

Of course, she'd done well and the old man deserved it; it's not our place to complain or to judge His leadership. But the delight in her eyes as the man was taken away woke me with nightmares for weeks, imagining it was me she was reporting, with some made-up charge to have me taken away after she found out about me and her son.

But even as time passed and Sook and I spoke more and more, we never talked about or queried or commented on whatever it was we had together, growing and deepening. Even though whatever we had didn't have a future.

Not if either of us wanted a future that was safe.

Chapter Seven

Time passed. Winter passed. Spring drew away and summer arrived with long days and short nights.

We left school, both of us, and while Sook was allowed an hour's walk to the nearest town every day to work in an office, I was given a job on the land. And as summer came, we met later, waiting longer for the dark to come and for the house to be sleeping.

That night, the one I remember so well, the air was warm and humid, close around us as we walked. We pointed out things to each other that sparkled in the moonlight, watched it dance on our faces, still with not a touch, or a kiss, or a hold of a hand. We lay next to each other on the grass, and the sky began to lighten as the sun came back round, and the first glimpses of orange and red reached up from behind the trees.

Eventually, in our sleepy way and with no regard to the consequences, we strolled back towards the village with dawn at our back and the song of birds as they woke, and we said a goodbye to each other that lingered perhaps a little too long.

He had become my best friend. With him, I felt wanted and needed. I felt awake and alive. I felt invincible.

I had become careless.

I stepped through the door and straight into the glare of my grandmother's eyes staring at me from her bed mat. I paused, my palm still resting on the handle behind me, watching as she shook her head, waiting for her to shout at me, or call my mother from the other room, or throw something at me, or jump up and hit me. She lifted a finger and beckoned me towards her, and I tiptoed across with my insides on fire. I crouched down, sure she'd be able to hear my heart trying to thump out of my body.

"Sook?" she questioned.

I didn't say a word, but I felt my face flush and my eyes widen before I could stop them.

"You stupid child," she hissed.

My jaw clenched and I lowered my eyes.

"What do you think his mother would say? What do you think she'd do? You think she'd approve? Wish you luck and welcome you into the family?"

I didn't reply.

"Or do you think she'd be disappointed and angry that her precious son would want to spend time with someone like you? And want to get back at you, at us?"

Reluctantly, I nodded.

"Of course she would, a woman like that. She'd destroy you. And it's not just your life you're putting in danger – you know that, don't you? It's all our lives. Mine, your grandfather's, your mother and father's. The more, the better for her. Even if we've done nothing wrong, she'll think of something, make something up, and she'll be rewarded for it. For rooting out reactionary elements or destroying the bad blood."

I didn't move.

"Do you understand how selfish you're being?" she spat, and even in the half-light I could see the ferocity in her eyes and feel it eating into me. I wanted to cry. "She'll find out, if you keep seeing him, if she hasn't already."

"But we're not doing anything wrong. We're not reactionary."

She sighed, shaking her head. "Don't you listen? *It doesn't matter*. But anyway, of course you are – you're seeing her son. In secret. And she's the *Inminbanjang*. She's only got to look at us and we could be taken away. What class are we, Yoora? Have you thought of that? We're at the bottom, we're the hostile class – we're *beulsun* – tainted blood. Everyone already thinks of us as suspect; we're watched by neighbours; parents tell their children to watch you at school.

"Why do you think you're working on the land, a clever girl like you? We'll never be allowed better jobs, never be allowed to join the Workers' Party, never be allowed any of their privileges. Never leave this village. We are *nothing* to them. Or to anyone. And *nothing* will ever change. Not for you or your children or your grandchildren. This is it. There is no way for us to move up in social class. It doesn't happen. You're born into it, you can't marry out of it and you die in it."

"But Sook is—"

"What? What do you think Sook is? As low as us?" She shook her head. "Not quite the core class, not the best, or they wouldn't be in this village. But not far off. And there is *no way* that she, Min-Jee, will ever let you and Sook have a relationship."

"We could run away," I breathed.

She laughed at me then. "Wake up to yourself and don't be so ridiculous. You need government permission to move, a permit to travel out of the village. Where would you live? How would you survive? No one's going to give you a job. They wouldn't be allowed to. If she finds out," she lowered her voice again, "she'll destroy us. You know how it works: the sin, the crime, travels in the blood for three generations. Anything you do, three generations will be punished for it. She *will* find out, Yoora, if you carry on seeing him. One day she will. That's if he hasn't told her already."

"He wouldn't—"

"Don't be naive. You have to end it. For all our sakes." And she turned away.

I climbed back into bed, but sleep eluded me and I watched the sunlight grow brighter through the window and change my sleeping parents from vague silhouettes into real people, with worries marked on their skin in heavy lines and deep wrinkles.

All the while my grandmother's words played over and over in my head and I thought about our family, how small it was, how we were *beulsun,* though no one had told me of it before. I wondered why. I wondered why no relatives were ever talked about, and no aunts or uncles, or other grandparents or cousins, ever visited. I wanted to know, I wanted to understand.

★

For the next few days I skulked around, avoiding Grandmother's eye, avoiding Sook, putting off telling him the decision she was forcing me to take. The truth, the honest, painful, selfish truth, was that I didn't want to stop seeing him. By that time, silently I loved him and, I believed, he loved me.

I missed those night-times that were a world away from my daytimes.

★

I saw him again a week later strolling towards me down the path with a spade in his hand and a smile edging his lips.

"Tonight? Same time?" he breathed.

I thought about telling him, thought about what I *should* do, but as I looked up and met his eye, as we watched each other for a second too long, I realised I couldn't physically say the words. So I nodded.

I didn't care about the threat. I didn't care about the danger. Because by then I trusted him to keep me safe.

But, in a country where one person in five is a

government informant, where, for a crime possibly not even committed, neighbour reports co-worker, pupil reports teacher and child reports friend, trust was a rare and reckless thing, a stupid and naive emotion. I knew that, but I didn't think it applied to me.

My stupidity, my naivety and my guilt followed me over miles.

Chapter Eight

Winter arrived, and still I had not broken off my friendship with Sook. Then finally the night came when I had my dream, my impossible dream, filled with images of a city of lights, a place unimaginable, unseen and unknown to me.

And so too came the conversation with Father and all the worries I had for him.

Was he a traitor? Because if he was, then I should report him. But then all my family would suffer. Or was he ill? Delusional?

Nothing made sense any more. I felt tricked into having the dream. I felt soiled from the words Father had said. And I felt a traitor to my country for not reporting him. But more than anything I felt so very, very alone.

I wished I could share it with someone.

★

That night, a year after I first met Sook, when I could hear my father's snores and my mother's slow, steady breathing, when I knew Grandmother would be sleeping and I could creep past her, I pulled my clothes round me and slid from the house. The moon was the thinnest slip of a crescent, and the darkness of the countryside swallowed me as I moved through it.

There was barely a sound, an eerie stillness, the trees half dead, motionless with no wind, the earth dry under my feet, the dust slipping behind me with every step.

I saw his outline, saw him turn to me, smile, felt warmth in my chest, heard myself sigh. Then a sudden screech came from above us, and next to me Sook jumped, and I heard his intake of breath as he stifled a scream.

City boy, I thought.

"It was only an owl," I whispered. I stopped, and the smile on my face slipped as I felt pressure on my hand and squeezing at my fingers. I looked down – Sook was holding my hand. I stared at our fingers, blurry, indistinguishable in the half-light, and I looked up at his face so close and felt my cheeks flush.

Neither of us moved, or said a word, but so much

passed between us as the moment stretched on: a conversation unspoken, an intensity in the air, an understanding somehow reached as it drew to an end.

"Let's walk," he breathed.

And we did, together, hand in hand, so close our shoulders brushed as we moved, so nervous that I didn't dare move my fingers or acknowledge that we were touching. Something so simple and natural, but something I had never seen any couple do before. Not in public.

It was exciting. Rebellious.

"Are you hungry?" he whispered as we reached the village greenhouses. I nodded and reluctantly let go of his hand.

We sat with our backs against the glass and our legs tucked under us for warmth.

"Here," he said, placing a bun in my hands.

"Your mother's baking?"

He took another from his pocket for himself. "She won't notice."

I struggled to believe that was true, not with so much hunger, with people who could offer good money for this bun in my hands, money that she could use to buy more ingredients, to bake more, to sell more. We couldn't afford the ingredients even if we had the contacts to get them, and even if we had, we wouldn't be allowed a permit to sell them in the markets.

How would Min-Jee feel if she knew her son was giving them away? And worst of all, to someone *beulsun* like me? What would she say to him? What would she do to us?

She wouldn't care that I was starving and so was my family. She couldn't, just as I had to not care that my neighbours too were starving, that the baby girl next door died from malnutrition, not enough milk from her mother to see her into her second month. I only ever heard her cry the night she was born.

Too many people were starving for me to be able to care about any of them. Aid for them would have to form an infinite queue to stop them feeling hungry for just one night. One solitary act of kindness would make little difference.

So without thinking of them, I tore a piece off the bun and placed it on my tongue, watching Sook do the same.

"I can't stay long tonight. My mother's not well. I'm worried she'll get up and notice I'm missing."

"All right," I replied. "I understand."

We carried on eating, but said little. I was disappointed; I wanted to be with him, feel my hand in his again, see that smile on his face in the moonlight, have that excitement tipping my stomach.

"You want to walk back that way with me? Past my house?"

I hesitated. We had never gone that way before. He stood up and held out his hand to mine. For a second I stared at it, the long fingers, the short nails, the lines deep in his palm, and then I lifted my hand, placed it in his and felt myself pulled up from the ground.

I smiled.

We walked.

And too soon we were approaching his house. He pointed to the different windows, explaining what each room was, knowing, I suppose, that I would never be allowed inside. There was a kitchen for cooking in, with a sink to wash things, and taps that water came from. A room each to sleep in, with beds that stayed out all day. Another with comfortable chairs to sit on and a television to watch.

"No foreign channels though," he joked.

I told him about our two rooms for five of us; our one table and five hard chairs; our one radio with, of course, its one government channel to listen to; one bucket to wash in, brush teeth in, wash pots and prepare food in. No taps. No running water.

We sat together around the back of his house, under a window pulled closed, the dead trees of the old orchard like crumbling gravestones before us, no use even for firewood.

"The apartment we had in Pyongyang was better," he said. "There was more food too. Better conditions, people were happier, the streets and buildings were clean and tidy."

He sighed. "There were big, tall buildings too. And underground trains, the deepest in the world, magnificent, with chandeliers in the stations and..."

He was describing my dream and I couldn't believe it. Father *was* right, at least about that, there *was* a place like it. But he was wrong about our Dear Leader. I knew that. He must've been.

"And do the buildings stretch right up high?" I asked.

"Some." He nodded.

"With lights in the windows that are orange or yellow or white. And there are loads of cars in the roads, one after another after another, all different shapes and sizes and colours." My voice became louder and my words faster. "And bars where you can buy drinks, and loud music thumping out, and people dancing in clothes of all different colours and styles?"

He stared at me.

I closed my eyes and could see it again, just as if I was strolling down it in real life. "And there are restaurants with smells of food, and stalls that sell food already cooked that you can carry around and eat and... and... and my father says there's enough food for everyone, and he says there's medicine if you get ill, and he said that's where I'll live. That's where my future is."

My excitement flooded out of me. The relief that I could share this with someone, with Sook, my best friend, the person who meant so much to me. Who I wanted to be with, stay with, make a life with. And I could do it, couldn't I? Maybe? In that place? That place that must've been Pyongyang. And Father was right — about that.

"No," he said.

I opened my eyes.

"That's not Pyongyang. Pyongyang is quiet; there's government music through the loudspeakers, but nothing else. A couple of cars on the roads, but black ones mostly, police cars. And you know nobody wears clothes like that. What you're talking about sounds like Chinese clothes, and they're banned. Yes, there are restaurants, but not like that. And there are no flashing or coloured lights. That's not Pyongyang."

Chapter Nine

"But it must be," I said. "It must be Pyongyang. There are signs for cinemas and shops and rooms to let in hotels. People, loads of people, all sorts of people, wandering around, smiling and chatting, some on phones that they carry, some with wires in their ears for music."

"Where did you see that? How do you know about it? It's *not* Pyongyang. It's not this *country*. It can't be."

"But..." My face fell.

"Your *father* told you about it? Said you were going there? Going to live there? But that would mean... that would mean... he's thinking of leaving the country. He's planning an escape. That would mean he's a traitor, that he disrespects our Dear Leader. Yoora..."

I shook my head. What had I done? What had I said? "No, no, no, he's not. It was Pyongyang, it must've been. Maybe it was a part you weren't near."

"Yoora, what you described is not Pyongyang. I lived there all my life until I came here. That place that you're describing, however you know about it, is not in this country, it can't possibly be. And if your father—"

"He loves our Dear Leader. He bows to Him every day. He... he never says anything against Him... ever... he... he's a good citizen, my father. He's loyal... and devoted and... and..."

We both fell silent, and I realised how loudly we'd been talking. I felt my eyes prickle and I was scared, wished I could take back what I'd said, wished my stupid mouth hadn't emptied out all of that rubbish. But he was my friend, Sook, my best friend, and I could trust him not to say anything. Couldn't I?

I felt sick.

"Yoora." He lowered his voice, leaning close to me. "Tell me the truth. Tell me what's going on. What's your father planning? What's he told you? Maybe it's something you should report. You'd be rewarded."

I stared at him. I thought of what that reward might

be. Food? A better job? Living in that city? I thought of my father, my mother, my grandparents. "Don't do this to me," I whispered. "Don't make me choose."

He shuffled closer and rested his hand on top of mine, and his eyes, so deep, stared at me as if they were looking right into my soul. "You know, I wish we didn't have to hide away, only meeting at night, an hour here and there. I wish we could have a future together..."

I smiled at him and all thoughts of Father were gone. "I try not to wonder what will happen to us any more," I replied. "You know, if this will all have to end, us meeting like this, because I don't want to think that it has to. I want to believe in it and ignore that your family are a better class than mine, but... but really it can't happen... not even friendship. It wouldn't be allowed, Sook. I know that. So do you."

"But maybe," he said, squeezing my hand, "maybe if you tell me what your father said, then it could change things for us. We could tell my mother, she could help you..."

"What?" I stared at him, shaking my head. "No. That's ridiculous," I spat. "There's nothing to tell anyway. And even if there was, your mother would never do anything to help me or my family. She'd just have an excuse to get rid of me."

"She wouldn't do that."

I lifted a hand to dare to touch his cheek. "She would," I whispered.

And I knew she would. Honestly. Truthfully.

And I knew that one day this would have to end. I just never wanted that day to arrive.

"You should go in. Check on your mother. But please, Sook... please don't say anything... not about my father... he's not what you're thinking... he's just..." But I couldn't find the words.

I looked up to a lightening sky, morning approaching, and we motioned our silent goodbyes with no hint of a smile, but with the briefest touch of hands, and I turned away.

I headed home feeling sad and scared and worried. The conversation playing over in my head, what I'd said, what I hadn't meant to say, what he thought, what he might do. And then, through the silence of the village, I thought I heard something behind me and I stopped, listening, turning towards the noise. It came from Sook's house. Voices strained and mingling together, or early morning birdsong? Was that Sook standing at the window, watching me? Should I wave? Or shadows playing tricks on me in the half-light?

I turned and walked away. I didn't know I would never be back.

Chapter Ten

I woke to the same noises as always, and I peered out of the window at the same scene that greeted me every morning. As I ate my porridge, I glanced around at the faces of my family: my grandfather with his wonderful smile and his marvellous stories; my grandmother, quiet and drawn nowadays; my mother who worked so hard to feed us all; and my father, my dear father, who could take away my nightmares and make sense of my dreams.

All their kindness for me.

I remembered the warning words from Grandmother just a few months ago, and I replayed my conversation with Sook from the night before. Over and over I heard my voice echoing and shouting through my head, telling him secrets, betraying my father, my family. Words we could be arrested for. Words we could die for.

I wanted to cry, wanted to tell them what I'd done and for them to make it all better again. They could do that, couldn't they? Take me in their arms, sway me back and forth, whisper in my ear while they stroked my hair, tell me everything would be all right, really it would.

And I would explain that I hadn't meant to tell Sook, it just came out, and came out wrong. Because Father wasn't planning an escape because that city *was* Pyongyang, and Sook must've been mistaken. But Sook had lived there for fifteen years, and he had sounded so certain. And why would he lie?

I swallowed a spoonful of porridge, lifted my eyes back to my family and opened my mouth to speak. I felt sick again.

"Are you all right, Yoora?" my father asked.

"I feel a bit dizzy," I whispered, bringing my shaking hands to my head, watching his eyes, full of concern, looking at me; his thoughts, his most secret thoughts that he'd shared with me that night in confidence, hanging between us, the secret I should've kept.

Escape? I thought. *Really, Father? Is that really what you're planning? Is that really what you think of our Dear Leader?*

Escaping, or even plotting to escape, even thinking

about it, was a crime against the state, against our Dear Leader. A crime punishable by prison or death. And not just for Father – badness runs in the blood for three generations, and so does the punishment.

I had seen it before, maybe five years ago: a radio, broken away from its preset government station, tuned in to a Chinese one instead. No malice intended, no reactionary thoughts or plans, just curiosity about what else existed, and an appetite for music with guitars. But his intentions were irrelevant – his actions went against our country's teachings.

He was older than me, the boy who did it, but I remember standing close to him at school, hearing his feet pattering out a rhythm I didn't recognise, the involuntary hum of a song in his throat. I wasn't the only one who heard it, and I probably wasn't the only one to report him.

They arrived early one morning and the radio was found; that was all that was needed.

I remembered his family – his mother and father, his uncle, his grandfather, his sister; seeing them thrown on to the back of a truck. I remembered the boy's eyes staring down at the watching villagers, eyes full of fear and desperation and guilt and disappointment.

I wondered if he still remembered the song. I wondered if he hated it now.

"Get some fresh air," Father said, his eyes looking up at the smoke from the fire that had settled in a layer under the ceiling.

On trembling legs I stood and wandered to the door, stepping out into the biting cold, my body shivering as claws of ice reached round me. I closed my eyes and sucked in a deep, rasping breath. I exhaled long and slow, my shoulders sagging and my face relaxing, and I opened my eyes.

And there it was. Staring at me with its beady black eyes and cocking its head to one side, like it was trying to tell me something. A crow. No more than a few metres away.

He'll be looking for food, I thought to myself. *He'll start digging through the earth with his beak. You won't find worms there*, I wanted to tell him. *They'll be too far down in winter. And the insects will be huddled together in dark places under rocks, or crevices behind loose pieces of bark, waiting for spring to come and wake them properly.*

"You'd make a good meal yourself," I whispered. "My grandmother would strip the feathers from you and put you in a pot. And you'd taste good. And I could stick your feathers inside my clothes to keep warm."

But he just carried on staring – a black stain, a threat, an omen.

He hopped sideways, stretching out his wings, the feathers glistening oily blue and green, and he flapped upwards, veering towards me and cawing, a raw, harsh, grating noise that stripped through the air and screamed in my ears. His wings were so close to me that I could hear their beating and feel the change in the air as they blotted and flickered out the light, my eyes squinting against the flashing, my arms raised to protect my face.

I crouched down, tucking my face into my chest and stretching my arms over my head. For a moment I thought I felt his claws on my head, pulling at my hair, and I imagined him lifting off into the sky and taking me with him. And for a moment I didn't feel threatened by him or scared of him. I felt something entirely different. Like an understanding, or a need, a sense of urgency.

But as suddenly as he had arrived, he was leaving again, and I stood up, stared into the blue sky scattered with dark clouds, watched his black form and his flapping wings ease away from me, his voice cawing out all the while, like he was screaming at me.

Chapter Eleven

I stepped back inside. "Did you see that?" I asked. But four sets of eyes met mine with blankness. I sat back down. "There was a crow." I waited for some reaction, a question from Mother maybe, or an intake of breath from Grandmother. But nothing. And I realised the stares were blank because of the silence they had thrown themselves into as I came back into the house.

They had wanted me out of the way. They had needed me out of the way. But what had they been talking about?

I slurped the last few spoonfuls of thin porridge from the bowl, and still nobody said a word; the silence was as frosty as the air.

Had they been arguing? Shouting at each other in hissed whispers? Maybe, I thought, they knew, somehow, that I'd told Sook about my dream, about what Father had said to me. Maybe they were too angry to speak to me.

But, I reminded myself, *Sook sneaks food to me, he meets me, he cares about me. He won't say anything. And I can tell them that, when they start shouting at me. I can trust him.*

As I took my empty bowl to the bucket at the window where we washed the pots, I thought I heard something like a vague growl in the distance, and my eyes searched past the grime on the glass and away across the countryside and hills surrounding us. I turned my head to Grandfather and caught him staring at his wife, my grandmother. I looked to Mother and Father, neither moving, just listening. The sound grew louder.

I leant closer to the window pane. "No," I whispered, shaking my head, my skin prickling, my chest tightening and my head spinning. "There's a car coming," I muttered.

"Not here?" Mother whispered.

I turned to Father, his eyes filling with disappointment as he looked at me, his head shaking.

"I'm sorry," I mouthed to him, but he wasn't looking at me any more, and he wasn't listening.

He was on his feet with Mother and my grandparents,

staring through the window to the car that had now turned towards the village, clouds of exhaust fumes belching out behind it.

"It can't be coming here," Mother whispered.

I opened my mouth to speak, to explain what I had said to Sook, about my dream of the city with the lights and the food and the music, Father saying he would take me there, his plan to live there. But I clung still to the belief that Sook wouldn't have done that, wouldn't have betrayed me like that, and I didn't dare say the words that proved how much I'd let my family down.

So I stood. Just stood. Watching the car. Knowing it was heading to us.

"Get rid of everything quickly," I heard my grandmother say. And I turned round, wondering what she could be talking about, catching a look between the adults and realising I was missing something, that some secret was being kept from me.

"Father," I whispered, "I need to tell you something."

"Not now," he replied and the worry in his voice made me gasp, and I watched dumbstruck as he knelt at a cupboard, pulled a drawer out at his feet and stretched an arm into the space it had left. With my mouth open, I watched him draw out handful after handful of papers, and saw my grandparents grab them from him, toss them on to the fire and poke them into the flames as they shot looks back and forth to Mother at the window, then to the door and then back to the jumble of things spread out across the floor.

"But—"

"I said not now, child!" Father shouted.

I moved around them all, trying to make sense of what they were doing, staring at the papers: handwritten letters, photographs, some black and white, some colour, magazines, postcards, newspapers. I stared without understanding at the flames licking round the faces smiling out at me, devouring the words before I could even try to read them.

"Not that one... please... not that one... let me keep that," my mother begged, grabbing an envelope from the floor, a flash of colour peeking out, sheets of paper covered in scrawled handwriting. I watched her gulping back tears as she stuffed the envelope inside her top.

"What are you doing?" I asked. "What is all this stuff?" I bent down, picking up a postcard of a city at night-time, the sky a beautiful deep, velvet blue, the streets alive with colour, buildings stretching up into darkness, the windows lit different colours, shop signs flashing neon symbols.

My stomach turned. "This... this is the city I dreamt about." I felt breathless and dizzy, staring at the neon signs on the card in my hand that I didn't understand and couldn't read. "This isn't North Korea," I said. "It's not Pyongyang. Sook was right."

Everything stopped. They stared at me.

"I didn't... I didn't..." But I couldn't lie. Father knew, of course he did; he knew the second he heard the engine and saw my face. I had betrayed him. I dropped my eyes away from them, the pain of the guilt too much to bear, and I stared at the floor scattered with the secrets they had kept hidden from me for so many years, secrets I had ruined without a thought.

I saw my grandmother's feet stride towards me and I looked up. Her face wore an anger that was indescribable, venom I thought no one could ever feel for me. I didn't see her lift her hand, but I felt it across the side of my face, and I felt the floor as I landed in a heap.

I stayed there. My face stinging, the car engine louder, the shuffling of paper around me, the crackle of the fire as it destroyed their memories. My mother's sobs.

What had I done?

I could smell the car's exhaust.

I felt my grandfather's hand on my shoulder, a gentle squeeze, and I was so very scared. And I realised how stupid I'd been. How thoughtless and selfish and naive. Of course I couldn't trust Sook. Of course he would tell his mother. How could I have thought anything else? I wanted to curl up in a ball on the floor and disappear.

The flames destroyed the last of the papers and dwindled low to leave ashes, the delicate remains of destroyed memories, of knowledge and evidence of something I had never even been allowed to share. My father snatched the postcard from me and threw it in the fireplace.

Outside, the engine stopped. I heard the doors open. Heard them slam shut. Heard voices. Deep and male.

"I'm sorry," I whispered. And they all stared at me. All, that was, except my grandfather.

"You should've told her the truth years ago," he said. "They'll take her too. Think what they'll do to her."

My mother turned to me, her eyes raw, tears streaming down her face. Her hand lifted to me and touched my cheek. "Go, Yoora, go quickly and hide. Anywhere you can. Keep away from these men. Don't let them see you."

I stared at her, wishing she would hold me and hug me. "You have to go *now*," she hissed. "Out of the back window."

I stumbled backwards, watching the faces of my family, the pain I had caused with a few thoughtless words in the dark, and I clambered through the back window, pushed it closed and collapsed on to the ground below.

Chapter Twelve

From under the window I heard the shouts of the men as they entered my home, heard my family's quiet replies, but I didn't know where to go, or what to do. Couldn't think where I would be safe or how I could hide. They would know I was missing, come looking for me, hunt me down.

I couldn't go to Sook's house, or to the school, or to a neighbour. Or to a friend, or a colleague of my father's. Nobody would protect me. Nobody would risk their lives for me. I was the only person I could rely on.

But I was scared. So scared. They were going to look out of the window, they were going to find me, they were going to take me away and kill me. And it was all, *all*, my fault.

If only, I thought. A million *if onlys*.

But something took hold of me, some survival instinct or fear, some voice in my head, and forced me to think and to act. There was a gap under the house close to me, a hole that maybe an animal had dug, and I squeezed myself into it, pulling the soft earth around me, smearing it on to my face, scooping up mud and dead leaves and branches on top of me. Surely they wouldn't think I'd hide so close.

I pulled off a shoe, throwing it as far as I could, hoping they'd see it, think I'd lost it when I was running, think I'd gone in that direction.

My heart thudded and pounded in my chest and my arms and my head. Shouting came from inside the house. My grandmother's voice pleading. My mother's crying. Male voices barking, demanding – *Where is your daughter?*

Silence. A scream. A thud. A sob.

What have you been burning? they shouted. And there came no reply.

I was a coward, hiding in the dirt and soil from what I had caused, while my family suffered, protecting me.

Voices shouted about South Korea, about escape, about crimes against our Dear Leader. Threats of re-education through labour, prison camps, trials and execution. I shook with fear, tears stinging my eyes, my vision a blur.

What have I done?

I squeezed my eyes closed, wished I could block out what I could hear. I wanted to scream, run inside and tear them to pieces, shout and spit in their faces. There was nothing, *nothing*, I could do but sit and hide and listen.

Guilt tore through me. And I hated Sook.

With every part of my being, I hated him. With every breath I pulled, I thought of how he had betrayed me. How stupid I had been to trust him. To think he might actually care for me. I could see now how it had all been a trick, an elaborate hoax, a game.

I despised him.

Of course, why else would Min-Jee have let him have the food for me? She'd known all along. He had played me, and I was stupid enough to fall for it. I boiled with anger, at myself and at him. My mother's cries sounded through the walls, and I burrowed further into the hole, wishing I could escape from what I'd caused. I hid like an animal because I was one.

Yet they *were* traitors, just like the boy with the radio,

and they deserved to be punished. That was what I'd been taught for a lifetime.

But they're not bad people, my head screamed, *and I love them so much, and I know they're guilty, punishable in the eyes of our government, but they're my family, they just made a mistake.*

The guards shouted my name again, but no reply came. I heard the door slam, the traipsing of boots, the muttering of soldiers, heard them barge into the neighbours' house, questions shouted, orders given.

I felt terror. Pure, absolute terror.

I heard voices closer, feet nearby, frosty grass crunching underneath them, smelt cigarette smoke and boot leather. I opened my eyes a crack, peering out, watching two men, certain they would spot the whites of my eyes. I drew myself back, hidden so low, so small, that surely, *surely*, they wouldn't think I'd be this close.

Their feet came towards me, and I slowed my breathing, desperate for my thumping heart not to give me away. I could see the cigarette dangling in one man's fingers, the smoke curling outwards, drifting towards me, like it was hunting me down, pointing to where I was hidden. I felt it tickle my nose, irritate the back of my throat.

Don't cough, I told myself. I held my nose, cupped my hands round my mouth. My throat itched, I needed to cough. I watched the men. Watched them... watched them... waiting... waiting.

I heard the man's lips drag on the butt, watched his fingers flick the cigarette to the ground and saw it land in front of me. My throat burned, the cough stuck there, the cigarette smoke pointing me out. I was going to cough, I knew it, and they would hear me, and they would catch me, and we would be gone. All of us. A family stopped in time.

A boot squashed the butt into the ground and I watched the soldier turn, my hands clasped round my mouth as I swallowed and swallowed, and I saw them reach the corner. And I coughed. But they didn't turn. They had seen the shoe.

They walked away and I breathed again.

Chapter Thirteen

I stayed hidden for hours, my brain imagining what my ears thought they could hear – my family taken away, signs hammered into roadsides advertising tomorrow's public trial, soldiers threatening neighbours who might be harbouring me, gossip muttered about what we had done.

I didn't hear Min-Jee, and I didn't hear Sook.

The air grew more chill and I watched the sun set and the village seep into darkness. I emerged from my hiding place after more than twelve hours, my arms and legs creaking and stretching like a spider appearing from a hole.

I felt the eeriness around me as I walked, a million eyes from windows and doors, or behind trees and bushes, or staring down at me from the stars: my neighbours, my friends, our Dear Leader.

Watching.

Waiting.

The dark was my friend, holding me and hiding me, escorting me as I stepped round the block of houses, ducking low under neighbours' windows, hoping that every foot I put down was in silence. The half-moon slipped behind clouds, and with wide eyes, I reached my hands out in front of me, using my instincts and my memory to find my way.

I made it to the front of the houses, feeling along the walls without a sound, my breath measured and controlled. I counted the windows and doors as I moved across, my eyes closed as I concentrated, stopping at the third house along – my house.

Was it my house? Or was I about to open the door on my neighbours? I re-counted the numbers in my head, drew my hands across the wooden door, feeling the splinters, the flakes of paint, the knot in the wood that my fingers recognised – my home. I eased down the handle and stepped inside, closing the door behind me.

I didn't know what I had expected. For my parents to be there? Or my grandparents? Asleep on the mats as they always were, the noise of their breathing, the creaking of the house as it cooled from the fire? There was nothing.

I felt around the room – the table had gone, the chairs too. I edged to the kitchen cupboards, still there, creaked open the doors and put my hand inside – no cups, no plates, no bowls, no food. With my arms outstretched, I went into the other room, dropped down to my knees and crawled across the floor – the beds had gone, the cupboards, everything.

And my family.

All of them.

In the corner of the room I huddled my knees to my chest, making myself as small as possible. I wanted to fade into the walls and disappear into the background. I didn't deserve to be here, alive.

My guilt tore at me while the night drew on. I slipped in and out of sleep, dreams and nightmares haunting me, leading me through questions and scenarios, torturing me with memories I couldn't bear to recall while awake.

And of course I saw that city of my dreams again. The city on the postcard. And again I was walking through it, a lightness about me and a smile on my face. But how could I be happy? That dream, and my stupidity, had caused all of this.

I woke with tears on my cheeks and no breath in my chest.

★

I sat in silence as the sun began to rise again, watching the long shadows withdraw from the floor and a murky light begin to fill the empty house. Too many memories came back to me, and I rested my hands on the walls that had held my childhood and I knew it was all over.

It was no longer my home; my family were no longer there to fill it and never would be again. Soon it would be given to someone else, everything owned by the state, nothing by the individual.

I knew I had to go, and soon, knew if I stayed there, in the house, in the village, I would be found before nightfall. Could be dead by the next morning. *I should've gone earlier*, I thought, *when I could still hide in the dark*.

I stood up and found another pair of shoes: my grandmother's, old and worn and a little tight on my feet, but better than only wearing one. I rooted through cupboards and drawers for food as hunger clawed and growled inside my stomach, but there was nothing.

I can't leave, I thought. *Not without knowing what's going to happen to them*. But in my heart I already knew. Because there was no alternative.

With a sigh, I let my head fall forward and that was when I saw it. A hint of colour in a grey house: the orange of neon, the sparkling white of light, hiding in the fireplace, obscured by ashes. The postcard. I lifted it up, the edges singed and curled, and wiped the dust from it. That was it. I knew it was. That *was* the city in my dream, the lights, the signs, the shops, the people, all there. *But what did it mean?*

I shook my head. I didn't understand. And now there was no one to ask.

I turned the postcard over, the space on the other side filled with scrawled writing, no address, no stamp. I recognised my father's name at the top, but nothing else; I couldn't make out what language it was, couldn't even read what city it was.

But how...?

And all those letters and photographs and magazines and newspapers? All burned. All destroyed. *Where did they come from?* I wanted to ask. *How did they get here?* I crouched down at the fireplace, my hands tearing through the remains of last night's coal and wood, lifting up the burnt paper that disintegrated in my fingertips.

There was nothing left. Nothing, apart from maybe

the envelope I'd seen my mother stuff into her clothes. But where she was, I had no idea.

There was a noise outside: a door opening and closing, footsteps. I paused, clenching the postcard between my fingers and edging towards the window. For a second I saw my neighbour reading a sign posted on a nearby tree, then he turned and I dropped to the floor, my back against the wall, the window above me. I knew what it would be.

"What does it say?" I heard his wife shout from inside. "The trial," he answered, "it's today."

"You think he'll be executed?"

I didn't hear his reply.

Chapter Fourteen

I didn't move.

I stayed crouched under the window while the rest of the village learnt of my family's trial. The news spread quickly, but with little surprise. Everyone had seen it too many times before. Still, it was a spectacle, an event, a change from the monotony of daily life.

I thought about Sook. Over and over again. The first time we met, the conversations we'd had, the food he'd sneaked to me, our walks in darkness, the smile on his face, my hand in his. I thought I'd meant something to him. I thought I could trust him.

How wrong I'd been.

I felt so lost and lonely. So confused. I didn't know what to do or where to go. I wanted to sit and cry. I wanted my mother, or my father, my grandfather, or even my grandmother; for one of them to put their arms round me and hold me tight. Protect me. Whisper in my ear that everything was going to be fine. Even if it wasn't. I wanted to shelter myself in naivety.

But was that what I had been doing for years? Father was right about the city: it was real. And if he was right about that... then what else might he have been right about?

I heard the roar of engines and music, tinny and distorted by a loudspeaker. I came out of my thoughts with a jolt. I didn't need to look out of the window. I knew who it would be: the People's Safety Agency who carried out executions. And behind their car would be an old white van with my family inside, rolling smoothly along the road I had cleaned and swept, then bouncing along the rugged paths into the village. Paths I had walked along with Sook.

I put my head down and closed my eyes, but the music droned on, louder and louder, and more and more distorted from the loudspeaker attached to the side, the words discernible only because they had been pumped into my head since birth:

"Our future and hope depend on you
The People's fate depends on you
Comrade Kim Jong Il!
We are unable to live without you! Our country
is unable to survive without you…"

I whispered the words along with the high-pitched voices screeching over the village, and when the song finished I looked out of the window, and I saw them lining up on a hill near the fields. I squinted through the glass, watching the children running towards them, the adults dropping their tools to the ground or herding their animals into a pen before walking over.

My father was taken from the van, his hands behind his back, my grandparents too. I searched through the crowds, over the vehicles – where was my mother?

I had to get out, I had to watch. I owed it to them. I wanted to see their faces one last time, wished I could catch their eye, tell them that I was so, so sorry. I wished I could do something. Help them. Stop this. Save them.

My chest burned, my head throbbed, my stomach rose and dropped with sickness and panic. I paced back and forth in silence, rubbing my head, my breath shallow. *What can I do? What can I do? What can I do?*

I just wanted it to stop. My face was wet with silent tears of pain and anguish and hatred at myself and at Sook. I wanted to shout at him and hit him — shout out, *What have you done?* But it was me. It was my fault. My family were going to die and it was my fault.

I stopped and I breathed. And my dizziness passed.

They can't execute them, can they? Surely they don't deserve to die?

But it wasn't only the crime that mattered, and I knew that; it was your standing, your social class, if your life mattered to anyone important. Ours didn't.

I wiped away my tears and climbed out of the window again, dodging along the backs of the houses in our row, moving up and towards the site of the trial, keeping low, hidden from windows, even though by now everyone in the village should've been gathered to learn my family's fate. To cheer, as was expected, when they were announced guilty, as everybody always was; to watch them die, if execution was the punishment.

I dashed from the houses, across a gap to the public toilets, remembering the first time I met Sook. I reached the end, peering out from behind the wall, the crowd of people with their backs to me, soldiers standing around, watching.

Are they looking for me? Would they recognise me this far away?

One of them glanced my way, a rifle in his hands, and I waited, watching his head pan across the countryside. As he turned the other way, I walked out, my eyes flitting from one soldier to another, to another, and back. I made it to the greenhouses and I remembered crouching outside them with Sook, the night we held hands, the night I opened my mouth and betrayed my family. I felt sadness pour through me, the disappointment of realising it hadn't been even a friendship.

I reached the end of the greenhouses, skirted along the side and ran, heading for a bank to the side of where everyone was gathered. I threw myself down, hidden again, rolled over on to my stomach and crawled to the top, peering through a clump of dead grass.

The village children sat together at the front, a good view, chattering and pointing, excited, all with their school uniforms on of blue skirts and white shirts, red scarves tied round their necks to show their allegiance to our Dear Leader. The adults stood behind them, their faces drawn and quiet, their blank eyes betraying no thoughts or opinions as they took everything in, a reminder of the eyes and ears of so many being ever-present in every place. Of suspicion ruling with an invisible force.

I peered through the grass, squinting against the bright winter morning at the faces of my family, trying to will them to turn round, to see me. My grandmother so small and frail, my father with his hands tied behind his back, my grandfather with his head still held high. But no Mother.

The wind took away most of the soldier's words as he began to speak and I heard only the briefest snatches about anti-state crimes, plotting against our Dear Leader and mutterings of guilt as he turned to the crowd.

I didn't see any evidence given or witnesses heard. Didn't hear any defence or see a judge or a jury. Because there were none. He asked the crowd for their judgement and they shouted their replies, and although tainted with self-preservation, I knew they were right.

They gave my family's sentence of guilt.

They gave my father's sentence of death.

Chapter Fifteen

I knew what was coming, had seen it before, had sat at the front as a child and cheered, knowing it to be deserved.

But this was my father. A good man. Who wished nobody any harm. Who worked hard. Who loved us and cared for us. But...

Ever since that dream and that night and that conversation outside, there had been this *but*. He had shown me another side to him and I didn't understand how the two could exist together.

I peered across the field, watching the people. My chest was empty, my lungs burned, my stomach clenched; I tried to gasp in breath that wouldn't come. My eyes stung with hot tears, my head spun, the world, my world, turned and tilted in front of me.

This dreadful thing, this terrible thing. And all because of what I had said, and all because of Sook.

I hated him. *Hated, hated, hated* him. And I hated myself. *Why did I tell him?* my head screamed. *Why did I say anything? Why did I trust him?* I wanted to kill him, I wanted him dead. I wanted him to suffer, I wanted him to feel the pain that I was feeling for him betraying the trust I had given him.

I saw him in the crowd and watched him, my stomach turning over and over, my teeth grinding, my fists clenching with rage. I wished I had a gun, or a knife, or a rope to show him how angry I was and how much I hated every single piece of him now. I was a fool to think I had loved him, a fool to think he could have felt anything for me.

I shook and sobbed as I stared down at the scene in front of me. My grandmother crying as the soldiers carried a wooden post from the van, standing it up on end, hammering it into the ground. I closed my eyes as they forced my father to undress, embarrassed for him, but I heard the crowd's jeers and taunts, and when I looked again he was pulling on a thick grey one-piece suit, and I remembered what my grandfather had told me when we watched the last execution. "The suit soaks up the blood," he said. "Straight into the fabric. Makes it easier for the guards to clean up after."

My father's blood this time.

I watched them lead him to the post and I wanted to scream out at them to stop. I watched them tie him to it, a rope round his legs, one round his chest, and I wanted to run to him and throw my arms round him, tell him that I was so very, very sorry, that I wished I could take it all back, and that I loved him so very much.

At his feet they placed a large bag. Then three soldiers stepped back, loading their rifles, taking position, staring down the sights towards my father. Who had held me as a baby and clapped when I first walked, who cuddled me when I was ill and talked me through bad dreams. Whose hand held mine on the way to school and whose smile made me feel loved and wanted and needed.

Whose death I'd caused.

I didn't want to see this, what was to happen to him, didn't want to remember it. But I couldn't close my eyes, I couldn't look away.

The man in charge of the soldiers turned to the crowd. "You will witness how miserable fools end up," he shouted. "Traitors who betray the nation and its people end up like this." He looked to his men. "Ready your weapons!" he told them, and they lifted their guns to their shoulders.

"Aim at the enemy!"

They squinted their eyes down the sights. My father stood resolute, tall and dignified, not a word, not a cry, not a sound. I loved him.

"Single shot! Fire!"

The shots rang out as one, tearing into the ropes round his chest. I flung my hand over my mouth, stopping myself from crying out. Shaking and trembling. I could hear my grandmother, see my grandfather holding on to her, grief flooding them.

"*Now* he bows to us!" the man shouted as my father's body bent over, the ropes round his legs still forcing him upright.

"Fire!" he shouted again, and they shot at my father's head, the bag underneath positioned to catch everything.

It was too much; I swayed back and forth, rubbing my hands over my head, through my hair, my fingers clenching and unclenching, my anger and shock and disbelief clawing inside me like an animal trying to escape. I stood up. I didn't care any more. I didn't care what he was guilty of. He was my father and I loved him.

I wished I could've spoken to him before this, could've said sorry. Wished I could've told him for the first time, and the last, that I loved him, that he meant the world to me, that I was so proud of him, so proud to be his daughter. All those things I had never, never said, and now he would never know. My body shook and tears streamed down my face.

I couldn't look at him, couldn't look away, couldn't sit again to hide, couldn't move. I glanced at my grandfather and he caught my eye. And I watched him very slowly and very deliberately move his head from one side to the other.

But the words came again, and on the word 'Fire', the ropes at my father's legs were broken and he fell, limp and lifeless, into the bag at his feet.

My lungs and my chest emptied as I shouted out my anger from the top of the hill, my words, that I can't even remember, carrying across the villagers and the soldiers and the body of my father and my grandparents until I had nothing left inside me.

Everybody stopped and everybody turned and silence fell over all of us.

Out of all the people in the village, my eyes fell on Sook, and I watched the leer on his face slip as he saw me. I hoped he could feel my hatred pouring out to him as we stared at each other.

That face. That face I'd imagined in darkness so many nights, that I could recognise in bleary moonlight, that had given me dreams to wish for. *How could I have been so wrong?* I thought.

Mutterings gathered, the babble of children, the bark of an order, but it was all background noise to whatever was passing between me and Sook. But then I heard it, the one voice shouting to me. "Run!"

I turned and saw Grandfather on his feet. "Run!" he shouted again, and I shot a glance from him to the soldiers reloading their guns, to my father's body, and back to Sook.

And I ran.

With fire in my belly, and fear in my heart, I ran.

With my legs driving and pumping forward and forward, I ran. Down the back of the hill and over the grass, across the fields and towards the school. Shouting echoing behind me. My feet pounding on the dirt road, my lungs screaming at me to stop.

I ran past the greenhouses, a shot ringing out, shattering the glass at my side as it missed me. I tried to speed up. Didn't know where I was going apart from forward and away. Behind me I could hear the thudding of heavy boots, shouts of stop. But I carried on and on, my lungs burning, my feet stumbling on ruts and lumps in the path.

I ran.

I heard the bang of a gun again and I screamed, but felt no pain and knew it had missed. I was tiring, no energy in my legs of lead, no air in my lungs. I tripped and stumbled, staggered, fell to the ground. I tried to scramble away, the sound of feet closing in on me, tried to pull myself up. But something grabbed my leg and pulled me backwards, my skirt rolling up as I clung and struggled and clawed and kicked and screamed and shouted. Desperate to get away.

He spun me over on to my back and put his boot on my chest, and I looked up at him, the rays of the sun coming out from behind his head, like a poster of our Dear Leader, Kim Jong Il. But the brightness obscured his face into shadow, and I could barely see him, and for only a fraction of a second did I see the butt of his gun lift above my head.

Chapter Sixteen

"Where are we?" My voice was strained, my throat sore, my lips dry and cracked. A pain throbbed in my head and lights flashed behind my closed eyelids.

"Ssshhh, child," my grandfather's voice replied, and I felt the rough skin of his hand brush hair from my face. "Keep your eyes closed and rest."

I felt tired and confused, could feel a blanket wrapped round me, the rough fibres rubbing on my cheek, could smell exhaust fumes, sense the moving air, knew we were moving as my body jostled back and forth, and bumped up and down and an engine grumbled underneath me.

We're on the back of a truck, I thought.

My body ached and groaned at me as I tried to remember what had happened, and I moved my hand up to my head, felt a lump, bruised and tender. I winced in pain.

"It's good to see you awake," Grandfather whispered, taking my hand and stroking it. I curled up against him like a baby, my head lifting up and down on his chest as he breathed, slowly blinking my eyes open.

"What happened?" I asked.

I felt him shrug. "You were unconscious when he dragged you back."

"Grandmother?" I asked.

"She's here. She's next to me."

I waited for her to speak, but nothing came.

"And... and Mother?" I breathed.

I felt my grandfather's sigh. "She's been sent to Chongyong in the north, near the Chinese border. She has to divorce your father, and she can't have anything to do with you ever again. Or me. Or your grandmother. Your father took all the blame for what happened. He said it was all his doing, so your mother wouldn't be punished because she doesn't share his blood. Not like us. He couldn't do anything to protect us. Three generations. You know that." He paused and glanced down at me. "We were going to leave, Yoora," he whispered. "In a few weeks. Everything was ready. Planned."

So Sook was right, I thought.

"You were traitors," I breathed.

The sadness in his eyes was painful to see. "Only to you," he replied.

I turned my cheek into him, his warmth giving some comfort, his arms round me now, his fingers stroking through my hair. I didn't understand how he could bear to be close to me; I had caused his son to be killed. I had ruined his life.

"I'm sorry," I whispered.

He wiped away my tear. "So am I," he said.

I peered through my sore, swollen eyes to the blue sky above us, watching the clouds form and re-form, a tree branch wave, a bird flap its wings in freedom.

Freedom, I thought. *To be able to cross a border, to be able to choose. Choose where to live, or what job to do. Choose what books to read, TV stations to watch, radio to listen to. Or even choose words to question, or argue, or debate, or just to think with.*

Next to me Grandfather jostled me, moving his arm and reaching into his pocket, and I heard something crinkle and blinked away the blurriness as he held it in front of me.

It was the postcard, creased and charred with singed

edges and smelling of smoke. "This was in your pocket when you came back," he said.

I nodded. "I found it in our house last night. I wanted to keep it." I took it from him. "I dreamt about it," I told him. "I was there, in my dream, but it was so real." I ran my fingers over the lines of light, and the cars in the street.

"You know where it is?" Grandfather asked. I glanced up at his face and shook my head.

"It's Seoul," he said. "In South Korea."

I frowned. "South Korea isn't like that," I whispered. "Our Dear Leader told us. Nowhere is better than here, he said." Grandfather said nothing in reply, only looked at me.

I thought of my hunger, my cold house with ice on the windows, my neighbours' child who'd died, my father and my mother who I would never see again. I thought of how hard we all worked, how little we all smiled, and I looked up at my grandfather's face, so tired, so drawn, then down to the postcard. And I thought of Father's words.

"But... but I've never been there... How could it have got into my head?"

"Another time," Grandfather whispered. "When

you're rested." Kindness spilt from him as he wiped a tear from my cheek and tried to smile.

Seoul? Really? I thought. *A different country? A place better than here? But that's not what we were taught. Yet I can see it, here in front of me, this postcard, this place, and I can remember my dream so vividly. How can it not be real?* I questioned.

I held the postcard tight between my fingers, a piece of hope, a link to the outside world. A clue to the truth. I wished it might be a flash of a future that could possibly be mine. But how could it be now?

I watched the trees speeding past us, the countryside stretching away, towards whatever waited for us.

The only future before me now.

*

Hours passed slowly on the back of the truck, and the sky turned from the fresh, bright blue of the winter cold to orange and reds streaking across the horizon like bloodstains, to shades of grey, muting everything, making everything indistinct. We turned on to a smaller road, bumpy and potted, and the trees became denser and the air stiller, and I felt trepidation creeping through me.

I could feel something. Something in the air, in the stillness. A foreboding. A dread. A sadness.

"The Pass of Tears," Grandfather whispered. "The last stretch of road before the prison camp."

I struggled to my knees, ignoring my cuts and bruises and aches and pains, and shuffled around, leaning over the side of the truck to see the road ahead of us. The truck rattled over a narrow wooden bridge and I peered down and over the edge; a moat or a ditch briefly passed underneath us, a little water just visible at the bottom, dark and murky with weeds clogging the sides. And something long and thin, shining and glinting, sticking up into the air, lots of them, following the length of the ditch for as far as I could see.

Metal spikes.

My eyes automatically flashed to my grandfather – he had seen them too. "To stop people trying to escape," he whispered, then turned away from me as if trying to hide his fear, his resignation to the life, and the death, waiting for us.

I looked back again to the entrance that was now so close: a fence stretching away for miles on each side of us, no end in sight, the top at least two and a half metres high, electricity signs near it. A grey concrete building stood hard and angular and box-like;

a flat-topped watchtower next to it with two guards, both with guns slung over shoulders, and narrow eyes staring down at us.

Waiting for us to pass under, marking our arrival, was a gateway, a concrete pillar at either side, a slab across the top like a gravestone. I whispered the words carved into it – "Give up your life for the sake of Our Leader Kim Jong Il" – and I shivered.

My grandmother glanced at me for the first time since the execution, and the hatred in her eyes, her disgust for me, was frightening. But I understood why. And I didn't blame her. This, that waited for us now, and her son's death, her only child's death, were all my fault. And there was no way I could change any of it.

"Grandfather?" I whispered, looking up into his dark eyes, which I knew would never hate me. "Will we come out again?"

He didn't say a word. I watched his eyes fill with tears as he looked down at me, and I heard him swallow hard and felt his first tear fall on me. "One day at a time, Yoora. One step at a time. One foot in front of the other and maybe. Just maybe."

There was no reply I could give, or words I could say, no amount of apologies I could mutter that would make any difference.

I nodded and I took his hand.

Chapter Seventeen

I pulled a blanket up and round me, peering out from inside as the truck drove us further and further into the camp, as the gates and the fence and the watchtower and the world beyond withdrew and dwindled and finally disappeared.

A memory.

We passed guards with uniforms similar to those of the People's Army, the dark green of old moss, black boots still shiny despite the mud and brown belts pulled in at small waists. Their backs were straight like ramrods and their faces stern and harsh with expressions unchanging.

We passed rows and rows of huts, piles of soil or stones, dilapidated shacks and large brick buildings. Farmland and felled trees, office buildings and a factory, a school and a coal mine. The prison stretched on and on and on. It was huge and sprawling; as big as a town, no, bigger, bigger than a city, but it was a prison camp, and the atmosphere that hung over everything was the quiet stillness of dread and fear and control.

A chill went through to my bones.

The truck slowed near a group of wooden huts and when I saw the people by them my hand reached for Grandfather, searching his face, then my grandmother's, the shock so clear in their eyes, the same shock that was running through my body and pounding at my head.

These people were skeletons. Their arms and legs like sticks, their bones jutting out from their skin, their clothes threadbare rags hanging off them, their hair matted thick with dirt or falling out in clumps. I saw a woman with her lower arm missing, a boy with only three fingers on one hand, a man hunchbacked, hobbling across the rugged earth.

These weren't people – they were monsters.

I couldn't stop my mouth from gaping or my eyes from staring wide, and I clambered from the back of the truck with my whole body shaking with fear of these creatures.

A woman, of what age I couldn't tell, lurched up to me, sores and purple blotches on her face and scabs and cuts on her hands, and she leant into me with her breath pungent and stale. "We all looked like you when we arrived. It doesn't take long," she muttered. "Three months and you'll be just like us."

I turned away, disgusted and shocked. I wanted to run, to hide, to escape – or just to wake up from this nightmare. But there was no waking. This was reality.

I looked back at the people, the monsters, as they watched us new arrivals, leering at us, asking where we were from, if we knew their relatives or friends, if we had any news from outside, if anything had changed. But I couldn't look at their faces, their hollow, sucked-in cheeks, their eyes deep in their sockets, staring out at us with a mixture of curiosity and blankness. They were my horror and my terror and my fear. Yet one word from a guard and they were gone, scattering like dry leaves on a gust of wind. I thought of the boy from school, the one with the radio, wondering if he ended up in a place like this, and if he was still alive.

I wondered if he did deserve it. And I hoped somebody other than me *had* reported him.

The guards pointed their guns at us and we lifted

down the two boxes of our belongings from the back of the truck – cups and plates and pots that Mother or Father or someone had packed from the house – and they ushered us away from the path and towards a group of huts.

As I walked, my eyes flitted around, taking everything in: the mountains flanking us, snow dusting the tops, the banks of trees leading up them, the barren earth at my feet, the camp stretching out in every direction, and that terrible feeling draped over everything, of quietness with no calm. Stillness and emptiness. Trepidation and danger.

I didn't feel like the adult I nearly was; instead I was a child again, naive and weak and useless. My guilt tore away any maturity I thought I had.

The guard led us to a wooden hut. "This is where you live," he said. "The other huts around here make up your work unit. You attend roll call at six in the morning, where you are instructed as to your day's duty. You work until six at night when there is another roll call. You work seven days a week. There are no holidays.

"You and you," he pointed to me and Grandfather, "your ration is five hundred grams of corn as you will be working, the old woman gets four hundred and will be in charge of preparing food. Outside your hut is a small piece of earth where you can grow vegetables.

"You are lucky," he continued, as he opened the door to the hut. "The furniture from the previous family has been left, and the bedding. Otherwise you would have had nothing." He paused for a moment, and I took a step into the hut.

"What happened to them?" I whispered.

Without a breath, he strode across to me, and before I'd even thought to move, he'd hit me across the face. My cheek stung, and I wanted so much to cry, but I stood firm, with my face fixed and my eyes blinking away tears that I would not let fall.

"Someone from your work unit will be along with your corn," he said, then left.

I felt my grandfather's arm going round me, and his slender hand on my face.

"I don't know how we're going to keep warm in here," my grandmother said. "Look at the roof – you can see the sky through the planks of wood. And the walls and the floors," she continued, "they're just mud."

"I'm sorry," I whispered to my grandfather.

"No more, Yoora," he breathed.

"And how do I light this fire? We have no matches. How will we keep warm tonight? What about our clothes? We didn't bring any of our clothes!"

Panic lifted in her voice and Grandfather took her in his arms and held her, stroking her greying hair away from her face, whispering in her ear words of comfort private to them. I turned away.

He was an old man, his hair and his body worn thin from years of work and worry, whose care now, according to our custom, should have been the responsibility of his son.

But I had killed his son.

We stared round at our new home: one room, like a shed, with dirty bedding strewn across a few mats on the floor, an empty furnace to one side with no coal or matches or wood to burn, a table with a few chairs, a chest of drawers and a cupboard. The air was cold and icy and stale from whoever had been here before.

The morning, waking in my home, seeing that leer on Sook's face, watching my father being shot, running away from the guards, felt like such a long time ago, and now darkness and gloom and shadows stretched over us and swallowed us whole, weighing down heavy on our thin shoulders.

Grandfather pulled a cord and a bare light bulb hanging from the middle of the low ceiling flickered a dim light, casting ghosts of shadows around us and bags under our eyes as if we were already skeletons.

We just stood, without a word, in shock maybe, and I felt the freezing wind blowing through the gaps in the roof and the door, ice reaching into me and shaking me from the inside. I had never known cold like it.

"We'll sleep together," said Grandfather. "Keep each other warm."

I heard footsteps in front of the hut and stopped moving, stopped breathing even, tried to stop trembling so I could listen. I hoped it wasn't the guard coming back, and visions flashed in my head of guns and sticks and fists.

The door creaked open and a face that looked older than Grandmother's appeared. "I'm from your work unit. I've brought your corn."

I breathed again as she stepped into the hut and we all watched her as she headed to the furnace. "I've brought you some wood too, but you'll have to find me some more in return – I can't give it away. Here," she said to Grandmother and bent down. "I'll show you how to light the fire without matches and how to keep the flame burning. And how to prepare food using the furnace. There are no cookers anywhere."

The wood began to pop and burn and I sat down in front of it, rubbing life back into my cold hands, feeling the heat from the flame on my sore skin, and watching it dance and flicker on the walls of mud.

The woman looked old, thin and drained, but said she was in her forties. "I've been here ten years, but ten years in here ages you like thirty out there. I'm lucky to be alive, but I will die in here."

She didn't ask why we were there, or offer her story — she was abrupt to the point of rudeness, but she'd survived for ten years. "I took some of your corn," she added, pouring some of what was left into a tin with water and placing it on the furnace. "In payment for helping you."

My surprise must've shown on my face because she opened her eyes as wide as they seemed able to go and glared at me. "I'm not here to make friends. Not enemies either though — there are enough people in here who would accuse you of anything to save themselves, or to earn favour with the guards, or to get a bit of extra food. That's not me. I was a nurse before, but in here I don't do anything for nothing. Nobody does. Keep your head down and do as you're told and you might survive long enough to get ill enough to die."

We all stared at her.

"Does anyone ever escape?" My words were quiet.

She huffed, shaking her head, moving towards me and leaning close, her missing teeth obvious now, as were the pits and scars on her skin, and her thinning hair. "You'd have to be crazy to try it. The fence is electrified, and even if you dare touch it, sirens go off, and the dogs come out, and the guns. On the other side of the fence is a ditch that runs all the way round, wide and deep. And at the bottom of the ditch? Spikes stick up. You don't jump far enough..." She shrugged. "There are guard posts at intervals around the camp, lookout towers too and there are roll calls twice a day. And even if, *even if* you managed to avoid the guards and the towers and get through the fence and over the ditch, where then? You seen the mountains? You going to get over them?"

She shook her head. "You know what happens if you're caught?" she continued. "You're executed – shot or hung. I've never known anyone get out alive. No, you'd have to be crazy to try." She stood up to leave. "Mind you," she said, stopping and turning round to face us all, "a few months in here and you'll be crazy anyway." And I'm sure I saw the ghost of a smile flicker across her lips.

Chapter Eighteen

We spent a cold night shivering under blankets left by the family before us – blankets that smelt of rot and decay and death. I could imagine their bodies around me and over me; I could imagine them breathing.

Maybe their last breaths.

Maybe they died under those blankets and I was breathing in their suffering and their disease.

Are there lice in here? I thought. *Fleas that sucked on their blood before ours? How many families were in here before them? How many will be after us?*

But in the side of the mat I found a hole, and I slipped the postcard inside. My hope, my secret, that I wanted to keep safe.

★

The following morning we ate our breakfast of cornmeal, not enough to take away the hunger, and headed over for roll call with the rest of our 'village', our status as new arrivals turning heads and attracting stares. I wondered whether they were curious about what had happened to us, or just curious as to whether we had any food to barter with, perhaps for information or tips about survival.

We answered our names, we heard the others, voices pale and quiet in the expanse around us, and we changed into the uniforms we were given – deep purple, itchy fabric, heavy on our bodies and chafing at our legs and arms. I tried not to react when Grandfather was told he would be working in the coal mine, or when I was told to head up the mountain to help with logging and felling trees.

I watched Grandmother turn back to our hut, a bucket she had been given to collect water hanging from one hand, the clothes we had just taken off, in the other, her head hanging low, her feet shuffling along the frozen ground.

It was clear from the explanation given at roll call that Grandmother's life was going to be hard, even though she had not been given a job. She would have to walk half an hour to the stream, break the ice if it was frozen, fill the bucket with water and walk back again. Then repeat the whole thing. And again. She would have to climb into the mountains to look for something edible to bulk out our rations, or we would simply not survive. The bark from trees perhaps, leaves that weren't poisonous yet still alive in winter, half-dormant insects, herbs that could be added to the corn.

But, as I looked up at the hills around us, I could see that so much of the mountainside was already bare. How many people in this camp had already stripped what they could from the ground and the trees and the wildlife? Higher up there were banks of frosted green, but that was a long way, a steep climb, and I doubted my grandmother would be able to manage that far. She was old and frail, and I watched her tiny frame struggle off into the distance, and I felt pity for her.

Grandfather watched her too and I could see in his eyes the same guilt I had in my heart. But why he felt like that, I had no idea.

The only two words I could offer him – I'm sorry – I'd said too much already and the words couldn't change anything, not even my guilt. I turned and headed to my work detail with a handful of other prisoners, hoping I would still be alive in twelve hours to see Grandfather and Grandmother again, hoping they too would survive.

I shut off and shut down as I walked, not worrying about Grandmother clambering along the mountainside in the freezing cold, or about Grandfather shut in the mine with so little air, or about how old and frail and weak they both were.

Because that would make it harder.

Instead I thought only of one step at a time, as Grandfather had said, and one log at a time, and one minute at a time, and somehow, with arms of lead and legs I could barely move, the end of the day arrived, and somehow I made it back to our hut.

And somehow so did they.

★

We sat in silence round the table that had been pulled up close to the furnace, the wind whistling through the holes in the door and the cold leaking down through the gaps in the roof. We pulled blankets round our shoulders as we spooned cornmeal into our mouths, into stomachs that wanted, and needed, much, much more.

Twelve hours' hard labour. No break. No rest. No lunch. I was cold and tired and hungry, and the reality of what our lives had become hit me hard. I could see Grandfather's head nodding as he fought sleep long enough to eat, but I didn't dare look into his face. I wanted to cry. I wanted someone to save me. I wanted to wake up and be back at home, looking into my father's eyes as he asked me if I'd had a bad dream.

"Yes," I would say. "The worst. You weren't there. And it was my fault. It was all my fault." I would just be able to make out his smile in the moonlight, and I would feel his fingers on my cheek as he told me it was only a dream. Only a dream.

And when I woke it would be the morning of the day I first met Sook, and I would go to do my chores, and after I'd shown him where to take the night soil, I wouldn't take the bun from him. I would never agree to meet him. I would never walk with him in the darkness. I would never smile at him or hold his hand or look into his eyes that I thought had cared for me.

I would never, never fall in love with him.

And I would never, never trust him.

My spoon scraped the bottom of the tin that was empty of cornmeal too soon. I hated cornmeal. Even the soup Mother had cooked at home was better than this.

"I wonder what Mother's doing now," I whispered without thinking.

"I'm surprised you care," Grandmother hissed back to me.

I felt my cheeks burning and wished I hadn't said anything. "Of course I care," I replied, keeping my eyes away from her. "I didn't mean for this to happen."

"No. You were just thoughtless. Even after I'd told you to stay away. You knew who his mother was. You knew the dangers. *Why* did you tell him? How could you have possibly thought that he wouldn't tell his mother?"

Her anger bore down on me, but I didn't say a word.

"Everything now is because of you. Your stupidity and selfishness. Why my son's dead. Why we're stuck in here. And will die in here."

"But... I didn't... I only..." I sighed. "I told him about that place in my dream. I thought it was Pyongyang, but he said it couldn't be because he used to live there, but in my dream..."

"Dream," she scoffed. "How do you think all that stuff got inside your head? It wasn't some *vision* of some future. It was stuck in your memory from all the letters and postcards, and the stories your grandfather used to tell you. It's his fault too. Him and his ideas and decisions."

I saw my grandfather look up, saw his mouth open to speak, to defend himself perhaps, then he closed it again and his gaze drifted away.

"What?" I asked Grandmother. "What are you talking about?"

She leant towards me. "I made him stop telling you. I told him you wouldn't be able to keep a secret. And I was right."

"But—"

"He should never have told you anything. It's all stayed in your head all that time and then come flooding out like that."

I rubbed my hands across my face, over my forehead and my eyes. My head was buzzing, tiredness blurring everything, nothing making sense to me. "I don't know what you're talking about," I repeated.

She pushed her bowl away and leant towards me, her voice low, her eyes blazing into mine. "The crime they accused your father of, that he was planning an escape – they said they knew all about it from Sook's mother, the woman I told you to keep away from. You know about *that*? She could only have learnt it from you; from you telling her son."

I shook my head. "But... but I didn't tell him that. He just thought it because... because..." I couldn't think straight, couldn't remember exactly what I had said to Sook. I didn't want to argue, didn't have the strength or the will. I didn't need any more guilt, or to carry any more blame. I wanted to ask about the letters, what they were burning that morning, what she meant about the things Grandfather had told me when I was younger. But I didn't.

"I loved him," I whispered, and I saw her, from the corner of my eye, standing over me, overbearing and overpowering, shaking her head, then turning to her husband.

"Love gets you nowhere," she hissed. "Believe me."

Her words were low and cold and they hung in the air and over me and Grandfather, and I watched his hands pull back from the table and his fingers curl inside his palm. I heard the gentle sigh of his breath and saw the shadow of his head as it tipped forward.

★

I had loved Sook.

As I tried to sleep that night, our second night at

the camp, his face loomed up behind my closed eyelids, and I saw his smile, felt his warmth and listened to his voice as he spoke to me on those nights as we walked. But I pushed them out and I tried to forget them, and in my head instead I watched his leering grin at my family's trial, heard the shooting of the guns that killed my father, remembered my mother's arms around me.

I hate him, I told myself. *And if I ever get out of here, I will find him. And I will track him down, and I will take a knife, and I will kill him.*

Because yes, it was my fault, my stupidity and naivety and some romantic notion that hid inside me, but I wouldn't be killing him for me. I would live with my guilt and my anger.

It would be for my family.

Chapter Nineteen

I wished I could take the thought of him out of my head. Wished I could stop the conversations we'd had and decisions I'd made from replaying over and over in my mind.

For days it didn't stop, not as I pulled at logs and branches and my fingers began to blister, or as I clambered up the mountainside with my legs aching and my muscles screaming. And I'd cringe at myself for things I'd said, torturing myself as memories, still so fresh, came again and again, of the last morning at home, my father's expression when he realised I'd betrayed him, my mother's voice as she told me to run and hide.

And even though by the end of the day I was so tired I could barely lift a hand or keep my eyes open, and my body screamed at me for rest, my mind would repeat it all, and sleep would stay far from me.

In those first few long, tired nights, when everything was still new and daunting and strange and shocking, and despite the thousands of people in huts and buildings around me suffering just as I was, I felt so isolated and so alone, and the only way I could stop my anger and frustration for long enough to fall asleep was to imagine myself killing him. To see the glint of the blade in my hand, the look of pain spreading across his face, his eyes growing dim, growing heavy. Hear the words I whispered to him, the last words he would ever hear – *That's for my family.*

So many times I thought it, imagined it, that when finally sleep did take me it sneaked into my dreams too, but playing tricks on me, and as I said those words and looked down at the blood on my hands and seeping through his clothes, and the light in his eyes turning dim, I felt nothing but sadness, a terrible draining sadness, and I watched as he shook his head, and I listened as he whispered back to me – *But I love you.*

I woke, sitting bolt upright, covered in sweat and staring at my hands, rubbing them together to make sure they were clean. And I felt so ashamed and so full of guilt and confusion.

In silence I cried for everything I'd lost, and everything I'd caused. And I waited for the sharpness of that pain to dull, and the clarity of that memory to fade.

★

Through trees showing the first buds of spring on their branches, and over grasses looking a little greener, we struggled up the hillside, a herd of us, my work unit, silent but for our heavy breathing and our trudging feet.

Time, I realised, was disappearing around me, days blending into one another. So quickly, I realised, years would pass, and how easy it would be to forget how long I had been there, how much older I had become, how I had had, before this, a home that was decent, if sparse, a mother who loved me and a boy who lit up my world with his smile.

And how easily it had gone.

My arms ached and my legs were heavy. My back creaked and my fingers clicked. I could move, though barely, but I carried on because I had to. Because exhaustion or hunger or pain were no excuses. There *were* no excuses. How quickly would the day pass? But then there would be another. And another. And another.

I stepped forward one step, and again, and I thought about the people around me, what they had done, how long they had been here, what names they had, what they were thinking then, at that very moment. If they were thinking at all.

I watched their feet shuffle in their split shoes and worn-out boots, one or two barefoot, and I lifted my eyes, though not my head, to look at the girl to my side, her uniform old and torn, the arms too short, the legs frayed and with holes at the knees. I looked at her face, her skin stretched over her bones, her hair a tangled mess. I looked to the next person and the next and the next: they were all empty, their humanity, their personality, their heart and warmth and their very being missing.

All obeying because there was no choice. Because if you didn't, you would be tortured or beaten. Unless you were released. But this was so unheard of, so rare, it was like a myth.

Much less rare was death. I wondered how welcome its arrival would be, if it came for me.

The girl next to me glanced my way, then back again, ignoring me. I wished I could talk to her, ask her questions, find out more about life here, what you could do, what you couldn't, how to find extra food, how to keep warm, which guards were worse, how to live, how to survive.

But I knew that behind me was the guard, listening and waiting maybe for a chance to prove he was in charge, that him we had to obey. What if he heard me talking? What would he do? Would it hurt, his punishment? Would I make it back to the hut? See my grandparents again?

I glanced back at the girl and took a breath. "How long have you been here?" I whispered.

Her eyes shot to me for a second, her face tense and stern, warning me without a word, and from the corner of my vision I saw the guard marching towards me, lifting his gun, pointing the muzzle towards me, resting his finger on the trigger.

I dropped my head back down, waiting for the bang, staring at my feet, waiting for the pain, my face burning, my heart racing, waiting to fall to the ground, for blackness to cover me. His footsteps came closer, his breathing louder as he neared me, and I felt the gun jab me in the shoulder. But there was no bang.

"No talking," he barked.

Was this truly fear? Every second of every day living in the anticipation of pain and suffering and death?

I could feel the guard, right behind me, his breath on my neck, his eyes boring holes into me. I wanted to slow down, to look around or up, to stop, or to shout at him. Instead my eyes focused on the ground and my feet kept their rhythm. Because I didn't want to know what he would do, because obedience was hard but less painful, because survival was my instinct and so rebellion was no option.

And so throughout the day, the hard, physical, demanding labour, I spoke to no one. I chopped down trees with an axe so blunt it was rusting without saying a word. I stripped branches from trees with hands sore and split, not making a sound. I sawed up wood and carted it, blisters cracking open on my palms, back down the mountain, with not a moan or a gasp, a cry or a complaint.

I was too scared, not just of the guards, but of saying something in the wrong tone, or in the wrong way. That the other prisoners, whoever they were, would hate me or judge me or ridicule me. Report me. And while I wanted a friend or an acquaintance to be able to talk to and ask questions, I didn't want to owe anybody even a smile.

I would do my work and I would go back to the

hut. As I would the next day and the next. For as long as it took. Whatever *it* was.

At the bottom of the mountain I dropped my pile of wood and, trying to forget my shoes rubbing on my ankles and squeezing at my toes, began the walk back up again, realising as I stared off into the distance, that the treeline would be for ever receding the more we chopped down, that the walk would lengthen and lengthen as the months stretched by.

I was thinking of the wood when I heard it, the shout. I was wondering, in my head, what happened to all the wood because it certainly wasn't to keep us, the prisoners, warm, when I heard the scream that followed. My stomach turned and my step, for a second, paused in the air; then my feet carried on, back to the trees, and towards the shouting.

I didn't want to know what was happening. Not to see it or hear it or let it into my dreams to wake me through the night. But as I neared, as I went to collect my axe from the ground, it was in front of me and no matter how I tried, I couldn't move away.

The boy. So small. Younger than me and smaller than me. Skinnier, bonier and weaker. His arms trying to lift a log that was so big and so heavy; the skin where his muscles should've been stretching and tautening; his face grimacing as he struggled in pain and frustration. And fear.

The guard stood over him, shouting in his ear. "You're lazy. You're weak. A disgrace to our country. Kim Jong Il and His father before Him have given you so much and this is how you repay Them."

The first blow hit and I froze. That terrible sound of knuckles on skin, banging on cheekbone, and the thud of his body on the ground.

I watched the boy reach a hand to his mouth, blood on his fingers, saw his eyes full of fear look up at the guard towering above him, and then away, whatever it was he saw staring back at him too shocking, too harsh to bear. I could've cried for him.

The boy struggled back to his feet, reaching down, his fingers scrabbling at the log, pulling it towards his chest. But his body and his arms and his legs trembled and shook, and the log fell back to the ground.

"You're useless!" the guard shouted. "And weak. A waste of my time and the air you breathe."

He swung the gun from his shoulder. I watched. Unable to move. He flicked off the catch. The boy's mouth fell open, his lips quivering, his eyes silently pleading.

The guard lifted the gun to his shoulder, leant his head to one side and peered with one eye down the sights. Horror stretched and contorted on the boy's face. Fear, shock and disbelief. His eyes wide, his hand lifting up. I heard the guard draw a breath, and I saw his finger on the trigger, squeezing, squeezing.

"No," I whispered.

Then a click. Not a bang.

And I saw the boy's shoulders droop as I felt my own do the same. But he didn't move or try to run; he just stared at the guard. As did I. Until the guard moved, turned and stared at me.

I thought at first he must be watching someone else, someone behind me or to my side, someone watching this scene as mesmerised as I was, though not wanting to be, wanting to look away, walk away, but unable to do so. Watching not with curiosity, but with a feeling of responsibility.

I needed to remember this. For the boy, I needed to remember. But the guard *was* looking at me, and at the axe still in my hand, and I knew he must've heard my whisper. He strode over to me, and at first I thought he was going to shoot me instead. But he didn't – he seized the axe and tried to pull it from my grasp.

Suddenly, horrified, I understood what he was going to do. For a second, only a second, I held on, struggling to keep hold of the axe. I looked at him as I strained to stop him taking it. Straight at him, and I felt so small and insignificant. So useless. He slapped me hard with his other hand. And I let go.

I let go.

I listened through my own sobs as the boy begged and cried, and I watched through eyes blurred with tears as the one blow struck. The one blow with my axe.

I hope shock kept him from feeling it. I hope he was unconscious before the pain registered in his brain. I hope he was dead before his body hit the ground. But I don't think he was. Because as a scream left my lips without even thinking it, as the guard's head flew round to me, as he grabbed his gun and strode towards me again, I looked into the boy's eyes as he lay on the floor, and I saw the life still in him and I didn't look away until it had faded. And all the time I muttered silently in my head, *I'm sorry, I'm sorry, I'm sorry.*

Suddenly the guard was in front of me, a grin stretched over his face, and the muzzle of his gun under my chin, and nobody was watching, nobody would see me killed and remember it, nobody would watch the life fade from my eyes.

"Shall we see if it misfires this time?" he asked.

I thought of my father, his courage in those last moments. *Are these mine?* I thought.

Somewhere inside me I felt angry. And I felt that rebellion again that I had tasted when meeting Sook in the darkness. Something I couldn't resist, that burned and itched inside me. Something, I knew, I was bound to regret. But...

I took a deep breath and then I spat in his face. I felt the adrenalin and the anger and the rebellion and the hatred course through me. I stared at him, straight *into* him, then I slowly closed my eyes and I waited. And behind my eyelids my imagination didn't show me the guard's face; my memory instead showed me Sook's.

As I looked at Sook, into his brown eyes, across his face, down on to his lips, I felt the click of the gun close to my chest, and felt the muzzle taken away from my skin. I opened my eyes and Sook's face was gone. The guard stared at me still as he threw the gun to the ground, and I saw a hint of triumph behind his eyes, and the specks of blood on his face, and I felt the wooden handle of the axe touch my fingers, then my palm. I held it as he turned away from me, my fingerprints replacing his, the stickiness of blood on my hand, and I looked over at the boy's body.

"I'm sorry," I whispered. I stood waiting for something, although I didn't know what, and there was nothing I could do, and I asked myself – *Was there anything I could've, should've done to keep you alive?*

A girl's hand touched my back and her face looked down at mine, the girl I tried to speak to before.

"What was his name?" I asked.

But she shook her head. "It doesn't matter," she said. "You have to turn away."

And she did, she turned away from me.

Is that it? I asked myself. *Is that how you survive this place? You turn away from compassion and humanity? From empathy? From caring?*

But I couldn't imagine not caring.

Chapter Twenty

The guard watched me for the rest of the day, pushing me over or kicking me to the floor, hitting me in the face, and though never for nothing, it was never for anything much: a slip perhaps, a weak blow from the axe, working too slowly, walking the wrong way.

Every second his eyes were there, anticipating every mistake even before I'd made it. Waiting, it seemed, for some excuse, though never needing one; he was playing with me, teasing me and torturing me with this constant threat of punishment, of violence, of pain and repercussions.

It was a long day, a hard day, passing slowly as if it was a week, my head swimming and flashing with images and thoughts and memories, of my father, my mother, of Sook, of that boy killed with my axe. I felt sick, whether with exhaustion or shock or guilt or frustration I don't know, and I ached and hurt so much that every step I took, or every lift of the axe or the saw, I thought would be the last.

I thought I would collapse.

Somehow I made it to the end and if I could get through that day, I thought to myself, I could get through however many days stretched out into my future.

Still the guard's eyes were on me as I picked up the axe again, and took a few steps down the mountain, a few steps nearer to my hut and my grandparents, to whatever food we had, and to my bed mat so welcome.

"You!" he shouted. "Come back here."

I stopped and turned, my body and my breath frozen.

"And you," he added, pointing to the girl who'd spoken to me earlier. "Both of you, get rid of the boy."

I didn't breathe, I just watched him, his back disappearing, imagining the look I felt sure must be on his face, a look of smugness and relish. He had the final say; he had the only say. There could be no arguing with him; I would always be the loser. He hated me. Maybe he hated us all. But I wasn't anonymous to him any more and that felt dangerous.

And the boy... I sighed. I didn't want to look at him,

touch him or carry him. I was going to walk down the mountain and back to the hut and forget about everything.

"Come on," the girl whispered to me. "We'll have to take him away from here."

"I can't," I replied, shaking my head.

"You don't have a choice." She walked over to where his body rested. "Come on," she repeated.

"What are we going to do? Where do we take him? Shouldn't we... shouldn't we take him to his family? Tell them?"

She shook her head. "Only do as you're told. Nothing more, nothing less. You'll learn. You have to. If you don't, you'll die. Simple as that."

"But... it can't be right... what he did... surely..."

She shrugged. "What does it matter? Who are you going to complain to?"

The whole thing was beyond comprehension. *How can people be so cruel?* I thought. *Because they're told to? Or because they can? Because there's no one to complain to, nobody who'd find out?*

I looked down at the boy, his body splayed out on the earth, his legs at uncomfortable angles, the dry grass bent over under his fingers, the features that made up who he was still visible. But he was pale, grey almost, and nothing was behind his eyes, no glimmer, no spark, just an empty shell. Life so fragile, taken so easily.

Yet I looked at the girl by my side, so thin and so frail, and I thought of the other prisoners, those I'd seen when I arrived, clinging to survival.

Life can be so tenacious. But it's always lost in the end.

★

We struggled deeper into the trees, further than I thought the camp extended, carrying the body of that poor boy between us, dragging spades that we'd tied round us. His body felt so heavy, and so many times he slipped from my grasp, or I would drop him to the ground with no strength left in my arms.

Every time he fell I cried, and every time I apologised to him, and the girl looked at me as if I was a child, shaking her head at me with impatience and incomprehension. But I cared. Still. Dead or alive, I cared. Finally we came to a patch of earth where the trees thinned out and we stopped, letting the boy down to the ground.

"Nobody usually comes this far out," the girl said. "Unless it's to bury someone."

I looked around at the mounds of raised earth here and there. "Is this where...?"

"Not all of them. There are fifty thousand people in this camp, or so I was told. There are more areas like this."

I turned and stared down the mountainside towards the camp. The rows of huts that were our village, the path leading away from them, a clump of buildings, a dirt road, the mine in the distance, more huts further away, hills lined with trees on the other side, snow-capped mountains away in the distance. We were held in a valley. The mountains and terrain imprisoning us just as much as the fence. No wonder nobody ever tried to escape.

"It's so vast," I whispered.

She gave a sigh, nodded and turned to me. "It'd take you a day to walk to the other side," she said. "I've been here with my uncle and father eight years, since I was eleven, with no explanation or trial. But I've hardly seen any of the camp, only know our little bit. And a few of the buildings. You're not allowed any contact with the other villages, but notes are passed now and again, about which guards are worse than others, or about food, or new arrivals.

"Are they still alive?" I whispered. "Your family?"

She looked away. "My uncle died the first month we were here. I don't know why, he just didn't wake up one morning." She shrugged and looked down at her feet. "The following month my father was put in a sweatbox for two weeks for looking at a guard the wrong way. He came back, but I hardly recognised him." She paused, drew in a long breath and looked at me. "Some days I think about dying. Some I dare to think of release. Mostly, though, it's better not to think at all."

I stared at her, her skin taut against her bones, the lines and wrinkles on her face, yet she was still a teenager.

I turned round on the spot, then stopped. A short distance away I could see a mesh of silver reaching up into the sky and a tall concrete tower to one side. "Is that the perimeter fence?" I asked.

I watched her gaze drift away and her head nod in reply, and for a moment, just a moment, we didn't say or do anything. In my head was just that fence, what it meant and what lay on the other side.

Then, without the need for acknowledgement, I lifted my spade and followed her to a place to dig. We jabbed and jabbed into ground still cold from winter, while behind us the sun dipped below the mountains, leaving a trail of orange over us and the earth, the boy and the tops of the trees, and down to the valley and the huts and the prisoners.

We struggled on and on, darkness growing and a chill spreading. And by the time we'd finished digging a hole that was barely big enough, we had only the light from the moon to show us where we had left his body.

"We need to take his clothes off," the girl said.

I stared towards her outline in the darkness. "You're only given new uniform once a year," she said. "Sometimes not even that. We can't bury them, they're worth too much. And his boots."

"Shouldn't we give them to his family?" I asked.

But she scoffed, shaking her head. "You won't survive long in here if you don't think about yourself first," she said. "I'll take his clothes, you have his boots. If they don't fit, you can swap them with someone for food, or seeds, or a cooking pot. Check his pockets too."

I crouched at his side feeling so callous and cold, so selfish and disrespectful. His colour was gone and his lips were blue, and taking a deep breath, I stuffed my hands into his pockets that were stretched against his stiff arms and legs. But there was nothing there. We pulled and tugged, twisted and grappled and yanked until his clothes were off.

I had never been so close to a dead body before, touching it, watching it. I looked at his skin prickled by moonlight. I'd never even seen anyone naked. He was undignified not peaceful, awkward not beautiful. Vulnerable.

We lowered him into the shallow hole and I paused with a shovelful of dirt in my hands. I couldn't do it. Couldn't drop it on to his face, which I couldn't see but knew was down there in the darkness, so young and so innocent, looking out at the world that had been so cruel to him.

But I did. And I convinced myself that he would be glad to be away from this place of suffering and pain and unhappiness.

How unfair it is, I thought. *What a short life he lived, and what sadness he endured. Nothing, no crime, no guilt, could warrant this.*

I imagined, as we stumbled back down the mountainside, feeling and scrabbling our way, his life before this camp, his childhood. I imagined it happy. I imagined the house he lived in and the food he ate, the brother he played with and the parents he loved.

And I saw him laugh, and I saw him smile. And I hoped it was true.

"What about his family?" I whispered as the ground grew level and the outline of buildings guided us one way then the next.

"Their hut's close to mine," she replied. "I'll tell them."

Where our paths split, we stopped a second, and I was surprised to feel her hand rest on my arm, and although I could barely make out her face, the seriousness in her warning was clear.

"Look out for that guard," she whispered. "He'll make trouble for you."

And he did. Every day until my decision was made for me.

The decision he forced on me.

Chapter Twenty-one

The camp felt eerie and quiet as I made my way back, a strange blue moonlight touching the roofs of huts as I passed by. So many of them – the family quarters – some with only three people like us, others with far more, parents and grandparents and children and aunts and uncles, but barely a sound coming from any of them; a tiny whisper through the thin walls, or a sob so quiet I could barely hear it, the scrape of a bowl, the crack of a piece of wood.

Nobody walked about, nobody sang or whistled or raised a voice. They were – we were – kept like animals, put to bed at night, controlled through fear. It wasn't just sadness I could feel in the stale air around me, it was apathy and hopelessness.

I creaked open the door and my grandparents' eyes

flew to me. Grandfather leapt to his feet, tears in his eyes, throwing his arms round me, then holding me back again, his gaze flickering over my face and my body, the mud on me, the streaks of tears down my face, the cuts and bruises on my skin.

"What happened?" he whispered.

But I didn't want to go through it again, didn't want to remember it. I shook my head. "I don't want to... don't want to... talk about it, Grandfather. Please."

He nodded, staring at me, touching his palm to my face. "But you're all right?"

I tried to smile. *I'm here, aren't I?* I thought. *I'm standing in front of you. I'm still breathing.* "Yes," I replied, nodding, my eyes filling with tears. "I'm all right now."

He held me. "We were worried," he whispered into my hair. "Both of us."

And I wanted to stay there for ever in the safety of his arms.

★

They'd saved me some cornmeal and we sat at the table in silence, Grandfather watching me struggling to lift the spoon to my mouth.

"I have stomach ache," I told them, my eyes closing between mouthfuls, sleep dragging at me.

"So do I, Yoora," replied my grandfather. "It's eating corn all the time. Your body will get used to it."

"Is there nothing else?"

I heard Grandmother huff, but I was too tired to wonder if I'd insulted her or said the wrong thing. I just knew how weak I felt, how hungry still, and that nagging pain in my belly.

"What do you expect me to do?" she said. "I don't have any seeds to grow anything, and I have nothing to barter with."

"Maybe something could be found further up the hills. Some bark off trees to boil down. Some leaves. Insects," Grandfather suggested.

She glared at him, but didn't reply, her face fixed into a look of disgust and anger.

"I've been there today." My voice was a mumble and I stood up from the table, staggering across the room to the door. I picked up the boots I'd dropped when I came in and slid them across the floor towards the table.

"Here. Use those to barter with. They're too small for me. He was only tiny."

I sat back down, tired, hungry and cold. And sad. I'd had enough. I looked at Grandmother, then at Grandfather. And I took a breath.

"Tell me about Seoul," I said. "The letters, the postcard, everything. Tell me why they were in our house. What they were to us." I wiped my hands across my eyes. *I'm not going to cry*, I thought, *I'm not going to show Grandmother how sad I feel, and useless. I'm going to be strong.* "I have to understand," I said slowly. "I have to know how... how... they got us in here... in this... this *place*." I waved a hand around at the walls that held us. "You owe me that much," I whispered.

Grandfather stared at me. And my grandmother too. But nobody spoke a word.

"How do you know about it? The world outside?" I asked, breathing heavy and deep, trying so hard to keep calm, keep in control.

"We... we..." he stammered.

"He doesn't know anything," Grandmother interrupted.

"He *must* do," I hissed at her. "Because you told me, Grandmother, you told me that he put stories and ideas in my head."

"Huh," she scoffed. "Your memory's tricking you, girl."

"No," I said. And I was so angry I wanted to shout and scream at her. "It's not. Because you said that when we first arrived here."

"I told you," she said, leaning across the table to me, her voice low and angry, but her face full of sorrow. "He doesn't know anything about Seoul."

Her eyes flashed a warning or a threat to Grandfather, but as I looked at him, his head was already lowered and resting in his hand.

I stood up and leant over the table towards her. "You're lying," I breathed, my finger pointing in her face. "I know you are."

I expected Grandfather to tell me off. Tell me to respect my elders, or not speak like that to Grandmother, but he didn't say a word, didn't even lift his head to look at me.

I've waited this long, I thought. *I can wait a while longer.*

★

I collapsed on my bed mat without taking off my clothes or washing the dirt from my skin. I didn't tell them anything about the boy or the guard, although I wanted to tell Grandmother, go into every detail with her about what had happened and what I had seen. Because I wanted her to know how much I'd suffered that day, that I was taking the punishment I felt sure she thought I deserved.

Before I went to sleep, I lifted a splinter of wood

from the floor, and in the mud walls I scratched a marker, next to all the others I'd scratched since we arrived, one for every day. How many now? Thirty? Thirty-two? I was too tired to count. How many more would there be? We had never been told. A lifetime's worth? A lifetime wasted.

My life, it seemed, was a single breath in the vastness of time that would never be heard, or seen, or remembered. My life meant nothing, to anybody, anywhere.

I had no reason to exist. And I was waiting to die.

Chapter Twenty-two

The rains came, heavy and continuous.

So much fell and for so long that I thought the sky couldn't possibly hold any more, and trying to keep dry was ridiculous. Every part of me was soaked: from the hair pasted to my head, to the clothes stuck to my skin, to my feet skidding inside shoes that did little more than hold together small puddles.

I struggled up the mountainside watching the rain pour off the ends of other prisoners' noses like a bad cold, running down their faces in rivers so fast that wiping them would've been pointless. It was strange, yet it was mesmerising. It was the rainy season.

I tried to work, but so many times the saw would stick in the logs, or my feet skid in the mud, or the logs slip through my wet hands and to the ground. Over and over. And every time my hands failed me, I remembered the boy and I looked for the guard who had killed him with my stomach turning somersaults. So much time I wasted stopping, sighing, wiping my hands down my wet trouser legs, staring at everyone else struggling just as much as I was. Desperation clawing at us all as we realised we were not going to make our quota.

I stopped to wipe my hands yet again, and next to me the girl who I'd buried the boy with paused too.

"Look at that," she whispered. The first words she'd said to me since that night.

I turned to see. And there was the guard and for a moment I thought she was warning me, as she had done before, but I watched as much as I dared, and I saw what she meant – there was the funniest of sights in the worst of places.

He was struggling up the hillside, his feet slipping every few paces, taking him back to where he started. Over and over.

I glanced back at her and saw the hint of a smile dance across her face.

"Don't stare at him!" I hissed.

"Look at the mud all over his boots."

I turned to the side slightly, scared he would see me and of what he would do to me, but still watching, mesmerised, from the corner of my eye. "He's going to fall over," I whispered.

She looked at me with mischief in her eyes, and I knew that every bit of her was hoping he would.

I risked another look, saw his feet still slipping, his body lurching sideways, his hands clutching at the air for something that wasn't there. "Look!" I whispered. And as she turned, he fell forward, his knees landing in the sodden earth, his hands splashing into the mud, his whole body slipping slowly downwards.

We shot a look at each other and turned away, our attention focused on the log next to us as our bodies shook with laughter, our hands over our mouths, giggling like schoolgirls, stopping for a moment as we calmed, then glancing at each other again, and again laughter pouring from us. Laughter among madness; a ray of light in a place so dark.

And that day we didn't make our quota, but when it came to checking, the guard had disappeared.

I walked back to the hut, trying to remember the laughter and the smiles and that wonderful feeling of lightness in my chest. Trying not to remember that the last time I felt like that was with Sook. Hoping the guard hadn't seen us laughing.

Hoping we wouldn't pay for it the following day.

Chapter Twenty-three

We stood so long at the following morning's roll call, in clothes still wet and heavy, with rain still hammering down on us and around us, and puddles to our ankles, that my mind began to drift. I thought of the previous day, laughing with the girl, the guard falling over, and I was surprised when I saw his uniform was pristine again, and wondered how long it had taken him to scrub off the mud, or if he had someone do it for him.

Did he see us? I thought. *Is he planning some kind of punishment? Revenge?*

My throat, my chest, my stomach, everything flushed hot.

No. Don't think. Don't think, I told myself.

I forced my mind to wander instead to other things,

other places, lifting my spirits away from that place to somewhere better, happier, freer. Drier perhaps.

"Is there a rainy season in Seoul?" I whispered to Grandfather next to me.

"Shh," he said.

"They can't hear us," I replied. "And they're not looking this way."

"Yes." A different voice spoke, to my right I thought, and I glanced that way. The man nodded. "Between June and September. It's the East Asian monsoon season."

I turned to him, amazed. "How do you know that?" I asked.

"I've read..." But he stopped, his eyes leaving mine and opening wide as something over my shoulder caught his attention. And he turned his head back to face the front, staring away to a vague point in the distance, his face, his whole body, a statue.

"How do you know?" I repeated, louder this time.

"Yoora," my grandfather hissed, but it barely registered with me.

"Have you been there? Have you been to Seoul?"

But still the man didn't move. I paused. Everything was silent and everything was still. But something was close to me, so close I could feel it breathing, its eyes upon me, waiting. I held my breath and I turned. And there he was – the guard.

"You," he said. "Again."

I dared to lift my head, to look him straight in the eye, and I saw something... something that scared me, that made my skin crawl and my breath catch, and fear pound in my head and run down my veins and into every part of my body. Something so powerful, so wrong, that it hurt just to look at it and made my eyes close and my head lower away from it.

He grabbed me by the hair and dragged me forward out of the line to stand me in front of everyone. I lifted my head and looked back at every single face so blank, so vague, anonymous, like slaves. Among them, the girl I thought could be a friend. And Grandfather. And Grandmother.

Don't cry, I told myself. *Don't cry.*

I tried to breathe slowly in and slowly out, tried to calm myself, stop my heart banging in my chest, and my thoughts racing with visions of terrible things I was scared of happening.

I stretched up on tiptoe as his hand dragged my hair up and up, and I closed my eyes, trying to remember Mother and Father, their strength and their bravery.

But it was a memory of Sook that came to me. His face in the rain. Smiling at me. Laughing with me. An evening we spent together hidden among the trees, hoping, naively, that they'd shelter us from the rains. We were warm, but we were drenched.

How could I have forgotten that? I thought.

His feet were so wet he took off his shoes, standing with the mud pushing between his toes, telling me how nice it felt, begging me to come and do the same. Laughing at me barefoot and wading across the mud to him, standing in front of him, with him, our feet squelching and slipping and sliding. Together. Laughing at the sight we must've looked. And the strangeness of it.

Sook, I thought, standing in front of my whole 'village', waiting for whatever the guard chose to do. *Sook*. And I let that thought come to my head, let myself see it and listen to it – *I miss you*.

The guard let go of my hair and grabbed me round the throat. "I could kill you any day I choose." His voice hissed in my ear, low, secretive, menacing. "Any day or any time. I could kill you now if I wanted to. Nobody would care. Or I could let you go, let you think you're safe, wait until you're cutting down trees, or walking down the hills, or in your hut sleeping – I could wake you for a second before killing you. I can do whatever I like to you."

I felt his breath in my face as he moved in front of me. "Open your eyes," he hissed.

I peeled back my eyelids, but kept my head down.

"Look at me!" he shouted.

Slowly I raised my head to those eyes full of hatred glaring at me and into me.

"Because I will kill you one day. When I've had enough of you." His hand squeezed at my throat and I felt the pressure growing in my head.

"My face," he said, leering at me, "will be the last you ever see as you die."

No, I thought. *The last face I will see as I die will be of someone I love. Because you cannot take my imagination from me.*

His grip tightened further and blackness seeped across my vision, and I could see nothing but what was in my head, a face coming towards me, forming, smiling at me. Not Mother. Not Father.

Sook.

The guard let go and I fell to the ground, gasping for the breath he'd allowed me to take. And the face disappeared.

Through the mud splashing and the rain pouring I watched the feet of all the prisoners as they filed past me to work. No one, not even the girl I had spoken with, stopping to check on me, to rest a hand on my shoulder or to mutter a word of concern. Only my grandfather slowing enough to allow him to watch my chest rise and fall and to turn his empty palm to me as if trying to show me there was nothing he could do.

Because there wasn't. And I knew that.

I dragged myself back to my feet, took a deep breath and followed my work unit up the hillside when all I wanted to do was collapse and give up.

No, I thought. *Don't give up. Keep going, keep going.* And I thought of Grandfather's words – *One day at a time, one step at a time, one foot in front of the other and maybe, just maybe.*

I struggled through the rain coming down, trying to calm myself, watching the leaves and branches turning glossy and reflecting the light, listening to the drops hammering out rhythms on trees or bushes or hands or faces as if it was nature's song, and as it collected in puddles of mud and sloshed back and forth with the steps of prisoners' feet.

I heard someone close by and I glanced to one side to see the girl. All she did was look, but she'd done what so many others hadn't.

Chapter Twenty-four

I dared to hope that those small moments we'd shared, me and the girl, laughing at the guard, her glance at me after he humiliated me, would mark the beginning of a friendship for us, but it didn't. Not quite. Instead it was more of a companionship, an understanding, or a connection where we never shared our names, or our stories about why we were in there, or even spoke more than a few words together.

But we would nod to each other if we found berries hiding on bushes and help each other fill our pockets and our mouths with them, and we would point out purple stains on fingers or chins or lips that could give us away to the guards and all the starving faces around us.

They were moments of relief that kept me breathing.

Because every morning, and every roll call in the evening, that guard marched down the rows of prisoners, and every time he came towards me he would slow, and I would watch his hand move towards his gun, see his palm rest on the grip and his finger stretch towards the trigger.

And every single time it would make me feel sick. Every single time I would think I was about to die. Waiting to see him draw his gun, see that barrel pointing towards me and the flash of light in front of my eyes before blackness swallowed me. The power, the control he held over me, never once wavered. Never. Not through autumn or as winter came, or as I realised a year had passed.

I would lie in bed with the cold biting through me, and the wind howling around the hut and through the gaps, and I would listen for every noise, waiting for the day I would wake to his clammy hands round my throat or his gun cold against my head.

And the only way I could sleep, when even exhaustion wouldn't take me, was to remember those moments of some kind of friendship with the girl, replaying in my mind the snowdrifts lying thickly over everything and staying for weeks on end, taking turns with her to walk in front up the mountainside, the other able to follow the path of the first, legs and feet stretching through channels and stepping in gaps already made in the snow.

Maybe it is a friendship, I thought. *Or maybe she's nothing more than another prisoner.*

But whatever name I gave it didn't matter anyway. Whatever it was, it was helping me sleep, helping me breathe in and out every day and helping me stay alive. Because life was intolerable, although we tolerated it. It was hardship like no other. It was debasing and terrifying. So many people of all ages dying from illness or malnutrition or starvation. Or beaten to death. Or executed. Or experimented on, I heard.

I longed not to hear these things and not to see them, wished instead to hear tales of freedom granted or a successful escape, stories that might lift me or give me hope, help keep the face of that guard away from my eyes and his threat from echoing inside my head. But I exchanged a few words here and there with people from our 'village', and Grandmother spoke to some of the women as she climbed up the hills around us, and Grandfather whispered to the other men in the mine, and all we ever heard was of the most terrible things that you thought no human could inflict on another.

I thought of those who sanctioned this place I found myself in, and the idealised view I held of my country did its final unravelling. I remembered Father's words to me after the dream that marked the beginning of so much and wondered if all he was ever guilty of was of telling me the truth.

Because this wasn't right. Because no crime could be horrendous enough to warrant the punishments I knew were being meted out, and the only crime it seemed anyone here was accused of was against the state or against the leadership. And that was so vague, so manipulable. Even as I looked around me, and listened to snatched words and half-conversations, I realised that innocence was everywhere. But innocence was irrelevant.

Chapter Twenty-five

The thought of the postcard and the letters and photographs and magazines my family had burned never left me, not as the mornings became lighter and the days longer, nor as I heard the crack of ice melting on the frozen stream and knew spring was here.

And every day as I worked, I thought of different ways to ask Grandfather what it all meant, who'd sent them, where the rest of my family was, what his story was, desperate to know now in case something terrible happened to us and the truth could never be shared.

But when the days passed and evenings came and I sat at the table looking at his face so tired and so drawn, life falling away from him, I couldn't find the words to say. Every day, it seemed, my courage to ask him dwindled, and my reluctance to upset him grew.

I wished I had a photograph of us from when we first arrived so I could see how much we had all changed, at least on the outside. Even with the light fading I could tell my grandmother's hair was thinning and falling out, that her cheeks were hollow and that even the anger in her eyes was fading, as it seemed her life force was too.

I watched my grandfather's fingers bend round the spoon and noticed how his knuckles stuck out, and as he walked across the hut, I saw it was with a stooped back and shuffling feet. And when I hugged him that night before going to sleep I could feel his spine curling under my fingertips and his shoulder blades pressing through to my cheek. Tears sprang to my eyes and my heart ached.

I remembered the words from my father in the darkness – *I can feel the bones in your arms and legs... but I have no more food to give you... I stare at your pale skin and your blue lips... but I don't have enough fuel to keep you warm...*

I understand you now, Father, I thought.

How I had changed, the weight my body had lost, I didn't know. But I could see my ribs and feel my hip bones, could reach my fingers round the tops of my arms, and I could see the shadows and the sadness in Grandfather's eyes when he looked at me, and I wondered if he could see me fading as I could him.

We were skeletons, we were monsters, we were the living dead.

But I learnt to turn my head and my memory away from the bad things, although that was hard, and I learnt that although they controlled our bodies and our movements, inside my head was invisible to them, and my thoughts and imagination could take me wherever I wanted, and the smallest of things could lift my spirits even if only for a fraction of time.

And so as I walked back to the hut that I refused to call home after yet another day, my eyes searched across the dull earth, and my heart lifted as I saw a sprout of green poking through. Then my mouth tipped a smile when I noticed a sparrow balanced on a branch above me, a few twigs grasped between his beak for making his nest. I stopped as I saw a flower hiding in the dirt, a feeling of warmth and joy in my chest as I dug it from the earth with my fingers, the roots so fragile in my hands, its delicate petals of white and pink.

I hoped I could keep it alive, hoped it would grow

on the window sill of the hut, hoped I could wake to it every morning. For a while at least.

My eyes drifted across the land in front of me, my feet moving automatically towards somewhere to sit, to rest, to sleep so briefly until it all began again the following day. But with my flower to look at when I woke.

But a shout came. A noise. A cry. Thin and weak, yet pierced with fear and pain. And my senses prickled and I paused, my head jerking upwards and my eyes staring towards the hut where I knew it had come from. My hut.

It came again, louder this time, and frightened. The door flew open and I stopped, staring, watching helplessly. The guard, the one who hated me, the one who killed that boy, whose face I spat in, stormed out of my hut, his gun in one hand, his other gripping my grandmother's hair, pulling her along the ground.

My hand shot over my mouth to stop myself screaming. I told my legs not to move as I watched her arms lift and flail around, her hands reaching for her head as she tried to protect herself, and her legs scrabbling in the dirt as they tried and tried to get upright. And her face... oh, her face... so vulnerable... so weak... so ashamed.

Again, as with the boy, nobody did anything. No one stopped to help, or shouted in anger, or even paused what they were doing to watch in horror. All apart from one, my grandfather, who was now standing next to me.

We stood without a word spoken, watching her being dragged away, listening to her cries tearing through the air, knowing it might well be the last time we saw her and there was nothing, *nothing*, we could do. I could feel Grandfather's sobs pulling at his body as he stepped closer to me, and I felt his fingers touch mine, and I grabbed his hand and held it, holding him close, keeping him close, my grandfather. My loyal, my sympathetic, my kind and caring, my generous and affectionate, my wonderful grandfather.

We watched Grandmother disappear into the distance, towards the buildings whose threat hung over us all, with the tales we'd all heard of gas experiments or chemicals, solitary confinement or beatings, punishments from the cruellest of imaginations, and I felt her eyes boring into me, hating me, blaming me for everything since the day Sook's mother sent the men to our house.

Yes, I regretted it, with my whole heart I did, as I watched her go and as I felt the pain of my grandfather.

What had she done or said to be taken away from us? So little, it could be nothing. I didn't want, or need, to know.

She disappeared and then so did her cries, and the shouts of the guard.

Chapter Twenty-six

We waited in our hut, our cornmeal eaten, hoping to hear the door creak open, her footsteps across the floor, her moans about how many trips to the river she'd taken that day and how little she could find to eat.

I dropped the flower into an old broken cup and placed it on the window sill, my symbol of hope for her return. Darkness slipped over us, quiet and inconspicuous, and we lit a candle and waited. For what? Did we really believe she'd be coming back that night? Or ever?

We pulled our bed mats together and stretched blankets over us to keep warm, to find comfort in another body being close.

"You think she's dead?" His question was so honest it hurt.

"N— no," I stammered.

"I do."

I didn't move. Didn't reach my hand to his to offer comfort or support, I just lay there, the silence agonising, feeling his chest rise and fall as he breathed, and secretly, guiltily, selfishly, I was grateful it wasn't him who'd been taken from me.

"Tell me," I whispered. "Please. Tell me who sent the letters and postcards. Tell me what happened."

He shook his head.

"Why not?" I sighed. "Why don't you want me to know? Is it that bad? Are you worried what I'll think of you? Because you know, whatever it is, however bad you think it is, it won't change anything. You'll still be Grandfather."

He wiped a hand across his face.

"You'll still mean the world to me," I whispered.

He sighed, long and slow, then he closed his eyes and lowered his head. And I thought that was it. He wouldn't tell me; nothing would change. And next he would be gone, like Grandmother, and his secrets and his past would go with him. And I would never know, and I would never understand.

"I did a terrible thing, Yoora," he whispered, and he looked up at me with his eyes full of tears. "A dreadful thing and she never forgave me." I took his hand and held it, his skin so dry I thought it would flake away, his bones so pronounced I thought they would break.

"I said sorry so many times, but it never made any difference. Sorry can't take it away. It's not your fault, you see? That we're here, in this *prison*, this *camp*. I know you think it is. I know you blame yourself. But all you did was trust somebody."

"Grandmother blames me."

"No." He shook his head. "Ever questioned why our social class is so low? Why we're *beulsun,* tainted blood? We just are, aren't we?"

I shrugged.

"For years I told your parents that they should explain things to you, but they never did. Your father wanted to, but not your mother. But then what are mothers for if not to protect their children?" His face wrinkled into a smile so unfamiliar, but a smile that faded away with the longest of sighs. "All right, child, we start from as far back as I can remember. Yes?"

I nodded. "Yes," I breathed.

"I was six years old, standing on the deck of a ship, staring out at this expanse of grey sky above me, and this never-ending blue beneath me; I'd never seen anything like it. *It's the sea*, my mother told me. *It's wet and cold and don't fall in.*" He smiled at the memory.

"It lurched up and down and side to side, and while my mother filled my head with stories of the better life we were going to have, I emptied my stomach over the side, cried a little and searched across the blue for land. It was 1941 and we were heading to Japan. So many of their men had gone to fight in the war that they were short of workers, and so they offered Koreans like my parents all sorts of promises to lure them over."

"You went from North Korea over to Japan?"

He shook his head. "No. We were from the South." I stared at him.

"It wasn't split then. There wasn't a North and a South, it was all one big country. We came from a village near Seoul."

"But that makes you... that means you're..."

The candlelight flickered on his face and I tried to make sense of the look I could see on his face: sorrow or anger or disappointment.

"The enemy?" He snorted. "Do I look it? Or your grandmother? Does she?"

"She's from the South too?"

He nodded. I stared at him. "But... but... the South started the war against the North, so..."

He interrupted, his head shaking, his finger wagging at me. "No, Yoora. That's what they want you, want everyone, to believe. But that's not true. They rewrote history to fit what they wanted and nobody dares question it. People from my generation know, but they say nothing. How could they?"

It went against everything I'd been taught, and all the history books I'd read at school. But I realised I couldn't believe anything, about my country whole-heartedly or without question now. How much was lies? I hoped one day I could find out. I knew now that I believed Grandfather, as I believed those words Father had spoken all that time ago. Completely and utterly.

"We arrived in Japan with barely more than what we were standing up in, but with hopes and promises keeping our spirits high. It was going to be a good life, an easier life. We were going to be happy. But I don't remember it ever keeping its promises. We were always outsiders and we all tended to group together, societies of Korean workers growing in corners of cities. My father went from job to job, never settling, and I watched my parents' expressions turn from hope to frustration to apathy.

"Time passed, I met a girl – your grandmother – and more time went by, and all of a sudden I was in love with her; I felt like..." I watched him lift his eyes as if he was looking for the answer in the darkness of the ceiling. "Like I'd woken up... like I was alive at last."

He sighed and I stared at him over the candlelight, watching it flicker on to his skin through shadows dancing in the warmth of those memories in his eyes. I remembered Sook, how he made me feel – alive and awake – just as Grandfather had said, and I felt that horrible sadness clawing at me.

"But..." he continued, "you make plans, you think of the future, but then *life* happens. November the third 1959, Japanese Culture Day, celebrating peace and freedom, the day she told me she was pregnant."

My hand flew to my mouth and I stared at him. "You weren't married?" I whispered.

He shrugged, his smile lifting again as he glanced at my wide eyes of disbelief. "Still aren't," he whispered.

I was so shocked. It was unbelievable. My grandmother?

Pregnant and unmarried? Pretending to be married now?

"Nobody knows," he added, his face so close to mine I could see a spark of something in his eyes that told me he might always have been a rebel. But in hiding. And with a quiet voice.

"We spent a while trying to decide what to do and who we should tell and what we should say. What my parents would do, how hers would react. But in the end, we didn't tell them at all. I was so frightened her parents would take her away from me, that I would never see her again or the baby, that I convinced her to run away with me, to go back to Korea and make a life together for the three of us.

"By then the country was split in two. She wanted to go to the South, close to where we both had relatives. I wanted to go to the North. The North offered free health care, free education. The South didn't. And the North didn't have any of her relatives who I thought might take her away from me.

"Like a child I moaned and nagged, until she gave way. We arrived pretending we were married, pretending we were older and for a while things were good, things were great in fact, and I believed I'd made the right decision for us. We sent letters back to Japan, apologising, explaining, saying we would visit, and hoped they would visit us. We missed them.

"The country seemed prosperous. We were given jobs, somewhere to live, food every week – our rations. The streets and the buildings were clean; there was barely any crime. We felt safe and we felt happy. And our little boy, your father, was born.

"But gradually, and I don't know when, things started to go wrong. We were moved from the town into the country. Away from my job in the factory, your grandmother's job in the office, to work the land instead. Tough, physical work. With less and less food. We wrote telling our families we'd moved, but no letters ever came back. Again and again we asked the authorities for permission to visit them, but again and again it was refused.

"Years passed and, thinking our families had disowned us, we stopped writing. I watched the sparkle of life and beauty leave your grandmother, and I saw her hatred and anger for me grow. *What can I do?* I used to think over and over. *There has to be something… something.* I could only think of one thing – I wrote to all the old addresses I could remember in Japan, and all the ones I could remember of relatives in the South, and had the letters smuggled out. And I waited. Hoping. And waited. And finally, *finally*, after nearly a year, one came back. From my brother in the South, with tales of their devastation when I ran away, of them leaving Japan and heading back to Seoul, and the journey one letter made, passed from kind hands to kind hands, over thousands of miles."

I didn't wonder any more, as his story unfolded, why I had never been told about my family, or had it explained to me why we were *beulsun*. The candlelight showed me all the guilt and pain etched deep on his face as lines and wrinkles, running through his hair as grey.

"She didn't hate you," I whispered. "She loved you. I'm sure she did. Still does."

He squeezed my hand and I watched his eyes begin to glisten and his mouth turn down. "She told me every single day," he whispered, "that she blamed me and she hated me. And every *single* day I apologised. But it never made any difference. I took her life from her." His tears began to pour, and his words were gulped and uneven.

I opened my mouth to ask him about the postcard, if his brother had sent it, how it had reached us, but this wasn't the time. I wished I could take his pain away from him, but I was the wrong person to do that, so instead I put my arms round him and held him tight.

Strange, I thought, *that decisions made so long ago have led to this – us struggling with every sunrise and sunset to survive, hour by hour, minute by minute. With death on our shoulder, whispering in our ear, waiting for our day, our time.*

Chapter Twenty-seven

I dreamt that night, not of the guard, or of the girl, or of my parents or grandparents. It was of a person, a somebody, a boy or a man. And I followed him from a distance as he walked through streets, tired and broken and empty, his head down, his shoulders low, his scuffed shoes dragging along the path, his arms slack at his sides.

Rubbish blew along deep gutters and bodies lay face down in the road, and no music played or shops existed or lights flashed or colour glowed. Everything was a shade of grey and he was the only person there and the only person alive.

I followed him. Down one road, round a corner, down another. And again. In circles. Over and over. But after a while I stopped, waiting instead for him to come around again, and as he did, I saw his face.

Sook.

He looked at me with such love in his eyes that it took my breath away. He walked towards me and I watched him, and I felt myself smile at him, stretch my arms out to him.

"Sook," I whispered.

But hands and arms and bodies came from nowhere and grabbed him, pulling him one way then the other, tearing at him, dragging him away to what I knew was his death.

And I woke. Breathless and panicky and incredibly, *incredibly* sad.

Isn't that what you want? my head screamed at me. *Isn't that what he deserves?*

I lay down again, closing my eyes, trying not to remember those evenings we shared, the times we laughed, the smile he had that had warmed my heart. I didn't want to think of what he'd done to us, how he'd betrayed me. Or what a fool I'd been.

It hurt too much.

★

I woke in the morning to birdsong. To rays of light streaming through the slats of wood that was our roof and on to my face. To the flower I had picked, it seemed like in another life now, with its petals open to the sun. To peace that meant not remembering. To happiness that was ignorance.

I wished I could lie there for ever with no thoughts or memories or worries. Calm. Stillness. Forgiveness. Wished I could stay in that suspended moment of innocence. But I heard my grandfather's sigh, his rattling cough from too much time in the mine, and I jolted back to our life and sat up on my bed mat. Still there was no Grandmother.

I stared down at my shoes waiting for me, caked in dry mud that seemed to be holding them together, and my clothes that I had no choice but to wear, the armpits stiff with sweat, and covered in dirt and grime, stains and mud; never washed, too slow to dry and no spares to wear.

I had become the same as all the others. I was a living skeleton, with skin covered in sores and eczema stretched over bones threatening to snap and hair matted like a bird's nest. Despondency dragging at my legs and pulling at my shoulders.

We got up, me and Grandfather, and got dressed, with barely a word shared, and as we left our hut to head for work, I caught the look in his eyes as he pulled the door closed behind him, hoping, I'm sure, as I was, that she would be there waiting for us by the time we returned. Hoping, I think, that he could tell her again how sorry he was and how much he loved her.

And I hoped she would say it in return.

How sad it was, to be that age, to be grandparents, to have been together so long, and still be so in need of hearing those words, and of being so scared they were no longer felt.

I stood with our 'villagers', our work colleagues, our fellow prisoners, receiving orders and quotas for the day as if it was any other, and I stared at the space where she should've been, and didn't know what to think or what to do. I didn't want to consider the possibility that she might not be coming back, didn't want naivety to let me believe she might still be alive.

Why? For Grandfather because I didn't want to see his pain any more than I already had.

I caught the eye of the girl I thought of as a friend, watching as she nodded her head, looking first to the gap and then to me, and I gave the slightest shrug of my shoulders. But as the lines broke up and people moved away, I edged towards her, trying not to attract the attention of the guard as I altered my path to reach her. We passed, slowing, keeping our eyes away from each other, and she whispered with barely enough breath to make her words audible, and I nodded my head just a fraction to acknowledge I had heard.

"She's in solitary."

I walked away with no possibility of asking why or how long for, and without the chance of thanking her for saying three words that gave me some comfort, but risked her own life, even though she was barely ten paces ahead of me. And I was oblivious to the mutterings of the guard as I struggled up the mountainside, and the mood of the people around me, and even the sunlight flickering through the trees as I passed in and out of shade.

I knew what it meant – being in solitary. Not as simple as it sounded, not a normal cell by yourself. Of course it wouldn't be in this sort of place. Punishment was imaginative and for ever evolving it seemed, as they conjured more ways to make us suffer or to make themselves feel more powerful.

I don't believe they all hated us. One or two, I believe, left a part of themselves at the gate when they entered, unable otherwise to carry out orders. But most, and definitely the one who hated me, took pleasure in hitting us and pride in themselves when they caused us to cry out in sadness or scream in pain. Or when one of us died. They enjoyed us and the opportunity we gave them to do the cruellest of things.

I had seen some of what man is capable of when no threat of repercussion hangs over him.

I struggled onwards, the gap to the girl in front growing as heaviness and sadness and hopelessness pulled me down. Images flashed in my head of that guard dragging Grandmother away, her bare legs scrabbling in the dirt, her mouth gaping open as she cried out, her eyes searching over the people who were ignoring her. It shocked me still. And it scared me.

I could see her in the cell that was more like a box; too small to stand up or lie down in, forcing her to crouch on her knees, hands resting on thighs, heels pressing into her bottom. Spikes on the walls stopping her from leaning. Her frail body not making the slightest movement. For hours. For days. Sometimes, I had heard, for weeks.

She was an old woman before she came in here and eighteen months had aged her like eighteen years. What would this do to her?

It will kill her, I thought.

She will die.

And Grandfather...?

I reached the treeline with tears rolling down my face.

I owe it to them, I thought, *to at least try.*

★

Our work detail had changed a few days before. Medicinal herbs and wild ginseng were needed, they said, though I doubted any were for us. Maybe for the guards or their families in their living area with their houses and schools that were warm and clean and comfortable, with food that wasn't corn or tree bark or grasses, that didn't give you diarrhoea one day, constipation the next.

But this work gave us more freedom. We could wander out of earshot of the guard and away from where he could watch our every move. I wished he'd sit somewhere away from me, close his eyes and go to sleep and ignore us. I would work still, of course, we all would: quotas had to be met; punishments would still be inflicted if we didn't.

How nice, though, it would be to work without those eyes staring at me, without waiting for him to come along and kick my legs from under me, or give half my quota away to someone else, or point his gun at my head as he had done so many times before, watching the fear on my face, the sweat growing on my brow and the shaking of my hands. Not knowing if that would be the day he would pull the trigger.

I watched him that morning as he moved from one of us to the next to the next, checking our bags, making sure we didn't fill the bottoms with soil or the wrong leaves just to finish earlier. And I scanned through the undergrowth, thin and overharvested, searching for the right plants and the right leaves, but with my mind on other things.

An idea. A plan. Dangerous as it was.

I saw the girl again, my friend, bent over plucking at grasses, picking into the soil with her fingertips, and I made my way over to her, edging close, bending down, a glance over my shoulder to check where the guard was.

"How can I get her out?" I whispered. Her eyes flicked to me for just a second.

"My grandmother, how can I get her out of solitary?"

She shook her head. "Don't be ridiculous. You know you can't."

"But... if I don't... she'll die in there."

She shrugged. "Yeah. Or if not, she will when she comes out. Happens like that sometimes. There's nothing you can do. You know that."

"But—"

For a second she stopped working and turned on me. "No," she said. "Forget it. Forget I told you. I shouldn't have said anything."

"I'm glad you did," I whispered.

"I'm not." She plucked some leaves, lifted them to her nose and dropped them into her bag. "Because now you're going to end up getting yourself killed. Or me. I should've known better than to try to be kind. That doesn't help in here; you need to be selfish to survive."

"Selfish is how I ended up in here in the first place," I hissed.

She said nothing in reply and I edged away, feeling confused and sad. The only prisoner in this place that had spoken more than five sentences to me in over a year, that I shared something with, that I thought could be a friend – I didn't want to lose that. But how could I stand by and do nothing? When I knew what was happening to my grandmother? Because they might kill me? That could happen without me doing anything. I looked down at my empty bag, no herbs or ginseng in it.

I'll never make my quota, I thought. *He'll punish me for that anyway.*

As I edged further back, I caught my friend's eye, and I could see the concern on her face as she shook her head at me. But still I turned away from her and carried on because regardless of what she thought, or of what the consequences were, I needed to at least try.

Chapter Twenty-eight

Everything muted around me, and everything was gone. Just me. And the guard. And my grandmother somewhere at the bottom of the mountain.

I was so scared I couldn't even hear my heart trying to pound out of my chest, or my jittery, uneven breath.

I glanced over my shoulder towards the guard and saw him leering at some man, jabbing at his face, his mouth opening and closing as if he was shouting. But I could hear nothing. I pulled in a slow breath, held it and eased it out again. My decision was made. I edged towards the trees.

If I can just make it that far, I thought, *then I can hide. He won't be able to see me. Maybe won't even notice I'm missing. At least for a while. Then I can sneak down to the camp. I can find Grandmother.*

I paused, bending down, pretending to pick some plants as I peered to the side. He was walking further up the mountain now, taking something out of his pocket, lifting it to his mouth. He was eating while we starved.

I stood again, hurrying to the trees now, knowing this could be my only chance, hoping beyond hope that he wasn't looking, wasn't watching. That nobody was. Nobody's eyes were following me, wondering, questioning what I was doing.

We'd been told where to look and where to go. And I was not in a place people were looking. I was not in a place people were going.

I was nearly there. I kept my eyes on the trees, but the branches seemed thinner now I was closer, the leaves not so dense. *This won't cover me*, I thought, *won't hide me; he'll still be able to see me*. But my legs kept driving me forward and as I reached the treeline, I paused for the briefest of seconds. *I could still turn round. I could still change my mind, step back, step away*.

I paused. Thinking... thinking... I took one step into the trees. Then another. And another.

I wished the trees would wrap their branches round me, swallow me, hold me safe and transport me down to the camp. I trod through the undergrowth thinking,

I have no plan for when I get down... I haven't thought this through... What should I do? Where should I go? How will I find her?

And suddenly there was a gunshot. Just one. Tearing through the air. I stopped and ducked. Spinning around, trying to see where it had come from. I stared back at my work group, realising I hadn't walked as far as I thought. I could still see their outlines, make out who was who.

I hid behind a tree, low to the ground. I could see the guard with a gun in his hand, striding back and forth, back and forth, and I saw someone near him, her shoulders hunched, her body trembling. And I knew it was her, my friend.

I sighed and closed my eyes. He knew I was missing. Knew I must be nearby. Assumed she knew where I was. And I *knew* what he would do to her to find out. I heard him shout at her, a mess of jumbled words, and watched her cower.

My friend.

He would beat her, I knew, hit her, kick her, punch her, stamp on her, whatever he wanted to do, and when she told him, because she would, he would beat her again. Because he could.

Would he kill her? I bowed my head. I didn't want to hear the noises, or see whatever he did. Someone hurting again, and again it was my fault.

What am I doing? I thought.

But... I turned my back on her, took a breath and scurried through the undergrowth. My senses were alive and wide awake. My heart thumping so loud, my breath screaming in my lungs as I dodged in and out of trees, my legs shouting out with no strength in them. Twigs snapping, branches bending and leaves rustling. Thorns tearing at my clothes, mud slipping under my feet, bark damp and coarse on my hands.

And guilt. And determination. Banging at the sides of my brain.

Then something behind me. Breath heavy and low, panting. Feet thudding, speeding.

Closer.

And closer.

My legs kept going and going. Faster and faster downhill. So fast. Too fast. A hand on my shoulder, grabbing my hair...

And I was down.

Chapter Twenty-nine

I lifted my head from the ground and he was there. Standing over me, leering at me. Not even bothering to raise his gun. Hatred poured from his eyes as they narrowed. Spit flecked on his thin lips as they sneered at me. Specks of blood on his cheek.

My chest burned, and I lay with my mouth open, sucking air into empty lungs. He grabbed my collar and pulled me to my feet, holding me just too high so I balanced on tiptoe, then he leant towards me, his nose not quite touching mine, his breath on my face, stale and putrid.

"Where were you going?" he hissed.

I couldn't speak. My mouth and my throat were dry, my body trembling. I couldn't make a sound.

"I asked where you were going!"

I swallowed hard, took a jagged breath. "My grandmother," I gabbled, breathing in again, the trees around me tipping and spinning, the sky tilting forwards and backwards, and I felt myself rocking and swaying. "I... I... wanted to see... wanted to see my grandmother." I closed my mouth, trying to steady myself, to breathe normally, to think, think, think clearly.

I watched his head move from one side to the other as if in slow motion and I saw the sneer lift and spread across his face of evil. The power he held over me lifting his chin up and his shoulders back, and his laugh raucous and exploding into the air around us.

"Move," he ordered. His voice was low and vicious now, and he grabbed me by the hair, pulling and dragging me down the mountainside. My feet struggled to keep up. I tripped, the hair yanking from my head. He changed his grip, holding tighter, pulling harder, marching faster. I lifted my hands, trying to hold on to my hair and stop the pain, but every few steps I stumbled, and it would rip out again, and he would drop handfuls of it to the floor and grab me again. And still when we made it back to flatter ground, he didn't let go.

"Please," I said. "I'll walk. I'll keep up." But he didn't reply.

The stones on the ground tore at the skin on my knees and legs. I put out my hands, but my palms were shredded by the gravel, and all the while my mind was running madly with questions and thoughts. *Where is he taking me? What will he do? What did he do to my friend? Is she alive? Will I be by the end of the day? And Grandmother?*

We stopped at a door to a staff building, my hair clamped in his left fist, my head at an angle, so I couldn't move. With his other hand, he pulled out a bunch of keys and fingered through them for the right one. He was humming a song. I recognised it. I remembered it from school, and wished I was back there. I thought of the words, remembered the last time we sang them, my last day:

> *"The bayonet gleams, and our footsteps echo*
> *We are soldiers of the Great General*
> *Who can withstand us?*
> *We shine with fine assurance*
> *We are the army of the Comrade Leader."*

His humming stopped, and he leered at me again, dragging me through the doorway and throwing me to the floor. I looked around: this wasn't a place for punishment, it was some sort of office, but it seemed old and unused, dusty and dirty. And empty. We were alone.

He closed the door and stepped towards me. I struggled halfway to standing, but his fist hit the side of my face and I went down. I tried again, crawling backwards, but he hit me again. And again, and again.

I lost myself. I was nothing.

I stayed down, put my arms up round my head and pulled my knees to my chest. I had no more fight left in me. He came at me again, and I closed my eyes, waiting for the blow that I hoped would take me away from that place. But it didn't come. Instead I heard the chink of a belt, and my senses prickled. I tried to sit up, drag myself further backwards, get away from him, but there was nowhere to go, and his hand grabbed me and pulled me.

And from somewhere I found the strength and the will to fight, kicking and kicking at him, my arms flailing and my fingers scratching, but it did no good. He held me and I couldn't move. Couldn't. He was simply bigger and stronger. He leant towards me, his weight on me, his face looming in front of me, and I closed my eyes and put my head to one side, and I felt his mouth close to my ear, and the words he said echoed in me and around me.

"If you struggle, or shout, or scream, I'll go back up that mountain and I'll whip your friend until she dies. Then I'll do the same to your grandmother. And your grandfather."

I held my breath, trying not to cry out, or sob, or plead with him to just please let me go.

My tears were silent. My eyes I kept closed. I didn't want to see, wished I couldn't feel the pain and humiliation, wished I was somewhere else, far, far away from there.

In my head, my imagination, my memory, I drifted away, and I saw the fields of my village, the rows of tiny houses scattered here and there, the children walking to school with their uniforms on and red scarves flapping against the greying background. I stepped through the doorway to my house and sat at the table with my family, their faces smiling more than reality would've let them, and I loved them all so very much.

I watched night fall in a summertime heady and warm, staring out of the window from my bed mat, listening to my mother and father's breathing growing heavier as sleep claimed them. Stars pinpricking the deep blue sky and the light from the moon shining down. I listened to the insects, heard an owl. And I sighed with happiness and anticipation.

I strolled along a dirt path, the moonlight showing me the way, a warm silence cradling me, and there, on the corner, was a shadow, a silhouette, of him. And I saw him turn to me, his face smiling, welcoming, and I reached to take his hand with a rush of excitement and expectation as I moved towards him. I wanted to be with him. I wanted to hold his hand and touch his face, to smile and to laugh with him, to feel him at my side and know he was there with me and for me. I wanted to love him, and to feel love offered in return.

This was not memory. This was imagination; a dream I wished had been true, a happiness and satisfaction with life I had never known.

In front of me, behind my closed eyelids, Sook's face froze and his hand didn't grip mine. And slowly, slowly, the love and warmth slipped away from him, and his face turned from smile to grimace to leer, and his eyes filled with hatred and anger, mocking me and laughing at me: how easy I was to trick, how simple I was to betray.

I wanted to tell him I hated him, but as I opened my eyes to stare into those I had loved so much, Sook was gone. And I caught instead the guard's sneer as he towered over me. His laugh at me. His words as he barked at me, "Get back to work."

I was nothing but hated.

I was nothing.

Chapter Thirty

Grandmother didn't return that night.

And that night I didn't scrape a mark into the wall to count the days as they passed. Nor did I tell Grandfather what had happened to me. Did he guess, from the state of me, the smell of me, that I couldn't eat that night, couldn't speak, couldn't even look at him? I washed myself over and over, until, with his nerves already on edge, he scolded me for using too much water.

"How many walks to the stream do you think it took for that much water?" he said, pulling the bucket away from me. Yet still I felt dirty; I could feel the guard on my skin and in my hair, could smell him, see his face when I tried to sleep, wanted to scratch that image from my eyes and from my brain and pull at my skin until there was none of it left that he had touched.

I was done.

I was finished.

I wanted no more of anything.

★

I woke the next morning hoping to see Grandmother lying on her bed mat, hear the sounds of her breathing, her gentle snore. Or roll over and see her sitting at the table. For his sake more than mine. I was surprised what I felt for her when she wasn't there.

But instead as I turned round, I saw only Grandfather's eyes staring back at me, filled with the sadness his life had become, tears waiting to fall. And nothing was said, but a thousand thoughts passed, and I could see the hurt eating him, the guilt destroying him, and I wished I could do something for him.

"I'm sorry," I whispered.

"So am I."

I missed my mother. I missed my father. I missed my home and my past and my childhood stretching away from me. My memory was showing my old life as better than it had been, but even what it had been was an eternity better than this.

This was hell.

And I realised for the first time, as I lay in Grandfather's arms, avoiding the day in front of me, that keeping hope alive, that release might just one day be possible, was torture in itself. It was a hope so slim it barely existed. A chance so minute that only belief in it being there made it visible. Glance away and back, blink, an infinitesimal pause in belief, and it was gone. And finding it again, a speck, a grain, was impossible.

Life here was no life.

Who am I in this place? I thought. *What am I but waiting to die?*

Yoora, the person I had been, was gone. I was a shell. I was empty. I existed only for free labour, for their amusement and an excuse for their cruelty. I was surviving on an impossible hope that stayed with me because the alternative, freeing myself from this pain, had seemed unthinkable before.

Yet still, on the window sill, with its gentle petals of white and pink, stood my flower.

★

That morning I waited with my work unit to receive my orders for the day, my body bruised and beaten and aching, a bag of bones with no energy, my hair matted, bald patches across my scalp, my skin dry and cracked, covered in cuts and sores.

My friend stood to the side of me and I tried to get her attention, see that glint, a wink maybe, or eyes wide with concern for me, but instead she looked at me with scorn and hatred, a cut on her face that should've had stitches, an eye so bruised it was swollen shut.

I looked away, blinking and blinking to stop tears from falling. I wanted to collapse on the ground and sob like a child until someone came along and stroked my hair and whispered in my ear that it was all going to be all right. I wanted my mother to wrap her arms round me. I wanted my father's voice with its unwavering bravery, Grandfather's welcoming smile and compassion expressed in words that understood. Even my grandmother, with her honesty and astuteness, who would tell me straight that it wasn't all going to be all right, but we would keep fighting anyway.

Did I want Sook? Did I want to feel that love for him again? Or did I want to hate him? To kill him?

I trudged up the hillside with the sunlight reaching

across the sky with shades of pinks and oranges and reds, highlighting the different shades of green and brown on the trees that stretched tall ahead of us. The feel of the air with the promise of summer to come. It was calm, serene and beautiful. But inside it, underneath it, was such ugliness.

And I looked at the prisoners just like me. Hair that had not been brushed or cut or washed for a long time, clothes of rags, skin stretched over bodies of bones, ribs that could be counted, shoulder blades sticking up and out, rashes and blotches on malnourished faces. They were dying, all of them, of starvation or sickness or exhaustion.

And throughout the day, nobody spoke, or looked at me, or even acknowledged I was there; they hated me, for what I'd done the day before and the danger I'd put them in. All would've been punished for the actions I'd taken and my quota not being filled.

I had made so many enemies in such a short space of time, yet had achieved nothing. I felt disappointed with myself; annoyed for being so reckless; angry for not being faster. Ashamed by what had happened with the guard.

Would I do it again? I would've liked to have said yes because then I could say that at least I tried. And for that I could feel just a twinge of pride. But after what had happened, and not just to me, I wasn't sure.

Chapter Thirty-one

I dreamt again that night of my city of lights, but this time it felt like my mind was toying with me, playing with me, torturing me with things I would never know.

I would never stare into the white headlights of cars streaming towards me or up to those buildings with windows lit orange or yellow or white. I would never breathe in the smells of food drifting from restaurants and takeaways or feel the sweetness of the taste on my tongue. And I would never hear music blaring from bars or see people dancing in bright clothes with joy in their smiles.

I pulled the postcard from inside the mat and moved into the shafts of dusty moonlight filtering into the room, staring at its colours and images, watching them blur into one as tears filled my eyes and fell down my cheeks and on to the picture in my hand of that city called Seoul.

Holding the blankets round me, I stood up and with anger and hatred filling every part of me, I held the postcard over the last flame dwindling in the furnace. I watched it lick the corner, watched a line of orange creep along the white edge, watched the edge turn to black and crumble and fall away, watched that line of orange creep towards the buildings and the lights and my dream.

But I pulled it back, changing my mind, burning my fingertips as I snuffed out the edges, ash smudging grey on my hands. Again fire had nearly claimed it.

It was only then, as I turned round, gripping my postcard, that I noticed it: something lying on the floor, a crumpled heap that from a distance, in the half-light, was a pile of clothes, bloodied in places, dirty all over. Was this someone's gift to us? A pile of clothes? Some kind of threat to me?

I stepped forward, an arm extended, my hand stretching out, and I knelt on the floor and leant in close, my hand touching the cloth, pulling it back. It looked like a face, and I peered in, closer and closer... and I stopped... frozen...

Grandmother.

And then I saw, backed up to the wall, his knees to his chest, shivering in the night air, Grandfather, staring at her body.

"Is she...?" I breathed, then paused. "Is she...?" But I couldn't say the words. I waited for his response, watching him for some recognition, but he said nothing, his face a mask of shock.

I pulled back the material and touched her face; she felt cold. I placed my hand on her neck, feeling for a pulse, and I closed my eyes, concentrating through the silence, and I thought perhaps I could feel something. Couldn't I?

I lowered my face to hers, my cheek to her mouth, and was sure, sure I could feel breath, and I put my ear to her chest, listening, feeling, waiting. A heartbeat, I was sure, faint, slow, but a heartbeat.

"She..." I began, my eyes staring through the shadows of darkness to Grandfather. He shook his head, and I looked back down to the body in front of me, stroking away the grey hair from her face, touching my fingers along her skin. And then I saw her eyelids flicker.

I gasped, turning to Grandfather, no words I could say, staring at him, my head nodding. He moved, crawling forward, his eyes never leaving her, and he saw her mouth ease open, her tongue reach to her lips, her eyelids flutter. Like magic his face lit up, his smile stuttering to life, tears of relief springing down his cheeks, his body bending to her, his arms lifting her, cradling her head to his chest, rocking her back and forth, staring down at the face he had loved for so many years. Brought back to him. Alive.

I watched them together for a moment, then I shuffled to my knees to move away – I felt an intruder. But I glanced back for a second and saw my grandmother's heavy eyes looking at me.

She was trying to speak, but her voice was too quiet, rasping and painful. She was a pitiful sight. I scooped water into a cup and held it for her to sip, pausing for the briefest of seconds to look at her face of shadows and shades and darkness that was barely alive, then I lowered my face to hers to kiss her on the cheek, and heard the smallest whisper. "I was wrong."

I frowned. "No..."

But she opened her mouth again and I stopped. "I was proud to be your grandmother."

I couldn't reply to that, I couldn't speak. I edged backwards to my bed mat with tears streaming down my face and faded into the background, trying not to listen to their broken conversation of apologies and love and regrets.

I knew she wouldn't see the morning light, that she would leave with the darkness, but I was glad for those words she'd said to me, and the few hours she and Grandfather had together, that they could say goodbye and part with nothing unspoken.

I hoped she accepted his apology, though I thought it unnecessary. And I hoped he forgave himself.

Whether she still blamed me for the time spent in prison, or was angry with me still for my loose tongue, didn't matter – I wasn't important. *He* was important. What she felt for him in those last few hours and what she said to him as they parted.

Chapter Thirty-two

I must've closed my eyes. I must've slept.

I don't remember hearing their voices stop. Or her breathing. I don't remember him lifting her head from his lap, carrying her to her bed or laying her down. But when I opened my eyes sunlight was straining into the hut and her face and her body were covered as she lay peacefully.

I rested my hand on his, but he kept his head down, hiding his grief and his pain from me. And there were no words to say, or explanations, or apologies.

We were now two. Only two. And the two of us went to work that day because we had no choice and, it seemed, only the two of us grieved for her, or missed her.

There was no proper burial site, no place to go to

grieve, no system of dealing with the dead. It seemed the bodies disappeared, or sometimes the people, still alive.

Why we were given Grandmother back alive was a question we would never be able to ask, nor would it ever be explained; as with so many other things, it was the whim of the guards. But it was our instruction to deal with her body, and so, after twelve hours' work, with little food and no rest, we climbed back up the mountainside.

He carried her in his arms, clutched to his chest, her body wrapped in nothing because we had nothing, her clothes bloodstained and dirty. I wanted to help him, share the weight, but her weight was nothing; she was a doll, her stick arms and legs barely swinging as he walked along.

We moved in near darkness, and I guided him as best I could to where I had buried the boy with my friend, the perimeter fence a few hundred metres away. We dug into the earth with tin bowls from our hut, as we had no tools, hoping we had chosen a spot that was still empty, hoping the cold, dim light from a distant watchtower swinging intermittently near us would help us see if we had not.

Some hours later we sat, exhausted, at her shallow grave, with my flower replanted on top. The silence, for once, was beautiful, reminding me of evenings at home, of sitting with someone I cared for, and just being, quietly. I wished I could stop time at that moment.

I moved closer to Grandfather and felt his arm go round me, and I watched and waited for the swing of the light, hypnotic in its timing.

"Tell me more about my family," I said.

"Yoora, I..."

"Tell me how all that was in my head, that dream of the city. Tell me before this happens to me." I nodded towards the shallow grave. "Or you."

His shoulders drooped. "Oh, child," he sighed, then he looked up at me, shaking his head. "I shouldn't call you that, should I? Because you're not and haven't been for a long time. And you shouldn't be here. I wish to every god in every land that you weren't. I wish you were a long way away, somewhere safe.

"The postcard of Seoul," he said, "is where the rest of your family live. My brother's children and their wives and husbands, and their children too. Like I told you the other night. That's where the letters came from. And the magazines and newspapers. And all the photos.

We've been writing to each other for years, since we first heard back from them when your father was a boy. The letters smuggled out across the Chinese border, smuggled back in again. They know all about you; we sent them photographs when you were born and as you grew up." He touched my hand.

"When you were little I would read the letters to you, show you the photographs, share with you this family you had in a different country, a different world. I told you all about them. Their names, what they did for a living, what their houses were like, what they liked to do, and you loved it. But when you started school you mentioned to your teacher that you had an uncle who'd been on an aeroplane, and a cousin who liked pop music.

"Those things we managed to talk our way out of. We told her you had an active imagination and thought Kim Jong Il was your uncle. But it made it clear to us that it was too dangerous. It was a risk we couldn't afford to take, so we stopped talking about them, and if ever you asked questions about them, we changed the subject.

"But somehow it stayed in your head and you had that dream, all those years later. You know what that dream was? It was made up of everything you'd seen or heard about South Korea and your family. All of the postcards we had, and photographs, and letters describing the buildings, food and music and the people. All that you saw us burn, apart from the ones your mother hid, and the postcard you took."

I nodded. I remembered. I understood.

"You know we've been lied to for years. You know we *don't* have it better than any other country," he whispered. "We *do* have a lot to envy. There *are* places with more food than here, where prisons like this are against the law. Don't you?"

I nodded. I did know that. But somehow hearing it spoken out loud, from someone else's mouth and not my own thoughts spinning in circles, made it more real, made it daring, made it feel scandalous.

"And you understand that so much of what you were taught at school is wrong."

I nodded again, and we fell silent. I did understand, had suspected, or known that much for a while now, but the scale of it felt so shocking, and that made it difficult to believe. How much there was, over these prison fences and across this country's borders, that I knew nothing about. And how much I had believed, for a lifetime, that was wrong, that was lies, that was made up to manipulate and control.

"I wouldn't lie to you, Yoora."

I stretched my hand out to his. "I know." And I really did.

"I wish you could get out of here somehow, some way, and live. I wish you could find your mother and the letters she has, with the addresses, and escape this country. Oh, I wish, Yoora, wish you could live your life. You could meet them, you could finally see them, your aunt and your uncle, your cousin, Jin-Kyong—"

"No." I shook my head. "That's enough. I don't want to know any more. Don't tell me their names. Don't tell me what they look like." It was all so useless. Thinking like that, even realising the truth – there was no point. There was no way out and there was no hoping for it. My life was here, as my death would be. I had accepted that now. But still he, Grandfather, had hope left inside him, and he was supposed to be the sensible one, the mature one, the adult. And it felt as if I should be telling him to grow up and face the truth.

How could I do that to him?

"But, Yoora, I thought..." He didn't finish his sentence. Suddenly his body tensed next to me and he pulled me closer, and I heard what he must have before me: rustling in the undergrowth around us, snapping of branches, soft footfalls on wet earth. My heart pounded, my mouth went dry and I was scared.

"The guard?" I whispered.

But as I moved my head around, the light swept in front of us and I saw it. Its eyes staring at me and Grandfather, unblinking, its body quite still, waiting. But then the light was gone, darkness around us again and in that space between us and the animal I was sure I'd seen, a space that could be getting smaller. It could be creeping towards us; it could be next to us, in front of us, a paw raised, its mouth open.

The tiger.

Chapter Thirty-three

We waited in time that stretched out eternally for a movement or a sound or a glimpse, the threat of a growl or its breath in our faces. Again the light scooped over us, and I saw the animal's massive head, its round face and its staring eyes still watching us, as if it could see right into us and read our every thought and feeling. Unblinking and fearless. And I didn't feel scared now. I could breathe again.

And it turned and strolled away from us. "Follow her," Grandfather whispered, grabbing me by the arm, pulling me along. "How did she get in here?"

"Follow her? What if she kills us?"

In front of us the tiger speeded up, her massive paws moving noiselessly and effortlessly through the snow.

"She won't live in here. There wouldn't be enough food for her."

"But then...?"

We followed at a distance, her shape the only thing moving. And the light flowed over her again, catching her, the power in her shoulders, her fur made of colours I had never seen before, spreading around and across her. She was beautiful. But... I knew where she was heading.

"No." I shook my head, slowing down, Grandfather pulling at me. "She's going to the fence. We'll be seen. They'll catch us."

"We've got to see how she gets out," he hissed. "Come on!"

I stumbled forward, thinking, worrying, wanting to turn back. But... There was the fence. And I could see it. In darkness and in shadow, but I could see it. We were so close, so close to the outside.

The tiger stopped and looked back at us for a moment. Then she lowered her shoulders and pulled something from the ground with her mouth: a cub, so small, so young. I caught my breath, pinpricks running over my skin and down my back, and I watched her turn away from me, lower herself to the ground and drag herself forward and under the fence.

We froze. We stood without a word. Watching. Waiting.

For what? To wake up? To realise it was a dream? For a guard to appear, laughing at us for believing what we thought we could see? I don't think either of us knew. But finally, finally, we stepped forward, dodging the light by timing, and we stood, staring in disbelief at the gap in the bottom of the fence, the hole in the ground underneath and the tiger and her cub on the other side of it.

"We can go," Grandfather whispered. "We can escape. We can follow her through there and run. We'd fit through that gap. If she can, then we can."

I was shaking. "Isn't it electrified?" I asked.

"Maybe not this bit. Maybe the gap in it means it's not working. She did it," he repeated, pointing to the tiger.

I looked back at her. "Why is she still there? Why doesn't she run?" We were so close. I stared at her, could just make out her white whiskers flickering in the moonlight, the different shades of her fur, her teeth, so big and so powerful, gently holding her cub between them. And her eyes, like pools, yellowy and glistening, staring back at me.

I took a step closer and she turned, and it was only

then that I saw what had been stopping her. The ditch. I sighed. Of course, the ditch.

But I watched as she jumped it, that huge, powerful creature, with all that muscle in her body and her legs, her innate desire to protect her cub. She flew over it. And I held my breath, remembering now, of course, that at the bottom of the ditches were spikes sticking up as a final attack on any who might dare to make an escape.

No problem for the tiger. She disappeared into the darkness and away from us, as free as she'd always been. Just an animal, but an animal that could walk out of here, cross borders, do as she pleased.

"I can't, Grandfather," I whispered. "I can't. I daren't." All I could think of was the spikes. Falling on them. The pain. The humiliation. Guards finding me, standing over me, laughing at me. Watching me die, slowly and painfully.

"Yoora, we could be free."

I shook my head, it seemed so impossible. "But... but... it's only a few hours until roll call. How far could we get? Even if we made it over the ditch. And... and... we don't have any food. No," I said. "No. It's too much."

What had happened to me? Where had my courage gone? My daring? Was I creating excuses, or were my worries legitimate? There it was, staring at me one minute through intermittent light, disappearing the next into darkness – an escape. What was I waiting for?

Before that moment, I hadn't realised the control that this place now had over me, holding my head prisoner as much as my body. *Is it electrified?* I thought. *Can we make it over the ditch? Do we have enough strength to run far enough away into the night? Will we be found? What will they do to us if we are?*

I turned and I ran. Because I couldn't stand being there, so close to the fence, that hole, and to escape, so close to the memory and the smell of that beautiful creature, who had looked right into my very being and turned away to freedom with such ease.

And because, I realised, now that I was faced with a real chance, I didn't dare. My fight, my spirit, had gone. I couldn't do anything else foolish. I had learnt my lesson and I had lost a part of me. I had become a coward and that I couldn't cope with.

"No more," I whispered, shaking my head. "No more."

Chapter Thirty-four

The thought of that hole in the fence stayed with me like torture. Tempting me back up the mountain, daring me to push my body through it, taunting me with thoughts of freedom and the life that could await me beyond, and ideas of heading for the protection of my mother. And the thought that I couldn't do it, couldn't risk it, didn't dare.

It stayed with me more than the memory of my grandmother.

Maybe, I thought, *if it was just me, just my life. Then if I didn't make the jump, if I fell into the ditch, landed on those spikes, at least it would end it all, release me. But what about Grandfather? How could I give him another person to say goodbye to? How could I leave him by himself?*

It made such a difference, having someone with you, even if it was only to share a look of exasperation as the sun rose on yet another morning, or to hear your sigh as you came home exhausted again.

I was staying alive for him and, I believed, he was doing the same for me.

★

A few weeks after we buried Grandmother, I began to get sick.

I threw up everywhere, all the time. And when I had nothing left in my stomach, I would retch and retch, dropping on to my knees with my arms gripped round my body, pulling up dregs of yellow bile, and feeling like my stomach was turning inside out. I would sweat and I would shake. My chest sore, my back stiff, my throat on fire.

And my head would throb, and the white of one of my eyes turned red with blood from the pressure. It was a sickness like I had never felt before. One that never stopped, that I could never forget, that consumed me day after day after day.

Grandfather would hold me and rock me, wipe the sweat from my face and kiss my forehead, hold a spoonful of food to my mouth, or a cupful of water. I had been tired for so long, and now I was exhausted; I was draining away, disappearing and weakening.

Dying?

We went through all the possibilities: poisoning from food or some leaves or plant I'd eaten, or a virus, or a stomach bug – but it could've been anything. Every day someone died from some illness, something, no doubt, that could've been cured with the right medicine, prevented with clean water or proper toilets. But we had none of those. Not even a doctor. I was sick walking up the mountainside and I was sick coming down it, and eventually the guard, that awful guard whose face I couldn't bear to look at, took me from my work unit and swapped me for someone else. Maybe he thought someone might find out what happened. Maybe he wanted someone stronger or fitter, who could work better. Or someone different to pick on and to harass. Or maybe he was just done with me. I hoped that would be the last I saw of him.

They put me instead into the shoe factory and I didn't know whether I felt happy about it or sad. I would never again see the girl I thought had been my friend, be able to make up for what had happened, or apologise any more. But I would be away from the guard, wouldn't have to walk so far or work so hard, and when winter came back again I'd be inside.

But I went through the doors on that first day and into a wall of heat and noise, and realised how much better the outside was.

Steam rose from huge vats of melting rubber, heat billowing out into clouds of hot air that hung around, obscuring everything from view, drenching the floor and the people and the equipment as they cooled. And the smell of the rubber flowed over and around me, a foul, acrid stench that made my head feel thick, my throat close up and my stomach pull as sickness plagued me again. Huge cutters thundered on to sheets of rubber, threatening arms or fingers that were too slow, yet were always tired. Blades were scratched and sharpened before slicing away at leather, machines groaned, doors slammed and pots hissed. But nobody said a word.

My head spun, sweat poured from me, my body tipped and tilted with dizziness, the heat bearing down on me, the humidity.

With two other people, I tilted a vat of boiling rubber, still so heavy, watching the black liquid, like tar, bubbling and oozing into the mould, the smell overwhelming, my stomach turning and my body retching, but I couldn't let go. If I did, the vat would fall, the rubber would be ruined and we would be punished. All of us.

But the second it was down, I would run outside to throw up, or the smell would overcome me and I would pass out, waking sometime later, propped in a corner, or left on the floor with people stepping over me. There was no concern, or doctor to be requested, or leave granted; only complaints that I had not worked hard enough or long enough, or punishments given for not meeting my quota.

But how could I?

Grandfather's work changed too. It was a piece of good luck for us, a small change but a blessing. He was out of the coal mine with the narrow tunnels that were making his back crooked, away from explosives that the children were forced to light and then run away from, and leaving behind the black dust that he breathed into his lungs every day and tried to cough up every night.

Instead he was on the land in the fresh air, preparing the crops, or the ground, or tending to the few farm animals. And now, instead of sneaking out one piece of coal if a guard wasn't looking, it would be a handful of animal food here and there. Anything to eat we were grateful for, even more so if it wasn't cornmeal.

I saw the change in him, however subtle: his eyes a little brighter, his skin a little clearer and his back a little straighter.

We sat down at the table to our bowls of corn one evening, still muttering the thanks we had to give to our Great Leader for the meal in front of us, and although I tried to eat, every time I lifted the spoon to my mouth, I could feel bile turning in my stomach. Grandfather would look at me with such concern on his face, the same concern he had worn for a long time now, but more intense lately, more lines on his face and worry in his eyes.

"I've got something for you to eat," he said. He reached into his pocket and pulled out a couple of cockroaches, some worms and a few bugs. "It's good protein. It'll help build you up."

I stared at them, for a moment disgusted. I had no memory of when I had last eaten meat, but if it helped me to feel better, gave me more energy so I could at least work and make my quota, then there was no reason why not. But still I stared at them.

I picked up the worm, holding it between my fingers, watching its body writhing. "I wish it was dead already," I whispered. "I feel like he's watching me."

"He is," Grandfather said. "He's shouting, *Don't eat me, don't eat me.*"

A smile crept across my face. "You eat one as well," I said.

He paused and I watched him, waiting for him to say that I needed it more, or he would have some tomorrow, or some other excuse. But he didn't. He picked up a woodlouse, its tiny legs wiggling in the air, and he popped it into his mouth. I watched him swallow, open his mouth, stick out his tongue and prove to me it had gone.

And he smiled at me. "Your turn."

I nodded, took a deep breath, opened my mouth wide and dropped the worm straight down my throat, swallowing before I could even think what I was doing. "It's like a noodle," I spluttered. And this strange thing happened, this noise I hadn't heard for so long, that I thought I would never hear again – my grandfather's laugh. Not a snigger or a chortle hidden behind cupped hands, but a laugh, big and booming and hearty.

A smile lifted my face, and I laughed too, the sound like honey, like warmth and family and love.

"The cockroach now," he said.

With a face of disgust, I picked up two brown

bodies, passing one to Grandfather, its legs itching away, trying to find the ground that had disappeared from under it.

"And you have to chew this time," he said.

I glared at him with wide eyes, my mouth clamped shut, the creature dangling in front of me. I looked across to Grandfather. He opened his mouth, stuck out his tongue, placed the cockroach on it and drew it back inside his mouth. My eyes stayed wide as I watched his mouth move up and down and side to side, saw his throat swallow and again his mouth was empty.

He lifted a palm to me. "Come on."

I opened my mouth and with shaking hands put the cockroach on my tongue, and I could feel its legs moving in my mouth, feel its antennae on my lips. I shook my head.

"Yes, you can," he urged.

I closed my mouth. Grandfather leant towards me. "Imagine," he whispered, "that the cockroach is Kim Jong Il."

My eyes widened further.

"Imagine you can crush him with your teeth. Destroy him. Get rid of him for ever."

I couldn't open my mouth to tell him that he shouldn't say that.

"Or the guard," he continued. "Or Sook's mother, or..."

I didn't wait for him to list any more names. I bit down on that cockroach with every piece of hatred inside me. I chewed it and destroyed it and swallowed it, and I looked up at him with a smirk on my face. "Let's eat the rest," I said.

Our laughter turned into giggles like schoolchildren, echoing across our walls of mud. Whatever the neighbours thought, I didn't care. A laugh was not a sound heard in this place, only perhaps from a guard, but then a laugh of cruelty, of pleasure taken in someone else's suffering. This, with Grandfather, was of sharing, of humour, of love, but most probably a sound few would still recognise. That was the true sadness.

For the first time in what seemed like months, after eating those insects that day, I wasn't sick, and as we finished our mixture of creatures, I caught the look of relief on his face, a glimpse of contentment in his eyes. The smile stayed on his face too, and he reached out his hand, scrawny and thin with skin like paper that had been left out in the sun for years, and patted my arm. "We'll make you better," he whispered, and I honestly think he believed it.

★

As time passed, we ate whatever we could find: cockroaches, worms, spiders, beetles and bugs. We ate leaves, though we never knew whether or not they were poisonous, bark that we'd peeled off trees and softened in water. Once we ate slops stolen from the pigsty, although only once, since a colleague of Grandfather's was seen licking it from his hands and was shot on the spot. We even ate gratings of leather I stole from the shoe factory floor, softening them as we did the bark.

Some evenings I would walk back from the factory past the fields where Grandfather worked, and I could smell the soil, freshly turned and covered with autumn drizzle, and I could feel my mouth watering, and I wanted so badly to crouch down, lift the earth to my mouth and take the biggest bite. Feel it filling my mouth and sliding down my throat. But I never did.

I once found a dead bird rotting away, and we picked off the maggots and stripped it bare to its bones. Then we ate the maggots. It was one of the best meals I had there.

I heard of prisoners eating clay, or swallowing stones

so their stomachs felt full. Others taking flesh from dead family members before they buried them. Roasting it, frying it, boiling it; they said it tasted like pork.

Would I do that? I asked myself. *Could I have done that? To Grandmother?*

I had no answer. Hunger does strange things to a person. Those who ate the clay died the same day.

We ate these things as a way of trying to survive, yet never knowing if they would kill us.

Chapter Thirty-five

The sickness came and went, but the tiredness stayed. I could've slept all day if I'd been allowed, and all night. In truth I could've fallen asleep and never woken again. I slept through storms, so my grandfather said, that made the hut feel as if it was being picked up and tossed around. I slept through screaming from the neighbour when her husband died. I slept through our door banging in the wind, and a visit from someone who hid a knife under my clothes.

Was it a threat? Or a warning? Was I being set up for something? I slipped it under my bed and carried on with everyday life.

And I didn't tell Grandfather.

★

Every morning, for however many mornings I didn't want to know and couldn't keep track of, I dragged myself out of bed and smiled at Grandfather, and every morning he did the same.

I never stopped to think how long I could keep this up for, or to think of the friend I had had, yet lost. And I forced myself never, *never*, to think of that tiger or the fence or the hole. That would've been cruel; that would've been torture.

I was thankful for small things – I was away from the guard, I was alive and so was Grandfather. Too thankful too soon. Because despite how tired I was, and how heavily I usually slept, that night I woke. Not slowly or gently or with my eyes gradually opening, looking around and realising it was still night-time and I could sleep a while longer, but suddenly. Like a slap in the face, or the bang of a gun, or a light blazing through the dark.

I could hear it, I could feel it. Something in the hut. I slowed my breathing, quietened it, listened across the darkness and the silence for something that didn't fit, something that wasn't right. I could hear Grandfather's laboured breathing – breathing in with a struggle and a rattle in his chest, breathing out with relief, then a pause and in again.

But something else was behind that sound. Something faster, sharper, cleaner.

A floorboard creaked and my head flicked round, and I saw a shadow move towards me so quickly. He was there. Above me. His face filling my vision. The unmistakable smell of him.

I wanted to scream, shout for help even though I knew none would be coming, wake Grandfather even though there was nothing he could do.

Help me, I wanted to shout to the sky, to the world, to everyone out there, *somebody please, please somebody care. Do it to somebody else, not to me, not again.*

His hand clamped across my mouth, forcing my head back on the pillow, and I kicked my legs and thrashed my arms, but he didn't stop. I remembered the knife hiding under the bed and tried to reach around to it, but I saw the shape of his head move back and forth and his finger lift to his lips to silence me.

"Move, or make a noise, and I'll kill your grandfather too," he hissed in my ear.

So I stopped. As he pulled away the blankets, I kept my legs still, and as he moved one hand down, and every part of me wanted to shudder and scream and grab that knife and bury it into him, I didn't move a muscle. Not even as his hand reached my stomach and silent tears rolled down my face.

I knew what was coming, but what could I do? I was stuck. I was helpless. And so I closed my eyes, resigned, sucked in one ragged breath after another, and waited. But his hand moved back up. And I felt his fingers at my face, forcing apart my teeth, and I felt something, some pill or tablet or capsule, drop into my mouth and fall to the back of my throat.

"Do you remember what I told you?" he whispered, one hand gripping my mouth closed.

I didn't move.

"That one day, when I'd had enough of you, I'd kill you? You remember that?"

Through my tears I watched his face distort from anger to pleasure. A grin, a leer on his lips, of satisfaction and enjoyment. And power.

"Swallow," he whispered.

I stared at him. I could feel the pill on the back of my tongue, big and wide and thick. *What is it?* my head screamed. *What is it?*

His other hand went to my throat, rough fingers stroking down it. "Swallow," he said again.

I sucked in breath through my nose and felt the saliva growing in my mouth. *No*, I thought. *No, no, no.*

"You want your grandfather to die too?" he whispered in my ear.

I looked away from him and closed my eyes. And the face of my grandfather came towards me through the darkness, and then my grandmother, and my mother, and my father, one fading to the next. And after my father came the last. And I stared at him, at his smile, into his eyes, and I thought of goodbye.

How long will it take? I wondered. *How painful will it be?*

And I swallowed.

Chapter Thirty-six

I didn't open my eyes as I felt him lift off me. Nor as I listened to his heavy boots across our floor, or when the door banged shut and silence grew around me.

I just lay there. I could feel the pill, huge and thick, like a knot in my throat, easing down so slowly.

How long? I thought again. *How painful? If only I could drift back to sleep and never wake. That would be so much easier.*

I calmed my breathing and drifted around in the blackness behind my eyes and in my head.

Not long, I thought. *Not long.*

I felt so tired, so tired, of fighting, of trying, of working, of struggling, of hunger and pain and death waiting for me. It would be so easy to just lie there, and wait, and everything, *everything*, would be gone.

Gone.

I opened my eyes, shaking my head, scrambling to all fours. "Grandfather," I said as loud as I could. But he was already coming towards me.

"What did he do to you? Oh, Yoora, I'm so sorry I didn't wake. I didn't hear him, not until he was going. What did he do?"

Panic was taking over me, my lungs burning as I sucked in breath after breath, my head spinning and everything blurring.

I don't want to die, I thought. *Not like this, not here.*

"Yoora, calm down, breathe, talk to me."

I lifted a hand and pointed to my mouth, touching my lips. "He..." I gasped. "A tablet... or... he..."

"He gave you a tablet?"

I nodded. Sweat dripped from me, as still I struggled to breathe; the room, Grandfather, everything was spinning and tipping and I could feel myself slipping from consciousness.

"Yoora, calm down, breathe. Or you're going to pass out. Look at me." He held my face in his hands. "Did you swallow it?"

I stared at him with my mouth wide, trying to concentrate on what he was saying, slow my breathing. I nodded. "I had to."

Suddenly his fingers were in my mouth and down my throat, and I was retching again and again.

"It won't have dissolved yet," he said. "If we're quick. If we can get it out."

My chest and stomach pulled and ached as I retched again, so little to bring back up. But I felt it rising up my throat and into my mouth, and I spat it out on to the floor. A big fat white pill. Grandfather's arms went round me, pulling me towards him and holding me.

"What is it?" I whispered.

He prodded it with his finger. "I don't know. Poison maybe." He shrugged. "But it hasn't started dissolving. You'll be all right."

"Why, Grandfather?" I asked. "Why do you think he did that?"

He looked at me for a moment, pushing back my hair from my sweaty face, wiping the tears from my cheeks. "Because he can," he whispered.

★

I don't think for the rest of the night that either of us slept. I closed my eyes and my thoughts drifted, but it was never to anywhere nice and was never without worries. The same ones over and over. The guard would be expecting me to be dead. There was no way to hide or pretend. How long would it be before he found out? What would he think then? What would he do? How many days would it be before he tried it again?

Chapter Thirty-seven

At the beginning of every day, I woke thankful to still be breathing. And at the end of every day, I sighed with relief, for that fraction more time, even in the most terrible of places.

I was certain the guard knew by now, certain he would be planning, watching, waiting, that he would come again, when he was ready.

Grandfather took to bringing something back with him from the fields every evening – a stone that was a strange shape or reminded him of something, a broken stick with bark the colour of our old front door, or a thick blade of grass that he held between his thumbs and blew on to make a noise. Things to cheer me, I think. I appreciated it.

I knew a week had passed since the attack because he brought home the seventh thing.

"Look, Yoora," he said with a smile on his face. "I found a feather."

I held it between my fingers, long and graceful and sleek, then brushed it down my palm.

"We need to leave, Grandfather," I said. "It's the only thing we can do. He's going to come back for me, and you too probably. At least this way we have a chance, we can try, we can find the hole in the fence again, and crawl through, and we can jump the ditch, and... and... we have to try."

"They've probably fixed it," he replied, turning away.

"But they might not have done. We can go and try, and if they have, we can come back."

His sigh was heavy and long and despondent. I watched his back as his head slumped and his hand ran through his hair.

"Grandfather," I whispered. "Please. We have to try."

He didn't turn to look at me; he just shook his head. "Not yet, Yoora, not yet."

Then when? I wanted to say. *When?*

Chapter Thirty-eight

I didn't know what month it was when I woke that morning, or what day. I had rubbed away all the marks on my wall, smoothed away the days and weeks and months I had spent there. I didn't want to keep track of my life disappearing as one season bled into another and another.

I woke that morning to find that the sickness was back, with a ferocity I could never have imagined.

I woke in pain. More than pain. With my stomach turning inside out and my back trying to bend me double. I woke certain I was dying.

I rolled on to my side and over to my knees, crawling and staggering from my bed and to the door, scrabbling at the handle and pulling myself outside. Crouching on the ground, I retched and retched, steam lifting from the puddle of sick at my feet, bile stinging through my nostrils. I couldn't move. Daren't move in case it hurt more. I just wanted to cry and curl up and disappear.

I felt Grandfather's arm sneak round my waist, and try to lift me to standing, my body coiled tight as he tried to hold me up and guide me back inside.

"Lie down," he whispered, and eased me on to the bed.

I stared up at him. *What is that look in his eyes?* I thought. *What is he keeping from me?*

"Grandfather?" I breathed. "I think I'm dying." Tears streamed down my face and my body shook and trembled and I clasped at my stomach again, lurching forward. "Please."

He leant towards me. "Sssshhhhh," he whispered. And with his face close to mine, he stroked my hair, his breathing soft and slow on my cheek, measured and relaxed. "You're not going to die," he said. "Not here. Not yet." His fingers rubbed down my cheek, so rough and dry, but so calm, and that calm seeped into me and I felt myself relax, and felt the pain subside a little.

I was hot and cold, clammy and shaky. "What did we eat yesterday?" I asked.

He shrugged and placed his hands on my stomach,

then on my sides, and I watched his frown grow and listened to his heavy sigh. He didn't smile, he just stared at me, with a thoughtfulness that worried me, and he kissed me on the forehead, stood up and moved to the window, staring out. "Snow's coming," he whispered.

I curled up on top of the blanket, my back aching, my body hurting all over. "I just want to sleep," I whispered. My eyes were closed, but I felt him next to me and I heard a bowl put in front of me, but I didn't open my eyes. I didn't want to see yet more cornmeal.

"You have to eat," he said. "Even if you throw it back up again. You have to try."

I opened my eyes a crack and through the blurriness I tried to focus on the bowl. It didn't look like cornmeal; it looked like, and I could barely believe it, noodles. A bowl of noodles. But no, it couldn't be, I knew it couldn't. My eyes peered open more. "Dried worms," I stated.

"I've been saving them." He sat next to me, his cornmeal in front of him.

"Why aren't you having any?"

"I'm not ill," he replied.

"But—"

His head was shaking. "No arguments." He eased me up to sitting and propped me against the wall, and with hands still trembling, I dropped a worm into my mouth and chewed. He lifted a cup of water to my lips and the coolness of it felt wonderful on my tongue and down my throat.

I knew I had to go to work and I knew it would be better, easier, if there was something in my stomach, some energy I hoped. And so one by one, I took each worm, chewed and swallowed.

The pain subsided, but still I ached, and still I felt sick and weak, but we walked together, me and Grandfather, along the path to work, quiet but for the footsteps of hundreds if not thousands of other prisoners, not a word from their lips – no gossip, no chatter, no news or anything. And not a word from ours.

I remember that morning so well. I was gripped by a fear so complete, a knowledge so unquestionable, that it would be my last. The words playing over and over in my head – *I will not take this walk tomorrow.* And no matter how much I tried to reason with myself, I couldn't shake it. I felt so ill. I was dying. I was certain.

Grandfather turned off at the fields and I continued away from him with tears stinging my eyes. As I reached the break in the path, I turned back to see him. He was standing, quite still, watching me go, and we held each other's gaze for a moment, the air stagnant as something unseen passed across the space between us, a knowledge or recognition, an answer to a question never asked.

"I love you, Grandfather," I breathed, and I wished the words would carry on the wind. I wished I could go back to him. I wished I could tell a guard I was ill, that I needed to lie down, rest for the day. But there were no sick days. There were just alive days or dead days.

We stared at each other across the empty fields, and I watched a guard march up to him. But Grandfather was oblivious to the questions even I could hear as to why he was doing nothing, or the guard shouting to get back to work, and I hoped he was oblivious to the pain gripping my stomach and feeding into my back, my body trembling as I tried not to stagger forward, or curl over, or shout out. Because I would not allow him to see what was happening to me or how much I was hurting.

Again the guard shouted, and he lifted his stick, and I watched it come down across Grandfather's back, but

I didn't move or shout or scream. I waited instead for him to stand up, then I turned and walked away.

Because I had to.

★

The factory loomed up in front of me, the smell of rubber turning my stomach as I headed through the doors, the heat like a slap in the face that took your breath away. My head was spinning, darkness in front of my eyes with lights speckling, a fuzzy head, a thick throat; the presses, the people, the vats of liquid rubber, the conveyor belts, the cutting blades, the strip lights high above me, all looming in and out of focus, back and forth in my vision.

The heat, stifling, constricting, suffocating.

Someone, a woman, loomed close to me, her eyes sharp and narrow, her face a skeleton, peering at me, frowning at me, her head shaking. *What?* I thought or maybe said, confused.

Sickness came again, and I ran outside, falling to the ground, retching and retching until a worm came up: my breakfast.

"You stinking dog!" shouted a guard and I felt a boot in my leg. "Get up, get back to work, you have a quota to make. You want to let down our Dear Leader?"

I felt my head shake, heard my words of innocence and saw, somehow, his boots trudge away from me. Then kind hands lifted me to standing, fingers pushing back the hair from my face, eyes filled with compassion looking into mine.

"Your grandfather loves you very much," she whispered.

The fog cleared from in front of my eyes and I saw her, an old face, the woman from near our hut who had helped us way back on our arrival here. Her eyes were full of pain, yet survival, her skin fragile like it would split if she smiled, her body so frail that if I breathed on her, I thought she'd fall.

"He asked me to look after you. To make sure you get back tonight. Promised me food, he did. And good food. Cockroaches, slops from the pigs."

I remembered her, remembered her daughter who had died not long ago. She was one of those who had eaten the clay.

"I can't remember your name," I said.

She shook her head. "You never knew it." And before we passed back through the doors, before we were surrounded by a million eyes watching and judging, she stared hard into my face and put a hand upon my stomach. "Hurt much now?"

"Eased a little," I replied.

She followed me over to the presses, the sheets of rubber formed, turned over, the shapes pressed out. "Happens like that though, I think," I muttered, more to myself than to her. "Food poisoning. Comes and goes, I think. The pain."

She gave me the strangest of looks from the corner of her eye, then she nodded, a slow, silent movement, her eyes flicking over me, watching me.

Chapter Thirty-nine

The day passed like a thousand hours. A blur of sickness and pain, of sweat and aches, of dizziness and spinning rooms. I moved with a deliberate slowness, concentrating on each movement, every one an effort both physical and mental. How I survived the day, how I made my quota, avoided the guards and walked out of there twelve hours later, I cannot even begin to understand.

Would I have made it without the help of the old woman? Her voice was a beacon of calm in my chaotic head, guiding me along the path a step at a time until the end came.

I can go back now, I thought, *to the hut that has become my home. I can lie in my bed with my grandfather next to me and with his hand holding mine. I can close my eyes and let myself drift away for ever. A better way to die than at the hands of that guard.*

I staggered home with the pain intolerable and unimaginable, the woman at my side, holding me upright, urging me forward. "Don't let any guards see," she said. "Stand up straight, look up, look normal, don't let them see, don't give them reason to stop us. Forward, keep going forward."

I couldn't see any more; kept my shoulder touching hers; stepped one shaking foot in front of one shaking foot, thinking not of the distance in front of me, how far it might be, thinking only of that step, that one, and one more now. One more. One more.

And I felt the wooden step beneath my foot, smelt my home fusty with dust and damp, heard Grandfather's voice so small.

"Thank you," he said to the old woman. "Thank you." I could hear the sob stuck in his throat and could imagine the tears held tight in his eyes. "Please stay, help me, I beg you."

Arms guided me in, laid me in my bed, and rough hands felt my forehead, tugged at my clothes, rested on my stomach. I heard a sigh.

"How long?" the old woman asked.

"I'm not sure. It was springtime. Maybe eight months."
He shrugged. "It was the guard. The one—"

"I know which one." She sighed again. "I'll stay and
I'll help, but when it's over, whatever happens, I have
to go. Don't tell me your plans, I don't want to know.
But you owe me."

I stretched my eyes open, staring at the shapes around
me through tears and sweat and darkness. I was confused
and scared. And the pain came again, tearing through
me. My back arched, my head flew back. I wanted to
shout out, to scream. I wanted to die.

"What's happening to me?" I sobbed. "Please, please."

Cold water dripped on to my head and down my
face, spindly fingers stroking my cheek, a kind voice in
my ear.

"You're having a baby," she whispered.

It didn't register at first. I didn't think it could be
true. How could it? Surely I would've known? But then
nothing was normal in here. Nothing happened as it
should. Nothing should be a surprise.

It was like I'd been woken with an electric shock.
Suddenly I was awake and aware and my eyes focused.
"What?"

"You didn't know?" Her question was kind and gentle.

"But..." I knew so little about life, no lessons at school, no talks with parents, had needed to piece everything together instead. I thought and I remembered, and it all fell into place.

The guard. He had made me pregnant.

The contractions came thick and fast, and with each one Grandfather held his hand over my mouth, frightened I would shout, would scream, would give us away.

Outside, the wind battered against our hut, snow swirling round us, a flurry through the gap under the door, a blanket dropping on to our roof, melting and dripping through the holes and making puddles on the floor. We had no windows so nothing lightened, and I was glad I could only see the horror around me, the scene I never dreamt I'd be part of, in flickering candlelight.

Reasoning and logic left me. I imagined, in my incoherent state, that this snow had been sent by Kim Jong Il, angry with me, his temper and disappointment in me manifested in this storm around me.

Visions passed in front of my eyes, as vivid as the real world. There was Father, his warm eyes upon me, muttering apologies – I couldn't imagine what for; my mother, her lips on my forehead, her hand stroking mine; my grandmother even, no longer angry with me. They all passed round me, stayed with me, waiting, waiting...

How much time passed, I have no idea; the air was stiff and warm with the heat of bodies and pain. Darkness smothered us, and candlelight flickered on us, and he was born so very quietly.

She lifted him to me with sadness in her face. I took him in my arms and looked down at this tiny, tiny being, his body so thin, his skin a pale blue tinge, his mouth puckered. I had never seen anything so sad, yet so wondrous.

I traced my hand down his face and his body, edged his cheek with my fingers; he was beautiful. I blew on him gently and I saw, was sure I saw, his head move, just a fraction. I brought him closer to me, blowing across his face, and his eyes flickered and his mouth moved and he breathed.

He was alive. Tiny and thin, fragile and delicate. Toes smaller than my fingernail, eyes swollen but when he peered out into the world, black as pieces of coal. And alive.

I held him to me, cupped in my hands, and cried tears of relief, of joy, of disbelief and of amazement, that this could happen, this little thing, this tiny miracle, this life in a place of only death. And I lifted him to me and I fed him as I had seen others do back in our village.

The woman gave a difficult smile. "Good luck," she said, but she was shaking her head. I stared at her, my hands cradling my baby to me.

"I only agreed to help *you* survive," she said. "Not the baby. It's pointless." She turned to Grandfather. "You know what'll happen to him, what they'll do. It would've been better if he was born dead."

I looked down at the tiny life drawing breath, and back to her, a frown of confusion on my face. Anger at her. How could she say such things?

She stepped towards me, her voice low, her eyes keeping away from the baby, staring straight into mine.

"Don't you judge me," she said. "I was a nurse on the outside. Came here and they got me doing everything from treating the guards' cuts and grazes to amputating prisoners' limbs and pulling rotten teeth. And delivering babies. Not many though." She shook her head. "Sometimes prisoners were pregnant when they came in and I was ordered to get rid of the babies. Sometimes by injections. Others, if they were born, we had to leave to die. In a box left by the mother's side as a reminder of the wrong they had done. They weren't allowed to feed them or hold them. They had to listen to their babies' cries until they died. Imagine that. Imagine the torture that is, listening and watching, but not being allowed to do anything.

"Others, what they did to others, I couldn't even start to tell you, gives me nightmares still, their little faces." She paused, her eyes closed for a moment, as if trying to get rid of images she didn't want to see. "So don't you dare judge me because I know, I've seen what they'll do if they find your baby, what will happen to him. Something shocking and dreadful is what he'll suffer, and what you'll suffer as you watch — because they'll force you to. Is that worth the few hours you might have before they find him? Because they will find him, you know they will."

She turned and I didn't know whether to thank her or order her to leave, whether to be grateful to her for helping me, or hate her for what she had just said.

So I said nothing. I just watched her back as she left.

And outside, the storm raged on.

Chapter Forty

"Now we *have* to go, Grandfather," I said with more certainty than I'd ever felt. "We have to escape. Tonight."

I watched him, waiting for him to shake his head, or tell me again *not yet*, or to try and argue with me. I was ready to argue back. But he just stared at me.

"If we don't, he'll die."

He dropped his head and I heard his breath wheezing through his old lungs.

"Grandfather, we have to try. We can't just give up; we have to give him a chance."

He gave an almost imperceptible nod. "Yes, yes," he whispered.

He began moving around the room, gathering things up and collecting what was hidden under cupboards or in corner shadows.

"Eat this," he said, passing me something wrapped in cloth. "All of it. But slowly. You need some energy." It fell open as I pulled at the edges, a mixture of dead insects, dried food, scraps of rat meat and leaves or bark, grains of some kind, some softened leather.

I frowned at him.

"I've been collecting it for a while."

"Did you know this was happening? The baby?"

He shrugged. "Thought," he whispered. "Just thought." He leant over me, touching the baby's head.

"I don't know what to do," I said. "But I know I can't give up. I know I can't let them kill him. I have to try." I swung my legs around slowly, looking down into his face. "For him. I have to try."

Grandfather nodded.

★

The snow swirled round us as we trudged away from our hut, up the hillside and towards the mountains. Our feet, with bags tied round them to keep us dry, crunched and left footprints, and I hoped so much that the snow was coming down heavily enough to cover our tracks.

Again I felt sick, but this time with nerves. It seemed ludicrous, impossible, hopeless, but then if we stayed, so was our survival. If we wanted to live past tomorrow, when we would be found, if we wanted the baby to live, we had no choice but to escape. Or at least try. So I took a deep breath, and I trusted myself, trusted that I would do everything I could.

"The ditch will still be there, like it was when we saw the tiger," Grandfather said. "And the spikes."

"I know," I replied, and in my head I saw myself jumping across it, clearing it – because I had to. "But there are hours and hours until roll call." I let myself think of the guard, and for a moment I let my imagination show me what he would do to me, to Grandfather, to the baby, and I walked on with strength and determination.

The baby was under my clothes, tied across my chest with fabric from Grandmother's old dress, rags wrapped round him to keep him warm. He was quiet, didn't cry, barely moved.

Every step we took I felt I was being watched, someone letting me make another move, get a little closer, let that glimmer of hope grow brighter in my chest, allowing me to believe that maybe, maybe... My pockets were stuffed with all sorts of things Grandfather had been collecting, and as we moved, I nibbled on them.

I was tired. So very, very tired. And I was scared, and now not just for myself. Now I had this tiny being relying on me and yet still it all seemed so impossible. I wanted to stop walking, go back to the hut, sit down, hold my baby and stare at him. And sleep.

And wake in the morning and find that everything was fine.

But that was the stuff of dreams. This was my reality. My baby in my arms. My baby who somehow, against everything, had grown in me, had survived childbirth and was alive. What he was a product of, I didn't care; it didn't matter.

We reached the treeline, and we walked together, my hand in Grandfather's, his strength pulling me along, willing me, guiding me.

"You remember what I told you about your mother, where she's living? The border town, Chongyong? That's where you need to go. You need to remember it, the town, and you need to head there. Straight there. Understand?"

I nodded. "But you'll be with me anyway," I said.

He ignored me. "Don't go back to our village. Not for anything."

I thought of Sook then, for the first time in a long time. I wanted to find him. Shout and scream at him. Demand to know why he did that to me and to my family. Why he hated me. Why he'd betrayed me.

What did I feel for him? Why did his face still come to me? Did I love him still? Did I hate him for what he'd done? Did it matter any more, after all this time? Could I walk away and never know the answers? Leave it, forget it?

No. I wanted to find him. I wanted to kill him.

"You hear me, Yoora? Forget it. Head to your mother and from there you can escape the country and over into China."

The trees were thinning; we were near the fence. "But—"

Grandfather stopped, staring down at me. "Whatever revenge you've been thinking of all these years in here, you need to forget. There's no point. It'll only get you found."

I looked down at the baby and back to him, nodding. This little one was more important now.

We walked a few more paces, stopping with the fence a few metres away.

"Head west from here," Grandfather said. "Think of

where the sun sets. The town's on a train line. If you can get to the train tracks, you can follow them."

I stared at him, snow melting and dripping down his face. "You'll remember that, Grandfather," I said. "You'll be with me."

"No, Yoora, you have to remember alone."

"What?"

He stared at me for a moment, and I could just make out his head slowly moving from one side to the other. "I'm not coming," he whispered.

I wiped the snow from my face and away from my eyes, searching through the darkness, wishing I could make out more of him, see his expression better. I didn't understand.

"I'll slow you down. We won't make it together."

"No, that's not true... I can't leave you."

"I'm too old and weak."

"But I'm weak too, we can—"

"No." His voice was firm. "I don't think I'll fit through the gap. I know I won't make it over the ditch, but even if I did, I don't have the strength to keep going."

I could feel the panic in my chest, the burning, the shortness of breath, my head dizzy, tears filling my eyes. "But... but... why can't you try?"

"If we both go, in about seven hours, at morning roll call, they'll realise we're missing, someone will go to the hut, work out that we must be trying to escape and they'll come after us. Seven hours isn't a lot when you're as tired as you are. You're going to have to rest when you get clear. If I stay, I can try and bluff them, tell them the other guard sent you somewhere, try and buy you some extra time, and maybe, *maybe*, it'll work. Even if it only gives you an extra hour, it's something."

"But... but..." My tears were pouring, looking up at the face of this man I loved so much, who had always been at my side, through everything, who never judged me for the mistakes I made, for his son being killed, for being in the camp, for what happened to his wife. "I don't want you to stay. I want you to come with me."

"I can help you more like this."

I stared at him, couldn't tell what were tears and what was melted snow, and I reached out my hand and held on to his. My head was shaking; my body was screaming at me to throw myself at him and snuggle into his arms and rest my head on his chest.

"I don't want to be alone," I hissed through gritted teeth.

"You're not," he whispered. "You have your baby now. Look after him. Get him to safety. Give him the future I could never give you. Please. Do that for me."

"What will they do to you?" I whispered.

His reply was a shrug, but we both knew the answer. A question I should never have asked. We stared at each other in silence, acceptance rolling over me. Tears fell from his eyes, but I could see the hope within them still. Hope he'd given to me. Hope for survival. Hope, and a chance, for a future.

And I loved him. I loved him so much.

Yet I was the tiger now, my young one in my arms, my eyes clear and bright, daring to believe that freedom could be mine. I was the animal.

He turned his face away from me, watching the security light swoop along the length of the fence, making sure we weren't in its beam. He waited, he timed the sweep of the light, then he grabbed me and scurried forward, stopping at the fence, edging along it, searching for the hole underneath it. When he found it he stopped. My eyes struggled to see through the fence, through the darkness, and across the snow to the ditch, and I looked back at him.

My head was screaming at me — *I can't make the ditch, I can't jump that far, I'll fall on the spikes, I'll die.* I looked down at the baby.

No, I reminded myself.

We'll die.

Chapter Forty-one

I was stuck between two choices, both life-threatening. One, a maybe – that ditch, those spikes, and if not them, the long journey ahead to a safety that was dubious at best. The other, a definite death for the little boy snuggled against me, this tiny thing that had driven me up this mountainside and had left me with this terrible choice that really was no choice at all.

"I could die," I whispered. *And so could this baby*, I thought. *A slow, horrible, painful death.*

Grandfather nodded.

"But I could've done earlier today. Or yesterday. Or last week. Couldn't I? Or the time the guard... or... or when I spat in his face, or my first day here, or when Father was shot, or with that tablet... or..."

I wrapped my arms round myself and the baby. I

drew in another deep breath, trying to steady myself, calm myself.

He nodded. "But out there, now, if anyone tries to hurt you, or threaten you, you must fight back."

"I know." I nodded, and from my belt I pulled the knife that I'd kept hidden under my bed. "I will."

He sighed, and I knew what he was thinking – *What has this place turned us into?* But I would fight back now. I'd do whatever it took.

He glanced through the fence and back at me. "And don't think about how far it is, to the border," he said. "Just think of one step forward. Always one step."

"I know, I know." I tried to smile at him, letting his words build me up, fill me with courage and confidence. "One step at a time."

He was nodding again. "And once you've made it to the town, you can make it out of the country and to China."

He bent down to the ground, scooping away the snow that had fallen into the hole, and pulling up the broken fencing.

"When you've made it to China you must carry on because if they find you there, they'll send you back. Keep heading south, through Laos, and into Thailand,

and there you can go to the embassy and claim asylum. They'll send you to South Korea, and then," he paused, standing up again, pulling something from his pocket and handing it to me, "you can find our family."

I looked at what he had placed in my hand – the postcard. "I forgot about this," I said. I tucked it into my pocket and crouched down. Then I took a deep breath and nodded at my grandfather standing above me.

The hole was small and the ground was wet and slippery and difficult. I crawled on to my side, driving my fingers into the snow and pulled my body forward, my feet slipping behind me. I glanced at the fence above me, the edges of the metal sticking down, tracing over my face, scratching at my skin, catching on my clothes; like tendrils, like fingers clawing at me to keep me, to stop me, to hold me still, until daylight came and I was found, or the light passed over us and we were caught.

But I kept going, kept pulling forward and the fence passed over me and I was out on the other side. I looked up, the light coming my way now, soft and sweeping, quietly seeking us out, and I dropped to the ground at the edge of the ditch and rolled on to my side.

Surely I'll be camouflaged, I thought, *covered in all this snow.*

The light passed over me, and the ditch with its spikes still visible glared up at me. A creature was impaled on one, its eyes empty and dry, its fur caked in dried blood, and I sucked in a deep breath and looked away. Darkness returned and I stood up, hurrying back to the fence, to Grandfather.

"Promise me something," I said, staring into the glint of his eye. "If I don't make it, come down there and kill me. Don't let me lie there dying." It was stupid and I knew it. He couldn't climb down there; he could never climb out again.

But still he nodded. "I promise," he said. "But, Yoora, you have to hurry now. Get across and don't look back, keep going. Remember, don't think about how far it is, just think one foot in front of the other, one step, then another, and you'll make it, and you can find your mother and a way out of this country. You promise *me* that?"

"I promise," I said quietly.

I turned. I looked in front of me and I could see the edge of the ditch, but not the other side. I could hear death calling me from the depths. I took a moment, trampled down the snow, dragged some away with my foot, steadied my breathing, cleared my head and moved the baby on to my back.

I was going.

And with everything I had, I would run at that ditch, and I would think only of survival. That I *would* make it. I *would* live. I *would* land on the other side and I *would be free*. And behind me Grandfather would be willing me on, urging me forward, holding his breath as I jumped, waiting for me to shout back that I had made it. Because I would.

I would.

I ran. Too quickly the edge came up and I jumped. Launched myself forward with a shout of effort and determination in my throat.

The ground left me. The air welcomed me, holding me, guiding me. My eyes wide, waiting.

And I landed. Roughly on my front. I could feel the ground underneath me, the snow on my hands, my fingertips digging into it. My legs dangled over the side and I scraped and clambered, grunting with effort, knowing those spikes were waiting for me. I felt my foot catch something, couldn't see what it was, and I felt my trousers rip.

I pulled and pulled, and slowly, gradually, I made it to the top. I stood up and moved the baby round to my front, next to my skin, my wet fingers reaching down to his feather-like hair, and I saw him breathe gently in and gently out, and I sighed.

I lifted my head and stared back through the darkness, to where I knew Grandfather's eyes still searched for me.

"I love you," I said, as loud as I dared.

A moment later his ghostly reply came to me. "I love you both."

I knew I would never see him again and it hurt so much, but I couldn't stop, I couldn't wait.

With the help of someone I loved, I had done something I had never heard of anyone doing before me – I had escaped. And yes, I was alone, *we* were alone, but we were free.

Chapter Forty-two

I walked.

I sat and I rested.

I ate some of the food Grandfather had given me.

I fed the baby, as yet unnamed.

I walked some more.

And as I walked, I thought of the prison.

I wondered if Grandfather was sleeping in his bed, or was staring at those objects he'd brought from the fields. I wondered how the hut now felt with only him in it, and if he felt as lonely and as lost as me.

And I remembered sharing laughter with my friend as we watched the guard slip over in the mud, our stifled giggles at each other as our cheeks bulged with berries, remembered watching her hands clasp against nothing as she tried to catch a frog, and the look of wonder in her eyes as we listened to the song of a thrush in the trees.

I thought about the flower I had found, the smell of pine trees around me, the leaves and branches often tipped with frost, the low morning mist over the fields.

And the woman who had helped me give birth.

And despite all the pain and the heartache and the suffering the prison had caused me, I felt strangely sad to be leaving it.

★

The snow and the wind stopped, and while the sun was still down I trudged along and up through the hills and mountains that had been my view for so long, and even though I looked out for gaps or detours, going around when I could instead of up, trying to make the walk easier or shorter, it was still so very hard. Up and up I climbed, over icy ground that I could barely see, my feet slipping as I grabbed at thorny branches, pushed through bushes that leered from the darkness and clawed out and tore at my clothes and pulled at my hair and made me wince in pain, clambered across rocks on my hands and knees with my skin tearing and my hands bleeding, leaving behind me a trail of bloody fingerprints. And all with my tiny baby held to me in the makeshift sling.

Yet he didn't cry, or even murmur. And countless times I peeled away the layers of clothing to stare down at his delicate and vulnerable face, placing my fingers on his chest to feel the heart that I hoped was still beating.

On and on I clambered, and my body screamed at me and my head spun and every few steps I wanted to stop. The woman's words played over and over in my head – '*You seen the mountains? You going to get over them?*'

Am I? I thought. *Am I going to get over them?*

I wanted so desperately to sit down, to lie down, to close my eyes, to sleep. So desperately. But what if I did? Would I wake again? Open my eyes agan? Stand up again? Sometimes, most times, every lift of a foot was an effort, yet other times I would suddenly find I couldn't remember the last few minutes, and I would wonder how it was that I was still awake and I was still moving.

Hours must have passed. Slowly my adrenalin waned and the cold came to me. I peeled off one of my layers, a shirt of Grandmother's, and wrapped it round my head and face, and I curled my stiff hands into balls and drew them up my sleeves.

On and on. Further and further. Higher and higher.

I'm so tired, I thought. *So tired.*

I stopped a moment, my head spinning again, my hands shaking, as I stretched them out to rest against a rock, and with the sky beginning to lighten, I turned around to see the red haze of sunrise lifting in the distance.

Are you looking up at that sky, Grandfather? I thought. *Are you thinking and worrying about me, as I am about you? Hoping I'm all right? Hoping I'm still alive?*

A gust of wind blew across the mountainside, lifting and swirling my hair around my head, waking me a little as the cold hit my face. I closed my eyes and breathed its freshness deep into my lungs, and I turned and took another step. And another. And another.

But I was so tired, and everything, every move of a foot or an arm, every breath in or out, every second with my eyes still open, was painful.

I'll rest a few minutes, I thought, and I sat down. *Just a few. I'll close my eyes for just a little while and then I'll carry on.*

I leant back and closed my eyes, and I could feel sleep pulling me and calling me and I don't know if it was cold, or snowy, if the ground was up or down or hard or soft because with my eyes closed I was no longer there.

I was drifting away. Drifting away to some place in my head. With food. And warmth. And lights. And there was my father coming towards me. Holding his hand out to mine and smiling at me. I smiled at him too, and held my hand out to his.

And I was drifting away.

I walked with him thinking we were speaking but couldn't hear a word, and I thought we were holding hands but I couldn't feel his touch. But he was with me, smiling at me, his love and compassion pouring from him as he looked at me.

I'll stay with you, Father, I thought. *For always.*

But his smile began to slip and the lights began to fade and the cold was growing again inside me and something jabbed into my stomach, then prodded at my arm and at my face. Suddenly I was awake again and I managed to open my eyes just a crack, trying to make sense of where I was and what was happening, but all I could see was the blur of colour and the mixture of darker and lighter. But I knew without doubt that I wasn't alone. Someone was standing over me.

Chapter Forty-three

Not a guard, I thought, *please, not a guard, or a soldier. Please.*

From my chest came the tiny cry of my baby and I draped my arm around him.

And I breathed slowly in and slowly out, and I tried to open my eyes further so I could focus, tried to blink and blink, to stay awake, to move, to stand up, to run, to keep going and find that escape.

But there were hands on my stomach and at my chest and touching my face. Hands at my mouth, water at my lips that was so good. Kind hands that brushed away my hair and wiped my sore skin and lifted my head so I could drink some more.

She sat with me as I slowly came round; an old woman with a drawn face, short messy hair and dark eyes that gave nothing away. She watched me like a hawk, but didn't say a word, and when I started looking around, when I opened my mouth to ask if this was where she had found me, halfway down the other side of the mountain, she put her finger to her lips to silence me and stood up.

I tried to remember what had happened, didn't think I'd even made it to the top, yet here I was, on the way down.

She couldn't have carried me, I thought, looking at her. *I would remember that, I'm sure. Then I must've, I must've made it this far.*

She beckoned me with her head and slowly I stood up, and with a hand supporting my baby, I put one careful foot in front of the other and followed her.

★

It never occurred to me not to trust her. She could've left me there, ignored and forgotten, a bundle of rags sheltering against the rocks. And I, we, would've died and nobody would've known.

So I followed her, alongside a field, past a few trees and down a frozen pathway, to a little wooden hut with a broken fence and tiles missing from the roof. I could feel the warmth as soon as I touched the door, and she led me in and indicated a seat by a small open fire.

"Thank you," I muttered, but she shook her head at me and again placed a finger to her lips.

I could feel the tears welling in my eyes but didn't let them fall, and as I peeled away my layers of clothing to feed the baby, I thought I could see the melancholy on the woman's face and wondered what past she had had and why she was being so kind to me.

The day went on in silence yet in more comfort than I could remember. She fed me every now and then, and gave me hot drinks, and slowly I could feel some strength coming back to me, and when the sun fell back down, she heated up some water so I could wash myself and the baby, and made me up a bed next to the fire. I slept feeling like the most important person in the world.

I woke twice in the night to feed the baby, and each time I saw the twinkle of the woman's dark eyes as they reflected the dying embers of the fire, but the last time I woke, with the sun straining through the glass, I glanced over to see her, and she was gone. On the floor next to me was an old bottle full of water, a bowl of grey rice and a warm coat.

Pulling the blankets around me and the baby, I stood up and tiptoed across to the window, and as I fed him, I watched the dark form of the woman walking away, the sunrise in front of her lifting the sky from deep to lighter blue, a hue of orange stretching up and away.

The countryside felt so calm now, the snow covering the mountains and everything in silence, frost glistening like magic on trees as the winter sun danced and played on their branches. It was beautiful. If you didn't know what happened back there, in that place over the mountains, you might never believe it.

Because the truth, it seemed, could be stranger, more disturbing and more shocking than anything you could possibly imagine.

Yet I was here. I'd made it over the mountains and I was on my way.

"Thank you," I whispered. "Thank you."

★

The sun was behind me; I was heading west. I had a warm coat on and some food in my stomach. My baby was clean, and so was I, and in the fresh breeze my hair flapped around in the wind, and I felt hopeful.

For miles and miles I walked on and on and slowly the snow thinned, the countryside changed from white to glistening frost, to frozen mud, and walking became easier if no less tiring. I listened to the air breathing through the branches of the trees, whispering to me sounds of comfort, but as the hours and the miles passed and tiredness and hunger came back to me, those sounds felt less like comfort and more like danger. A soldier hiding in the tree, perhaps, whispering to his colleague, watching me, waiting to catch me.

How far away from the camp I was, I had no idea. Had I been noticed as missing yet? Was Grandfather still alive? Unless I was captured, these were questions I would never be able to answer.

And what if the guards had found that woman's house? What if they'd found her, questioned her, threatened her? What if she'd told them she'd found me? What then?

They'd be coming for me. They'd be right behind me.

Yet there was nothing I could do but carry on. Keep going. Keep trying. So I sucked in a deep breath and shook the thoughts and worries from my head. Knowing I must eat, must keep strong, I bent down to the ground and turned over a large stone where I found a scurry of insects and, grabbing them one by one before they woke enough to hide, I chewed them all down.

The earth was so much more fertile here, hadn't been ravaged for years by starving fingers, and so I picked at whatever I could find as I went, feeding and filling myself, because I knew I must.

I picked and ate leaves off evergreen shrubs as I passed by, found the remnants of an apple that must've been preserved by the cold, underneath an otherwise bare tree, and ate it anyway. It felt so sweet, so soft and juicy, melting on my tongue and sliding down my throat. Oh, it was good.

I walked and I walked, all the time listening for the sound of a truck coming towards me, and every now and then glancing over my shoulder and scanning around me.

The sun reached its peak and began its way down again. I had to stop a while to rest my feet and to feed the baby, but before I set off, I foraged the earth for more insects, eating plenty and saving plenty, stuffing them inside a spare sock.

I was tired. Exhausted. I wanted to sleep. The soles of my feet were sore, my toes rubbed on the sides of my shoes and my heels were blistered. My back hurt, my body ached, my mind was a confused jumble of not just the last few days, but of everything that had got me to this point. Everything that had fallen into place from that one dream and that one person.

Sook.

Why did he still come into my head? Why when I thought of him did my stomach flip and my chest feel tight? I hated him. Didn't I? I wished I could forget him, wished I could at least understand this tie I felt to him. And as I stood again and one foot plodded in front of the other, heading, I hoped, still west, to the town where Mother was, I wondered in which direction my old village was, how difficult it would be to find it, what Sook was doing there right at that very moment.

I wanted to go back there. I wanted to see him. That face. That sneer. I sighed, deep and heavy. That smile when he looked at me. That warmth I'd felt.

Distance stretched out interminably in front of me. Dusk was coming and night-time would not be long after, and with it would come darkness that would swallow me whole. I was so tired. I wanted to stop, curl up on the ground like an animal and fall asleep.

What had got me this far? Hope? Or love? Or just plain luck? How far would it keep taking me?

The dying light played tricks on me, and Grandfather's face loomed from shadows and darkness, towards me and away again in front of me, as if beckoning me onwards and onwards. Watching him, and with that hope that I might, just might, find my mother, I kept one foot going in front of the other.

A vague outline of a town appeared on the horizon, slightly to my right, and I veered that way, through a field, along a dirt path, to the start of a pavement cracked and broken. There were no cars, a few bicycles, people heading home from work. I felt their eyes watching me. I felt a stranger. I felt naked and obvious.

I needed to stop for the night and rest. And in the morning I would need to find someone to speak to, to ask directions to Mother's town. Or find a railway station as Grandfather had said, and follow the tracks. I tried not to think of her not being there, but couldn't stop thinking that by morning I could've been seen, found, sent back, and I could wake up again in that hut, or in solitary. Or not wake at all.

If I was legal, I would have identification papers, I thought, *a permit to be in a town not my residence, a visa to travel there. I have nothing. What if they hear the baby cry, realise I'm a stranger, that I'm homeless?*

I wasn't free. And would never be while I stayed in that country.

They were all guards, just different types. Prison guards, policemen, government people, and all those like Min-Jee who watched everyone else, reporting back tales of crimes committed, strange activity, suspicious people, and many times, too many times, they were made up to save their own skins.

We were surrounded by them. It was one great big prison of a country, with borders for barriers and our Dear Leader, all-powerful and all-knowing, ruling over us unquestionably. A self-styled god. Controlling.

My eyes are open, Father, I thought, *and you were right.*

I knew the argument against – not even an argument but a belief, a way of life. What a good leader He was, how He provided for us, guided us, His wisdom, His skills, His knowledge, and I truly didn't know what to think of their, everyone's, commitment to Him.

Was it honourable? Was it right? I only knew what *I* thought now, what *I* believed after what *I'd* seen and experienced for myself – that *I* had no commitment to him; *I* didn't believe any longer.

I wanted the freedom to disagree, to put forward my own arguments, my own opinions and exercise my own judgement. To have choices, and for my choices to be respected. And more than anything, I wanted that too for this little baby clinging to me and relying on me.

And that I could never have, if I didn't escape.

★

I stumbled forward through the streets, hoping to find somewhere to rest, trying to avoid the glances of people walking home, all with a purpose and direction. There were no signs to tell me what town I was in, or how far it was to the next village, which direction the border was, or even what road I was on.

An apartment block loomed through the dusk, perhaps three storeys high, grey and old with broken windows on the ground floor, and curtains or blinds at others with the dimmest of lights leaking through. I glanced briefly over my shoulder and headed towards it, peering as best I could through dirty glass into a darkened room: it looked empty. On one side of the block was a large door, and I walked over, pushed it open and stepped inside.

A corridor stretched forward into dark and gloom, all concrete and hard edges: bare walls, but for a couple of doors, and the obligatory paintings of our Dear Leader and his father our Great Leader. A flash of colour, of red.

Their eyes followed me from behind the polished glass free from fingerprints or dust, watching me from their round faces and smug grins, waiting for me, judging me, laughing at me with silent pleasure for what they had done to me. Believing, I was sure, that they were absolutely, completely, totally correct in what they did, that I deserved everything that had happened, that I needed to be re-educated, to learn how to love them again and honour them and respect them.

I stared at their faces. I'd seen the worst of humanity in so many, and the best in so few.

I turned away, and pushed through the door opposite and into the ground-floor apartment I'd seen from outside. I felt around it, my feet shuffling, my hands stretching forward and exploring carefully. The last of the day's light filtered through the windows and glass dulled with dirt, showing me a room empty and dark and dirty. Particles of dust I'd kicked up swam in the dying light, tickling my nose, and the cold draught through the broken glass pushed them around in ever faster, then ever decreasing circles.

I moved through the other rooms, three in all. In one was a cupboard with doors hanging off, another had a wardrobe that had fallen to its side, and finally there was a kitchen with no cooker or fridge or even a table, just scratches deep in the floor, and pipes that groaned and banged when I turned on the taps.

I found nothing but a jumper with a hole in the shoulder and loose wool dangling from the cuff, but I reminded myself it was shelter for the night, somewhere to hide, and a jumper I could wrap round my baby.

I sat on the dusty floor and pulled out the mixture of leaves and insects I had collected on the way and some of what Grandfather had given me. And I pulled out the postcard too, resting it in front of me while I rubbed at my sore feet and aching legs.

I felt a glimmer of excitement, as if I'd been sleeping for years and finally now had woken. Ahead of me, waiting for me, I hoped, I believed, was my freedom, and somewhere, beyond that, was the city of lights.

Chapter Forty-four

Silence and darkness enveloped me. For a while I relaxed and rested, daring to feel safe, invisible and unknown. I knew the door behind me was blocked, the footsteps above me were only the neighbours and the scratching outside was only animals.

My baby snuffled and I worried about him: so small and helpless, his tiny hand clinging to my finger, his cry a whisper of apology.

He seemed impossible. A baby with no name because I didn't dare, because that would mean I expected him to survive. I *hoped* he would, but every beat of his heart I felt, every rise and fall of his chest I saw as he breathed, was a surprise. Was spectacular. Was frightening. I was a mother. *His* mother. I was responsible for him, his safety and his life. Yet I was barely holding on to my own.

I fed him as soon as he murmured, hoping he was getting enough to live to the next minute and the next hour. Questions mounted in my head: where would I find food for me? How would I survive? What would happen to him if I died? How was I going to avoid the authorities? Could I really find my mother? Escape this country? All with a baby?

I watched through the window as night fell. No lights sparkled in any houses, no streetlights twinkled. A darkness so complete, shrouding the town and the countryside further and the mountains in the distance. Any sense of peace or of safety left me. I was falling into a black hole: empty, ominous and frightening. My eyes played tricks on me, showing me images hiding in the shadows: Grandfather at the fence, the guard looming above me, my friend from the camp, faces of prisoners I'd left behind, gaunt and pleading.

My ears told me people were creeping into the apartment, stepping towards me, guns pointing, an axe raised, handcuffs, rope, ready for me.

They let me escape, I thought. *It was too easy. They followed me step by step, behind me in shadows, obscured by trees, hidden by bushes whenever I turned round. Laughing at me. Closing in on me now.*

My heart pounded and my body leapt with every sound. I shuffled backwards until I found the wall, carried on sideways until I could prop myself in a corner. I drifted in and out of a fitful sleep, an odd sleep, waking at the slightest noise, confused for a moment, before the memories of the last couple of days took hold and I could recall how I had got to this point.

Sleep was difficult, rest was uneasy. But morning did come, without enemies at the door or death in the shadows. And the room reappeared around me as sunlight stretched through what glass remained in the window frames, and the dust again danced in its rays without a care and still in the apartment there was only me and the baby. I tiptoed across the floor in my bare feet, footsteps muted by dust, a trail of prints behind me, the baby in my arms cooing as I rocked him.

I wished I could stay there, make a home for us. But how long would it be before neighbours questioned who I was? Before someone asked to see my papers? Before I was arrested again? A day? Two or three maybe?

There was no option. There was no choice.

The clothes that had got so wet the day before were still damp and cold, so I rearranged everything with the drier ones next to my skin and the baby, and the damper ones on the outside. I hoped they would soon be dry. I hoped for no more snow.

With a glance left and right, I stepped from the apartment and into the corridor and out on to the street. I kept my head low as I headed further into the town, my pace even, catching nobody's eye, hoping to look as if I knew where I was going.

I needed to know where I was, where the train tracks were, what direction I should be heading in, how far away Mother's town was, how long it would take to get there. And I needed to, had to, avoid the police, the authorities, anyone who might report me or ask me anything. But I had no idea where to start or what to do.

I walked. Thinking. Worrying. Panicking about when I would next have to feed the baby, where I was going to do it, how I was going to without being seen.

My mind turned somersaults, but my feet drove me forward into a town that was so much bigger than I had ever seen before. There were wide roads that were empty, tall buildings that were blank and stark, music piping through loudspeakers that were tinny, with children's high-pitched voices singing praises to our country. And people who had empty faces and few smiles.

There were no restaurants or stalls with the smells of food wafting from them. There was no music with beats and rhythms thumping. There were no bright clothes. No shop signs flashing. No cars with horns blaring and engines roaring.

But I saw train tracks to one side, and I followed them, and eventually they led me to the station. And high on the station building of grey concrete, two familiar faces again stared down at me: a burst of colour of pinked cheeks and shiny black hair, of red backgrounds and yellow sunbeams. A flash of warning to me, a flash of danger.

I stepped inside the station, thinking I could sit there a while, rest near people waiting for trains, and no one would be suspicious. There were no benches, there were no seats, so I wandered over to the busier side, thinking it easier to hide in a crowd, and sat down on the floor, my arms wrapped round my baby.

It had been so long since I'd seen anyone but prisoners or guards. I watched the people moving around, all so thin, and I saw the children, so many of them, lying on the station floor or drifting among the waiting, their eyes keen, darting here or there to the sound of something dropping to the floor or the rustle of someone's hand in their pocket. Their faces were filthy, their clothes not much more than rags, their bodies a tangle of bones.

I couldn't help but stare. Couldn't help but lean forward, catching the eye of one, lifting a finger to beckon him over, watching his eyes, sullen and empty, dart over me.

"You got any food?" he asked.

I shook my head and he started to turn away. "Wait... please."

His head turned back round to me, and I saw his shoulders droop with a sigh. His legs crumpled and he fell into a sitting position in front of me and I thought his bones would snap.

"What town are we in?" I whispered. He stared at me as if I'd asked if grass was green.

I reached a hand into my pocket, into the old sock, felt through and grabbed a dried worm, tearing it in half. I kept it hidden in my palm, stretched towards him and dropped a piece into his hand. He didn't pause for a second. The worm half disappeared into his mouth and was gone.

"Musong," he said, but it meant nothing to me.

"What about Chongyong?" I asked. "How far away is that?" His stare came back to me, not greedy but desperate, his palm up and open to me, waiting.

I dropped the other half of the worm into his hand, and it disappeared as quickly as the first.

He shrugged. "Couple of stops on the train, I think. Five hours maybe? Trains don't move fast."

I caught my breath, hot in my chest, nerves tipping my stomach. I tried not to stare at him. I felt relieved and excited, nervous and worried. Was it possible? Was it really possible? *No, of course it isn't*, I thought and I felt stupid. *I have no ticket. Can't get a ticket. Have no money. No visa. No permit.*

I sensed him watching me, waiting for the next question and the chance to earn more food. But I didn't need to know any more; it was pointless asking when the next train was due or how much it cost. I would have to follow the tracks, and I would have to hope I could make it that far keeping hidden and out of view. Five hours by slow train; how far was that? How long would it take to walk?

I felt the baby squirm in his sling under my clothes, heard his soft whimper and I peered down, loosening my top layers, but keeping him hidden.

"What you got?" the boy whispered and he skulked towards me.

My eyes flashed to him and away, back to my baby,

positioning him for feeding, his snuffles and murmurs the quietest of sounds. I didn't answer.

"What is it?" he asked again.

There was no way I could trust him; he would betray me for a sniff of food, or for his own safety. Wouldn't we all?

"You'll have to beg from someone else. I don't have any more." I shook my head at him.

"I don't beg," he said. "Even if you do, people don't give anything because they don't have anything." He paused. "Apart from you. So you must be desperate. Or just plain stupid."

"Why are you here if you're not begging?"

His brow furrowed. "Where else am I going to go? We all live here," he said, pointing to the other children around us.

I stared at him, as he stared back at me, taking me in, sizing me up. "You're not from here, are you?"

I didn't say a word.

He sighed. "They call us *kochebi*."

"Swallows?" I asked. *Kochebi* was the name for those small, swift birds that dart after insects in the summer.

"Yes. Because we're little, and we wander around in flocks — wandering swallows. None of us have parents or family. We have nowhere to live and nowhere else to go. So we stay here because it's dry, and because people pass through, and sometimes they drop stuff, and sometimes it's stuff you can eat. Sometimes kids just lie down and give up and die. Most do eventually. There's no way out, see? There's nothing for us but this."

I followed his sad eyes as they looked over the station, the adults waiting, the kids shuffling around or lying on the floor or propped against a wall.

"There," he said, his bony finger pointing to a heap on the floor. "That kid there, see? Near the wall? And the column?"

I nodded.

"He died yesterday."

I stared at what I'd thought was a bundle of rags, and I could make out a couple of toes, the outline maybe of a hand. My skin prickled. It was like the camp all over again. But with no work. Nobody cared about these children. Nobody moved their starved bodies. Nobody bothered to see if they were alive or dead.

"Why doesn't anybody feed you all? Or help you?"

"How? And who would?"

I tried to look at each of their faces. His question echoed in my head. How could you feed all of them?

There were so many. How could you help one and not the other? And keep helping? Every day?

"How long has it been like this?"

He shrugged. "Don't know. As long as I can remember. Worse now, though, since I've been by myself."

I nodded. "How long's that been?"

He was silent a moment, his fingers scratching through his tangled hair, his hand pulling at his ragged clothes, his face full of pain and his eyes full of memories.

"Two years, I think. Three? Not sure. Not long after I turned thirteen." He sighed.

I couldn't take my eyes from him. Couldn't believe he was any older than ten. He was so short, so skinny. Again I stared round at the other kids, the *kochebi*, as he called them. How old were they? Some seemed smaller. One or two slightly taller, but all with that gaunt look of hunger that had turned them into these walking ghosts.

I thought back to the camp, to our arrival and the faces looming towards us of skeletons barely living. Three months it had taken, for us to become one of them.

And I thought of life back in our village, back home, years ago, a life ago. We never had much food, but we had enough to survive, just. We could grow things, our own food, not a lot, but we had a little ground at the back of the house with enough space for a couple of rows of potatoes and a few carrots. Enough to ease away the clawing hunger the day brought and to help you sleep through the night without your stomach rumbling you awake.

Here in the town, there was barely any ground to grow anything, people lived in apartment blocks or tiny houses and you relied on what the government said were your rations, what you needed to survive given the job you did and the age you were.

"What about your rations?" I asked.

He looked up at me with his wide eyes, mocking. "I don't get rations," he said. "Because I don't live anywhere. And even those who do only get a handful of rice a day." He paused a moment, wiping his face with fingers like dried twigs about to snap. "It's the same everywhere," he said. "Doesn't make any difference if you sneak on a train and go to the next town. It's all the same. May as well die here as there."

Suddenly I saw myself, lying dead on the ground with my baby crying before his last breath left his body. What right had I bringing another hungry mouth into this world? How long could we survive?

No, I thought, *no, no, no. I will not let this be me. I will not let this be my baby. I'll move on. I'll follow the tracks and I'll make it to Mother's town. If it takes me days or weeks or months. I will not become one of these.*

I tried to stand, every muscle in my body stiff and unwilling, and I glanced down at the tiny bundle hidden in my clothing, his perfect face so calm, so trusting.

If only he knew how valuable, how important, how rare every breath he takes is. How fragile. How each one goes against what should be.

I ignored the pain in my body and I stood up. "I have to go," I said.

He looked away from me, thoughtful, nodding. "Train's coming," he said.

I sighed. I'd have to wait for it to go, watch it disappear into the distance so much faster and easier than me walking behind it. I strained my ears, thought I could hear it, not a powerful sound, thudding and beating and screeching into the station, but a tired, quiet chug of effort.

I turned and there it was. I had never seen a train before. It wasn't impressive and awe-inspiring, or shiny and new as I'd expected. And there was no sudden outpouring of passengers, no hustle or bustle, no whistling of guards or announcements over the Tannoy. It arrived almost apologetically. But I saw, and couldn't believe, that there were people sitting on top.

"You better hurry," the boy murmured. "You never know how long it'll be here. Could be hours, could be a few minutes."

"But..." I looked from him to the train and back. "The people... on top..."

He nodded.

"I don't have a visa. Or a travel permit."

"Neither do they," he said.

I stared, my chest tight, my stomach hot. "But... what if...?"

"Two stops."

I glanced back at the train. Kids were scrambling up the sides, and so much space was already occupied.

"Thank you," I whispered. And I ran. To the train, green and rusting, with faces peering out obscured and contorted by the glass. I held an arm across me, cushioning the baby, and I got to the train, staring up at the bulk of metal in front of me, the tiny faces of the *kochebi* trying to escape, dangling above me.

No hands were offered down to help me, to pull me up, and I glanced around, desperate to see how I could get up there. The engine breathed in deep and I started to panic. I ran to a gap between carriages and clambered on to the tracks, hoisted a foot on to the metal holding them together. Then I put both hands on a window frame, and one foot on a door handle, and my fingers grabbed on to a lip of metal at the top of the train. I turned my body as much as I could, scared for the baby, that I was going to squash him against the train.

I felt something. I glanced down and saw the gravel between the tracks disappearing. I looked to the side. We were moving. Slowly, but we were moving.

With every bit of strength I had left, I pulled myself up, my arms screaming at me, my toes pressing against the train, keeping my body from hitting the side, desperate for the baby to be safe. My feet found the window sill and my elbows scrabbled to the top of the train, and a push and a stretch from my legs and I was up. Lying on my back, staring up at the blue sky inching away above me.

I rolled on to my side, looking over the station, searching for the boy. I could see him, his back to me, his head lifted a little, watching people walk by, waiting for something to drop. I looked at all the others who had nowhere to go and no one to care for them. Their faces so young and innocent, staring up at the bodies passing by with their mouths open and their eyes full of wanting.

Like baby birds. Like swallows. *Kochebi*.

Chapter Forty-five

The town slipped away behind me. The houses, the streets, the apartment blocks and the people. I sat with my back to where we were going, sheltering the baby from the cold air that blew through my clothes and jabbed into my skin, lifted my hair from my head and pinched at my face.

But I had been so lucky. I had seen no police, no soldiers, no guards of any sort. Were they searching for me? They must be, surely? How long had it been since I escaped? Two days? Three? I stared at the mountains dwindling into the distance behind me, horror hidden behind them. Grandfather by now surely dead.

I had imagined trains to be faster, thought I would be clinging on to survive, but it plodded and chugged steadily onwards with little more speed than that of a fast bicycle, speeding up sometimes, slowing down at others.

I wished it would go faster and the countryside would be a blur at the side of me, hurrying towards me and away, further from the camp and those footsteps I thought were following me. And closer to Mother.

I tried to be positive, kept telling myself I would be fine now, *we* would be fine, that we would find her. Nobody was following us because nobody cared. But I couldn't believe it, and I pored over every piece of countryside as it came into view, over every house, every field and every tree. Looking, checking, searching. For a car, a tank, a soldier, a policeman, someone who would see me, know who I was, where I had been, what I was hiding.

It was written all over me. Wasn't it?

I'm an escapee. Wanted. Report me. Take me. You'll be rewarded. They will love you. They will kill me. And the baby.

Carriages stretched out behind me and in front of me, dark green bodies and rusted metal tops that stained the palms of my hands and the knees and elbows of my clothes orange. Kids sat and stretched and lay and sprawled; adults too, but not so many. All with blank faces and empty eyes. Nobody speaking a word or making eye contact. All of us lost in our own thoughts and reflections.

I hunched forward, my shoulders high, my neck and face disappearing inside my clothes to obscure my face. I swung my feet to one side, shuffling around and turning my back on as many of the others as I could, and I loosened the front of my clothes to feed the baby, hoping he would take it before his murmuring began. So desperate I was to keep him hidden and keep him secret from all those staring eyes.

I ran a finger along his cheek, his skin so fine, barely able to believe he was still alive, that he was mine. And he was. Just mine. Nothing to do with that guard. I didn't see his face when I looked at this baby's. I didn't replay what happened that day. I didn't feel the pain again, or the humiliation. He wasn't a reminder of that place of torture; he was hope in an impossible situation. He was a future.

★

The miles dragged on. We passed an old man walking with an ox and cart, watching us with little comprehension in his eyes and no concern on his face. We passed a woman on a bicycle, another carrying a bundle on her head.

The tracks, old and worn, led us on, until eventually we came towards a village. Too close to a village. It came like a storm on the horizon, deep and ominous, threatening and worrying. It looked so much like my own: rows of harmonica houses with white walls and corrugated roofs, children bent double in frozen fields, a van parked nearby with a loudspeaker spouting songs, tinny and distorted, of the greatness of our Dear Leader. Songs I knew by heart, my lips mouthing the words without conscious thought. Women struggled here and there with buckets swaying from hands, men with spades and rakes and hoes.

And soldiers. Their green uniforms with red collars, their oversized caps with shiny badges and their brown belts pinching in waists. Black boots marching. Eyes watching, scanning, waiting. Guns slung across shoulders. Fingers too close to triggers.

I slunk down, though I was the only one who did, laying myself flat on my side as we passed perhaps 200 metres away, one hand resting under my cheek, the other supporting the baby.

Watching them all: the women, the men, the children and the soldiers.

A few years ago I had been one of those, before my life had exploded around me. What a simple time it had been. Would I wish away everything that had happened since that day and be back there?

In a breath I would.

I felt the baby stretch his body, felt his cheek turn to me and I heard a murmur so slight.

I'm sorry, little one, I thought, *but in a breath I would. How could I not wish my family back? Or wish I'd never said those words, had that dream, met that boy?*

But there was no going back. There were no wishes. And I could never change anything, undo anything, bring anyone back to life. The guilt made me feel sick, and my frustration at Sook made my head pound.

That's not your village, I told myself. *He's not there.*

My eyes filled and my tears fell, but I didn't make a sound. I cried for everything that had gone; for the people in front of me struggling through life, for whatever lay ahead of me, and in fear that a soldier would turn round, stop the train, pull me down and shoot me dead.

I watched one soldier, with his olive green and bright

red and shiny black, through my blurred vision, past the trees with bare branches and across the fields empty of crops. And I saw him turn, saw his eyes fall on the train, following it from the first carriage to the last and back again. Was he focusing on us balanced on top? No visas, no permits, no tickets.

Murmurs flowed down the train, fingers lifted and heads nodded cautiously. Some sat down, some lay down, some stared right back at him. I didn't dare move, my breathing slow and shallow, my hands shaking, watching and waiting.

The music sounded louder, the words echoing in my head:

> "*Brought up in a brilliant culture*
> *The glory of a wise people*
> *Devoting our bodies and minds to this Korea*
> *Let us support for ever.*"

My body prickled, my head and my thoughts fuzzy and difficult, spinning and turning. The train seemed to slow and I wanted to scream at it to go faster, as fast as it could, to tear through this land and away from that soldier.

I saw him reach for his gun and pull it to his shoulder. Saw his head cock to one side and his right eye peer down the barrel.

"Please, no," I whispered. "Please. Please. Not me. Not my baby."

The sound came sharp. Rattling and belting through the air. A string of shots. Someone screamed. Someone else gasped. I held my breath and my whole body tensed and I waited to be hit. And I watched him wave the gun back and forth, pointing high to avoid the carriages.

He's not trying to hit us, I realised, *he's trying to scare us. Show us he's still in charge.*

The noise stopped and I watched him lower his gun. On the train nobody moved or screamed or shouted or even whispered. I looked back at the guard, his gun pointing now to a flock of birds in the sky, and the shots rattled out again.

No, I thought, *no matter how much I love my family, I would not have that back. Not in a breath, a second, a week, a month, or a year. Not ever.*

The train carried on, speeding up slightly, and the village disappeared into the distance until it was nothing but memory.

I breathed the air deep into my lungs, fresh and clean, and I loosened my belt and tied myself to the top rail with it. And with the weak winter sun trying to warm my face, and the train gently rocking me, I laid a hand on my baby and let my eyelids fall.

Chapter Forty-six

The rest of the journey passed long and slow and uneventful. I drifted in and out of sleep, with dreams vivid and frightening, made from memories left in my head and from threats challenging my future.

They woke me with a jolt: with fear, relief, trepidation or hunger.

I finished what food I had left: insects and bugs and bits of leaves I had collected, keeping them hidden from the starving eyes around me. And even when the baby gave his murmur and his feeble cry, few people heard, and fewer still turned to look. Nobody was interested in anything but their own survival.

The hours disappeared behind us. The first stop came and went and slowly my stop, the town where I hoped to find my mother, crept towards me, and the houses, apartment blocks, flat buildings and the concrete station loomed larger and grew more and more intimidating.

As did the nerves in my stomach.

This is it, I thought. *This is the all or nothing. I'm doing what you said, Grandfather*, I whispered to him in my head. *But what if I can't find her? What if she's not here? What do I do then?*

And that struck me for the first time as a real possibility. What *would* I do then? Escape by myself? Across the border a few miles away and into China? Then what? To Thailand, Grandfather had said. Then to family in Seoul. By myself?

With stiff legs and fingers so cold I could barely move them, I struggled down the side of the train, waiting as long as I could before dropping on to the tracks, watching and copying those around me. I didn't dare still be on the train when it pulled into the station, couldn't risk getting this far and soldiers or guards or police capturing me now. And all the time I was thinking how ridiculous this was, how I could even dare to hope to find her, or think of escape, or believe that things could work out all right for me and the baby. But I could either carry on walking and looking and trying, or I could give up.

I fled across the tracks, following the others like rats, half running, half stumbling, darting here and there as my legs came back to life, until we made it far enough, and then we scattered away from each other and disappeared.

I felt lost. And I felt alone.

Think, think, think, I told myself.

This was not like the first town where I could stay on the edges and all I had to do was find the train tracks. This was huge. This was like a city. And now I had to walk into the centre and down every road until I found her. And I couldn't look suspicious. And I had to look as if I belonged there and had a purpose there, when in reality every turn of the corner, or glance to the side, brought me to streets that led somewhere unknown, and houses full of strangers. It seemed hopeless and ridiculous.

Roads stretched into one another, wide and smooth, and everywhere I went it seemed I was flanked by grey and concrete, with that flash of red staring down at me from some poster somewhere; or a gleaming statue rising up so far into the sky above me that it hurt my neck to look at his face and I had to shade my eyes from the sun gleaming down at me from behind his head.

I wandered. I meandered. Glancing at every face, looking for those eyes I had last seen full of fear not for herself, but for me, begging me to leave, to run, to hide, to not be found. And here I was, after all that time. Did she know I'd been caught? Did she know Father had been shot? Did she know we'd been sent to a camp?

Or maybe all these years she'd been waiting for me to knock on her door, wondering what had happened to me, wanting to know where I was, why I hadn't been in touch.

★

I found myself at the edge of a market, and I tried to blend in with the other people; shopping bags in hands and coats of muted green or faded black, trousers all dull colours and drawn faces peering out from under hats or headscarves.

On every chest, in front of every heart, was a blot of red, the badge of our Dear Leader, his face round, his smile bright and wide with the happiness his leadership brought him. The widest smile and happiest face I had ever seen.

My feet crunched on frozen puddles alongside rows of stalls, all run by middle-aged women sitting on upturned buckets, their wares in metal bowls in front of them, or on plastic sheeting covering the ground.

Tiny children of indeterminate age trudged along, wide eyes flicking across the ground. One stopped and bent down, his oversized head looking like it would topple him forward, his fingers, scrawny and dirty, picking at the icy mud close to one of the stalls, at things too small for me to see. Grains of rice perhaps, or kernels of corn, which he lifted, still caked in mud, and put in his mouth.

I wasn't shocked to see it, had eaten things similar myself, but was shocked to see it here, outside the prison fences, where not so long ago food had been given in exchange for work, where markets weren't needed or allowed. I looked around at the sunken faces, the spindly legs of children and the sadness in the eyes of mothers. Hunger, it seemed, was now just as prevalent here as in the camp.

I stepped through slush that splashed on to a row of potatoes, and headed towards stalls set up on rickety tables. There was food: some, but not much. But I looked at the sacks of rice or grain, a few bunches of carrots, a handful of spring onions, and read the pieces of card placed on them, the prices glaring at me – sixty *won* for 200 grams of rice. A month's wage. One apple for ten *won*, an egg for five. How could people afford to eat? Or to feed their families and their children?

I looked at the faces and bodies around me. *They can't*, I thought.

I glanced at a bag of rice standing open on the floor, a cup inside to measure, a flag and red writing printed down one side. I tipped my head to read it. I knew that flag. Those white stripes, and red ones too. Those stars in their columns and rows, so neat on that blue background. The flag of our oppressors, our enemies, or so we had been told. On bags of rice in our markets. *Food aid*, it said on it. But it was being sold.

I took a step away, turned round and read down the side of another bag. This wasn't food to be sold, this was a gift to the people.

I didn't want to believe it and didn't want to think about the how and the why. I reached out a hand when nobody was looking, took a carrot and hid it in my pocket.

And at another stall selling rice, I took two spring onions, and at one more I pulled into my palm a small potato, and hid that up my sleeve.

I had become many things growing up in this country:

an informant, a killer, a gravedigger for my grandmother, a slave, a mother in the harshest conditions and a fugitive from the authorities. And now I had become a thief.

I strolled back out of the market and towards a main road, not caring what I had done, pleased that I would eat that day and hopeful I would be able to feed my baby.

At the main road I stopped, staring at a beautiful girl standing in the middle of the junction wearing a uniform of blue skirt and white blouse, her red scarf flapping at her neck. Her arms reached high into the air, directing traffic with black and white sticks, pointing first one way then the other.

A strange sight. She was mesmerising as she clicked her heels and stepped ninety degrees this way and ninety degrees that, around in a circle, a dance, a routine performed with meticulous accuracy. But, as I stared back and forth down the joining roads, I realised there were no cars, no buses, no trucks or even carts. Absolutely no traffic at all.

I was about to move on when I heard a rumble, distant and vague, deep and throaty, getting louder and closer. An engine. Suddenly I was back in my village two years ago, and I was standing at the window, staring through the dirty glass at the clouds of dust following a car as it made its way towards me, my parents and my grandparents, all the terror and horror I would see in my future stretching out in front of me. That noise, that rumble, and my memories overwhelmed me without pause or hesitation.

My body trembled. My hands shook. My throat was dry. My feet, my legs, wouldn't move.

The engine noise deepened, a growl of threat and power, and I turned for a second: a solitary car, slipping towards me down an empty road, smooth and gleaming. I had never seen a car like it, never heard the burr of tyres on tarmac, or watched anything move that fast.

This is it. They let me escape. They knew where I would go, knew I would head here to Mother. Of course they did. They just waited for me to arrive.

It came closer. Louder. And I stood still, with fear burning into me.

This is it. This is the end.

I could smell the exhaust. Could feel it in the back of my throat. I commanded my legs to move, one foot in front of the other, in front of the other. Everything blurring around me. Streets and buildings and...

This is it. They're going to kill me.

People and...

I'm going to die.

The noise was deafening. And the fumes. The car slowed and pulled alongside me.

Chapter Forty-seven

I turned my head away from the car window, let my hair fall over my face. Let my hair fall over my baby.

I made my feet move, waiting for the car to stop, expecting someone to get out, to hit me, grab me, shoot me, or pull me into the car and take me away again. I wouldn't let myself look or turn. I wouldn't let them see my face or know without any doubt that it was me.

A side street was coming up on the right, and I slowed slightly, letting the person behind me pass, and my feet turned me right as the car continued forward, following the other person instead.

Maybe it was coincidence. Maybe they weren't looking for me. Maybe I was nothing to them. Nobody.

I exhaled and felt my body relax a little and my shoulders droop. I lifted my head up, focusing somewhere into the distance, watching a man as he moved towards me, his eyes vacant and hollow, blinking and tired. For a second he looked my way, but he didn't see me, didn't focus on me. Yet in that second I knew who he was.

He took my breath away. He made my stomach flip and my head spin. My legs slowed and I watched him cross the road before he got too close. I couldn't take my eyes off him, and I stared at his face, his eyes, his hair, the way he walked.

It was all him. But how could it be?

I turned and crossed the road, watching him. He was taller and thinner, but it was still him, I felt sure.

I followed, getting closer. A block away. A couple of metres. A few steps. Struggling to believe that it could really be him.

I could hear his breathing. I could see his fingers curled into his palm, his black hair touching the neck of his shirt, his jawline.

Him.

The boy I had loved, who was now a man.

Sook.

Chapter Forty-eight

Sook was ahead of me on the street. I couldn't believe it. I remembered that feeling of warmth in my chest as I walked to meet him, his silhouette in the darkness, remembered the smile on his face he always had for me, remembered that last night we were together, my hand in his, his warmth as he held me. How happy I had felt.

I loved him.

But I remembered too that feeling of terror running through my body as I watched the car heading towards us in the village, the look of panic on my parents', my grandparents' faces, the shots that killed my father ringing out across the countryside, the weight of my grandmother's body as we carried her up the mountain, the look of sadness in my grandfather's eyes as I said goodbye.

Tears ran down my face and my breath sucked in and out as anger and hatred grew and swelled in me, as I watched him take step after step, still alive, still breathing, still living.

I hated him. With every part of me, every muscle and fibre and bone and breath of me, I hated him. For the treachery, the deceit, the lies, the fool he had made of me, the pain he had caused my family. The pain I would cause him. Now.

So I followed. Down streets, across roads, through alleyways. He walked and I followed. At a safe distance, so as not to be seen. As my anger drove me onwards, I thought of killing him. I wanted to make things even. For him to understand pain and to know how it felt to be the victim. Then things would be settled, and I would leave this country with my guilt somewhat assuaged and my redemption somehow earned. I could do it. Was sure I could. I had motivation and good cause. And the knife from the camp still in my pocket. I followed him. At a block of flats he slowed down, ignoring the front door, sliding round to the side.

I took a long, slow breath, pulled my arms round my baby, and stepped forward, peering round the corner, watching him pull open the door to a shack and disappear inside.

★

How long I stood there, waiting to make my mind up what to do, watching for that door to open again, I have no idea. Was I mistaken — was it someone else? No, it was Sook. I wanted to be mistaken, but I knew I wasn't.

I had decided as I left the camp, as I headed here to this town and not to my village, that my past with Sook, and everything that had happened, was over. But. There was always a but.

That was him.

That *was* him.

Everything, all the pain, the suffering, the death and loss in my family could be traced back to that night: my naivety and his treachery. My anger swelled in me, burned in my chest, pounded through my veins and drove down to my fingertips. Didn't I owe it to my family to make things right?

I ran my hand along the outline of my baby, down towards my pocket, the knife still there. Too many months the idea of this had been in my head. Festering.

Often I'd change my mind, forget about things, stop thinking it important, then back it would come. Over and over. And now I could do it. I could do it, then tonight I could find my way to the river, cross it and be out of the country before anyone found his body.

But then I wouldn't be able to stay and look for Mother. Yet was I really going to be able to find her anyway? My thoughts ran in spirals and out of control, faster and faster, losing logic on the way and coming up only with answers I wanted to hear.

Think of the future, I decided, *but first, rectify the past*.

I took a step and edged forward, my heart thumping in my chest, my baby murmuring next to me. I was so close now, close enough to reach out a hand and touch the wood of the shack, splinters like needles sticking out, warning me off.

Through the gaps in the planks I peered at him, as daylight strained through and flashed on his face. It was him. I was certain. I stepped around to the door, glancing through gaps as I went. At the door I pulled out the knife. Sickness washed over me and through me, nerves shaking my hands, my head thick with hatred. Through the gaps I watched him moving inside the shack.

I waited. And when, at the other side of the shack,

he turned his back, I eased open the door and stepped inside.

For a second light flashed across the shack from the open door and he spun round. For a second I saw his face in that light, his surprise and shock and confusion as the door swung closed behind me and we were lost to the half-light.

He wasn't the Sook I had loved, he was the Sook who had betrayed me and my family, and for that he would suffer. I charged at him, grabbing him by his collar, pulling him upright, slamming him against the wall, his face caught in a beam of light, mine hidden in shadows of darkness.

"Wh— who are you?" he stammered. "What do you want?"

My chest swelled. I felt powerful and in control for the first time ever. I drew my right hand up, easing the knife through the shafts of light and towards his throat. I watched horror dawn on his face and fear grow in his eyes, and inside I laughed.

"Who do you think it is? Who do you think would want to kill you?"

"I don't... I don't... I don't know. Please... please don't."

"I would've begged them not to kill my father. I would've got down on my knees and *begged*. I would've begged them to release me and my grandparents from that camp, begged them for food, begged the guard to leave me alone. But it wouldn't have made any difference. And it won't make any difference if you beg now. *You* may as well have killed them yourself." I touched the blade to his throat.

He was shaking his head. "No." His voice was a whisper.

"I trusted you." I wanted to be strong, wanted to slice that knife across his throat, thrust it into his stomach, watch his pain, but my hands were shaking and my voice starting to break, and tears welled in my eyes and blurred his face in front of me. I sucked in breath, steadying myself. "I loved you," I whispered.

"Yoora?" he breathed. "Yoora?"

I stared at him, stared into his eyes in that half-light, and I could've been back there, in my village, walking through fields and down empty roads, under trees with moonlight flickering through leaves and branches and on to his face. Looking at mine with what I'd thought was at least friendship, what I'd hoped was love.

How stupid.

I gripped the knife tighter, sucked in a jagged breath,

felt my anger and frustration grow again in my chest, looked into those eyes that had betrayed me and killed my family. But I paused. And behind me something rustled, someone groaned.

I leant towards Sook, my face looming into the shaft of light, letting him see me, what I had become.

I nodded slowly, deliberately.

"Yoora," he said. "I didn't... I didn't... honestly... I wouldn't have done that. Not to you. I swear."

"I saw your face at my father's execution. Saw your sneer. How happy you looked. How pleased with yourself. And your mother."

"No. It wasn't like that. I wasn't sneering. I was... I was... trying not to cry."

Why was I waiting? Listening to his excuses. Why didn't I do it? Push that knife into him? His face contorted in sobs, tears streaming down his face.

Don't listen, I told myself. *Don't feel sorry for him.*

"Please, Yoora, please, let me explain..."

"No!" I shouted.

Again behind me there was movement, of blankets perhaps, someone moving, a croak of hard-drawn breath, from someone weak and struggling, like those last words spoken by my grandmother.

"Yoora?" the voice creaked.

It was like a slap in the face, a splash of cold water, being shaken awake from the deepest of sleeps.

I hesitated. Loosened my grip on the knife. Turned my head instinctively towards the sound hidden in the dark. A shape on the floor, stretching and moving.

No, I thought.

"Yoora?" came the voice again. I dropped the knife.

How can that be?

I felt Sook take hold of my other hand, releasing himself from my grip.

It can't be.

I stepped away from him, a few paces across to the other side of the room with the wooden floor creaking and groaning with every step, and my head spinning and pounding with confusion and disbelief. And hope.

There was a mattress on the floor and on it a pile of rags. As I watched, the pile of rags moved. A pair of eyes opened. Eyes I knew so well, staring up at me.

My mother's.

Chapter Forty-nine

I sobbed silent tears into hands clasped round my mouth. It was too much; it was all too much to hear, to see, or to believe. It couldn't be true. Not possibly. I was dead and being led to my heaven or my hell; I was dreaming and would wake again in that camp, or worse, on the morning it all began, with no way of changing anything.

It was ridiculous. It was a trick. I was being watched for my reaction. To be caught. To be killed. My head, my imagination, was cruel, conjuring something that could not possibly be true.

I heard the strike of a match and the crackle of flame as Sook brought a candle to me, glued with wax on to an old tin plate. The light flickered and danced in the darkness and across my mother's face, thin and hollow, skin tight across bones, blue veins bloated like swollen rivers. Her eyes deep and sunken. Her hair clumped and matted.

I watched her struggle to draw in breath, saw her relief when she again exhaled. My mother, whom I'd not seen for more than two years, who had every right to blame me for everything. What would she say to me? What could I say to her but sorry?

Her face was filled with sadness and her body was so frail. I held my hand over my mouth while tears streamed down my face, and my body shook with every sob I tried to stifle.

The boy behind me was forgotten and the outside world was left behind.

The air was stagnant, the only sounds the rasping of her breath, the nervous juddering of mine and the snuffle of the baby. I watched her face; her eyes peered into mine, her expression changing, softening and smiling, and I leant forward, my hair dropping on to her, and I kissed her cheek.

Her mouth eased open, her lips split and cracked. "Yoora?" she whispered. Her head shook, almost imperceptibly. "No," she breathed. "It can't be. It can't be you."

I took hold of her hand, so much smaller and thinner than I remembered, and I nodded to her. "It is." I smiled.

And maybe it was the smile because then she seemed to recognise me, and I realised I must look as different to her as she did to me. Gently I placed her hand back down and carefully I pulled my top clothes to one side, and slowly I took the baby from his sling, still wrapped in the clothes that were his blankets, and turned him round for her to see.

"Your grandson," I whispered.

I had never thought that far ahead, never dared to dream it. I had hoped I would see her again, but never truly believed I would ever find her. I hadn't thought how to tell her about this baby, or what she would think.

"He's so small," she said, her shaking hand resting on his body. "But..." She looked up at me, those eyes that for sixteen years had chastised me, cared for me, disciplined me and loved me. Was I still *her* baby?

I looked away. "There was a guard." The words were difficult. "In the camp. He... he... I couldn't..."

Her hand held mine as if I was ten years old again and she was comforting me after a bad dream. I didn't need to say any more.

"He's beautiful," she whispered.

And I knew it didn't matter. I watched her eyes flick over his face, her fingers touch his hands, so small and delicate, and I saw the smile stretch across her face. She turned to me with the light of the world in her eyes. "He looks like you, when you were a baby."

For seconds that stretched into minutes that could've gone on for hours, we sat without a word shared. There was so much to say, to ask and to explain, but nothing mattered more, in that space, in that time, than being together. But when the silence that had been so complete between us for those moments began to fade, and pauses and hesitation came back, it was my guilt that made me speak first.

"I'm sorry," I said. "For everything."

She shook her head. "It wasn't your fault. None of it."

"But it was. I told Sook what father said about leaving..." I remembered the knife, what I was going to do.

She was shaking her head as much as she could. "No, you—"

"He must've told his mother. Grandmother warned me not to get involved, said no good would come of it, and I didn't listen. I was so stupid and thoughtless, and I'm so sorry. For everything. For Father and—"

"Yoora, is that what you've been thinking all this time?" Her voice was so quiet now, so strained and difficult, and she looked so weak and tired, her eyes dull, her breath rasping in and out, her skin like old paper that would flake into nothing if touched. "It was his mother, Min-Jee. She saw the two of you together that night, but she didn't hear anything you said and he didn't tell her."

"You can't know that," I said.

She sighed. "I do." She paused for a moment, her eyes closing, heavy and tired. "Min-Jee knew you two were seeing each other, had known for a long time, and she was desperate to stop you. That night, seeing the two of you together, must've been the final straw for her. What better way to stop it than to get rid of us all? She reported us on the off chance they could find something to blame us for." Her eyes peeled open, staring at me. "They did."

"But..." All I could think of was how she didn't understand, how it was still my fault. I shouldn't have spoken to him that first day, I shouldn't have met him again afterwards, I should have listened to Grandmother, I shouldn't have opened my mouth and told him about my dream or repeated what Father had told me.

"You can blame yourself, or Sook, for your relationship, or blame me and your father and your grandparents because we were sending letters out of the country, or because we wanted a better life for us all. Blame Min-Jee for reporting us because she was worried for her son. Blame everybody. They all did their part." Her shoulders gave the smallest of shrugs. "Or nobody. It happened. It's gone. Leave it be."

The candlelight flickered on her skin and she closed her eyes again. "He's looked after me well," she said.

I turned then and looked at Sook. He was standing there meekly, his hands clasped together, as if he didn't want to interfere in our reunion. Could it be true? Could it be that he wasn't a monster?

I turned away from him, back to my mother. I watched as her breathing slowed and deepened. "Grandfather helped me escape," I whispered and I thought I saw the edges of her mouth lift. "We buried Grandmother when she died," I breathed and her head gave the smallest nod.

I lay on the floor next to her with the baby on the mattress between us, and I lifted the postcard from my pocket and showed it to Mother.

"You still have it. After all this time." She smiled.

"You can do it, Yoora, you can get there." But her smile drifted away. "I don't have the letters. I'm sorry. They found them. Took them from me."

"It doesn't matter," I whispered. How could I be disappointed with her, or angry?

Behind me Sook cleared his throat softly. "You should stay," he said.

I gazed at him, remembering what I'd thought of him, what I'd planned to do, and I felt ashamed. I nodded. So much I wanted to say, to ask. But I sensed that my mother didn't have much time, and he seemed to know it too.

"Here." He came forward and held out a blanket.

"Thank you." I draped the blanket over myself and Mother, stretched out an arm and rested my hand on hers. Closing my eyes I imagined I was back home, lying next to my mother in the darkness was my father, and quietly sleeping in the next room were my grandparents.

And I drifted away into a blissful sleep.

Chapter Fifty

She was dead by first light.

Was it luck that I found her in time? Sook said not. Said it was like she'd been hanging on, waiting for something, and now had let go in peace.

There was so much I'd wanted to tell her, share with her, ask her. Sook held my hand, wiped my tears, put an arm round me in the silence that enveloped us, held us static. He cradled the baby in his arms, stroked his head and smiled at him, and I wished he had been the father.

The day passed in a strange but comfortable silence. We boiled up what food we had left, and the vegetables I'd stolen from the market, into a soup, and we ate it as if it was to be our last meal ever.

It was mid-afternoon by the time he finally spoke

to me in sentences of more than two words. "What have you called him?" he asked, rocking the bundle in his arms.

"Nothing yet," I whispered. "I daren't. Because that makes him more real. And if he's real, he's more likely to die."

He shrugged. "I thought you had more fight in you than that. That's like giving up before you've even tried."

I didn't reply.

"And if he did die, how could you mourn something that didn't have a name?"

I ignored his question. "Why did you do it?" I asked him.

"What?"

"Why did you leave the village and look after her? And how?"

He shrugged. "I owed it to you. And your family. I ran away, didn't care about the consequences if they found me. I didn't care what they did to me. What else *could* they do anyway? They'd already taken you."

He edged towards me. "I loved you. Always did."

I looked at that face and into those eyes that had followed me from the village to the camp, across the mountains and to here. Never knowing if they'd betrayed me, but always assuming they had. Never being able to let go of that hope that he did care for me and so allow myself to admit what I felt for him. Luck, for once, had been on my side when I walked into his town, guiding me and showing me maybe the right streets to go down, leading me towards him.

But still, *still*, I couldn't quite give him my trust.

"It's not safe here, though, Yoora. We can't stay. There are police everywhere," he said. "We're so close to the border. They look out for smugglers, people who've sneaked over the Chinese border and brought back things to sell, or people like me who've run away and don't have a visa or a permit or any papers. People without their badges pinned on their chests, or people wearing Chinese clothing or eating Chinese food."

"Are we that close to the border?"

He shrugged. "An hour's walk to the river."

I glanced at the body of my mother.

"She'd want you to go," he said.

"I know," I sighed. "But... but..."

He crept over to me, put his arm round me and pulled me towards him, my head tucked under his chin. "Scared?" he asked. I nodded.

"But you're the bravest person I know. Think what

you've done — survived two years in a prison camp, *escaped* from it, walked all those miles from there, keeping yourself alive, and this baby too. You're so strong and brave. You can't give up now."

But I didn't feel strong or brave. And I didn't want to fight any more. I didn't feel like I had anything left in me. Not even the energy to cry. All I wanted to do was curl up and go to sleep.

"I can't," I whispered. "I can't do any more."

"But you're so close." I felt his breath on my face, his hand stroke my hair. "We'll do it together."

I felt my head move with the rise and fall of his chest and I watched my baby's eyes flicker as he dreamt. *What could he be dreaming of?* I thought. I listened for a moment for sounds from outside, the chatter of people walking by or the bounce of a ball against a wall, girls chanting as they skipped or children shrieking as they chased each other around houses. But there was none of that.

"Will the river be cold?" I asked.

"Freezing," he replied.

"Will there be guards there?"

"I imagine so," he whispered.

"Will they shoot me if they see me?"

"If they don't, then they'll capture you and send you back to prison."

"And... and when we get across, *if* we get across, we'll be safe then?"

He sighed, long and slow. "No. If the Chinese authorities find us, they'll send us back."

I knew all of those answers before I'd asked the questions, but I wanted to hear him say it, wanted to hear if he'd tell me the truth.

"But they won't find us because we won't stay there," he said. "We'll travel through, get to a different country. Somewhere we can claim asylum. The three of us together."

I closed my eyes and nodded. I thought of Grandfather, and I knew I, we, must leave. I knew it was the best thing to do. Here, it wasn't a matter of *if* I was caught, it was a matter of when. It wasn't *if* my baby survived, it was when he would die. I had to trust Sook.

And I owed it to my family, to my baby, and to myself, to keep trying and to keep going.

"Let me rest a while first," I said. "I need to. I'm so tired. Just a couple of days."

"All right. Two days then. We should bury your

mother, say our goodbyes to her. Maybe gather some food and extra clothing."

I nodded.

It was decided. And on that day – leaving day – we would start walking as soon as the sun was down, the darkness our friend as it hid us from prying eyes, and the clouds, we hoped, would keep the moonlight behind it, and we would hurry across the river that should be frozen in winter to the safety that waited for us somewhere on the other side.

We hoped.

Chapter Fifty-one

I remember the air growing colder, I remember the sun beginning to set, I remember shadows creeping across the shack and towards my mother's body on that night. Sook trying to think where we could bury her, while, with guilt heavy in my bones, I looked through the few spare clothes she had for something warmer to wear.

I remember hearing the first scream. And that feeling of dread lurching through me. The look of terror in Sook's eyes as I spun round to him. Then another scream. And a sob. Doors opening in apartments above us, slamming shut again, feet on stairwells, voices in tears, gasping and crying and wailing.

"What is it?" I whispered to Sook, but he shook his head, lifting his finger to his lips to quieten me, moving across the room to peer through the gaps in the walls.

I closed my eyes and listened, but all the sounds and the words were mixed up and nothing made sense.

"Sook?" I breathed. "Sook, I'm scared."

We stared at each other a moment.

"Me too," he said and looked away. "I'll be back in a minute," he muttered and he was gone. Out of the door before I could even think about replying or arguing.

So I sat there, on the cold floor. Waiting. Listening to the outside world. With my dead mother and my tiny baby. Waiting for the door to open again. Wishing it would be Sook who came back in. Not a guard, or a soldier, or even a neighbour.

I will never feel safe if I stay, I thought. *I'll for ever be looking over my shoulder.*

I closed my eyes. And waited. *He's not coming back*, I thought. *He's abandoned us. He's reporting us. He hates me. He's tricked me. Again. And I fell for it again. What have I done? How could I have let myself trust him again? They'll come for us, take us. What then?*

My thoughts ran out of control, as flashes and memories and visions flew in and out of my head. The woman who helped me give birth. The stories she told me. The boy I saw killed. The guard who attacked me. The hunger. The desolation. The hopelessness.

What will they do to us? I thought.

Suddenly my head was clear and I had the answer. *I won't let them win. I won't let them hurt me or my baby. I will kill myself before that happens. And my baby will die at my hands, as quickly and as painlessly as I can do it. Not at theirs. They will not do that. I will not let them. I will not give them the satisfaction.*

I cried and I shook. I stared down at the tiny face staring back up at me. "I'm sorry," I whispered. "I'm so sorry." I crawled across the floor, brushing the ground with my hands, searching for the knife I'd dropped the day before, and at my chest I felt my baby's stutter of breath and I heard his tiny cry. "I'm so, so sorry," I breathed.

The blade touched my hand and I stopped. My fist gripped the handle and I lifted it. I sucked in breath ragged and desperate, my head spinning and sweat dripping from me in the cold air. Behind me the door creaked open and I paused, and I turned, and standing in the doorway was Sook. And next to him was nobody.

"What... what are you doing?" he whispered, closing the door behind him and dropping to the floor next to me.

I stared up at him in confusion and fear and dread,

and I realised what a mess I was. What an effect everything had had on me. The paranoia that had been drilled into me over years.

"I thought..." I sobbed. "I thought... I thought..." But I couldn't say the words.

I felt his hand rest on mine, felt him pull the knife away from me and heard it clatter to the other side of the room.

"Oh, Yoora," he said. I let myself be pulled towards him, and I let his arms go round me and hold me tight, and I let my body go limp as he rocked me from side to side. "I would never, never betray you, and I would never, ever let them hurt you again. Together," he said, "we're in this together. The three of us."

I nodded my head against his chest.

"But, Yoora, listen, we have to go. We have to go *now*. Kim Jong Il is dead."

Chapter Fifty-two

Of all the things he could have said to me then, that was what I expected the least. That was not even in my imagination, not even in my hopes and dreams and wishes. It was impossible. I stared at him.

"Listen," he said. "Listen to what they're saying outside. It's true, Yoora. This family, they showed me it on their television. I wouldn't have believed it myself otherwise. He's dead. He really is dead."

I stared still, waiting for it to sink into my consciousness, waiting to understand it. "How?" I asked.

"Heart attack."

"But—"

"I know, I know," he said, and he had such excitement on his face. "He's not invincible," he whispered. He stood up and started hurrying around the room, gathering things together. "We have to go, Yoora. Now. We can't wait. We can't..." He looked at the body of my mother.

"Why? Surely this means it can all be over. Things will get better. Things can change."

He shook his head. "Why would they?"

"Because... because it won't be him any more. We can have a new leader."

"Yes, you know who that'll be? His son," he spat. "Kim Jong Un. They're talking about it in the streets already. He's to be our *Great Successor*. Things will be exactly the same. Just as they were when Kim Il Sung died and his son took over. You remember? Nothing changed then. They're all the same, one son after another. They all think the same. They all do the same."

I stared at him and then nodded, still amazed, still shocked.

"Martial law's been declared," he said, "all over this province." He stood up, taking the few steps to the other side of the room and pulling open a cupboard. "We're supposed to report to the town offices and listen to speeches praising Kim Jong Il's greatness."

"What?" I stood up and moved towards him. "But—"

"And they're going to block the roads, post policemen on them to stop people passing or leaving the town."

"How do you know that?"

"Everyone's talking about it."

"Then... wouldn't we be better off waiting, hiding in here?"

"What if they see us? Or find us? Or hear the baby crying? What then? No. We *have* to go now, while we've still got a chance."

Outside our four walls I could still hear all the movement and the crying and the wailing. "They're grieving for him," I said. "All of them. Crying for him."

He nodded.

"I thought they'd be glad." I shook my head. "I don't understand."

I watched Sook stuff a few clothes into a bag and grab any bits of food we had left. I looked down at my mother, and I remembered my father, my grandmother and my grandfather. My grief seemed perpetual. "I can't just leave her," I said. "Can't we at least bury her before we go? I should give her that, a resting place. Please, Sook. Let me do that before we go."

He stopped what he was doing and he looked at me. He stepped towards me and he held my face gently in his hands. "I wish we could, but we don't have time. They're going to close the borders," he said. "Announce a curfew, post more guards. If we don't go now, Yoora, they're going to find us."

I didn't want to nod or agree with him. Didn't want to leave her there, my mother, to rot. Turning into something that wasn't her.

"That isn't your mother," he whispered. "She's gone now. All that is, is the body she lived in."

"She'd be disappointed in me."

"No." He shook his head. "She'd be proud of you. She *was* proud of you. She told me so."

★

In silence at first, down empty streets we walked, keeping close to the sides of buildings, peering round each corner, checking for guards, for soldiers, for police, for anyone. If anyone saw us, they'd be expecting us to be crying, to be heartbroken, to be on the point of collapse through grief – our leader was dead.

And if anyone spoke to us, they'd be telling us we

were heading in the wrong direction. We should be reporting to the town offices, we should be listening to speeches and stories of his greatness, we should be mourning.

I was. We both were. But we weren't mourning him.

Maybe it was coincidence, maybe someone was watching over us, or maybe, just for once, luck was on our side because every building we stopped at, every corner we glanced round and every street we walked down was empty. And so, slowly and cautiously, we edged our way through the town, leaving behind the buildings and houses full of their tears of grief, and the windows that we hoped didn't have faces peering out, watching us, and we headed away into the barren fields opening up wide to countryside.

It was a pretty country. It was beautiful, serene and calm. I would miss that. But I wanted to be able to eat when I was hungry, to be safe and to be free. To spend time with whomever I wanted, to think whatever I wanted and to be judged only for being me.

In darkness again I walked with Sook like all those years before, but this time in hope of a freedom that could be ours beyond the river.

★

In the hour it took us to walk there, keeping among trees, following a line of bushes, staying in the darkest pockets, he explained how he'd tried to stop Min-Jee reporting my family, how he'd told her that her plan to stop us seeing each other was ridiculous. He warned her he'd leave if she did, that he would disown her, and she laughed at him, telling him he was a fool, and would lose everything if he did.

And he told me how helpless he'd felt, how, when he watched my father being shot, he could barely stop himself from crying out, and how when he saw me stand up he wanted to scream at me to run, shout at me that he would be behind me, tell me that he was sorry. And that when he tried to follow me, Min-Jee knocked him to the ground unconscious.

He explained how he'd found out where my mother had been sent, that he left that night, with not a goodbye or even a note to Min-Jee. How he found my mother after two weeks of searching, and how they had looked after each other, comforted each other, and together waited and hoped for one of us to make it back. One day.

He told me how the food rations stopped and the starvation began. How they begged and stole, sold everything they could to survive to the next week, the next day, the next hour. How weak she became. How ill. And I trusted he was telling me the truth.

We held hands through the darkness, and I wondered if I'd ever really fallen out of love with him.

Chapter Fifty-three

I heard the river before I saw it; the clap of one wave against another, the slosh as it hit the bank, sounds so unfamiliar to someone like me who had never seen more than a stream trickling through countryside.

I smelt it too, a smell of freshness, like spring rain on mud; damp earth and wet grass.

We struggled up to the brow of a hill, pausing at the top, crouching so the moonlight couldn't show us to any guards, looking down at the sight below us.

There it was: heaving in from some faraway distance to our right, stretching fat and wide in front of us, gliding away on our left, drifting and flowing and splashing away to some distant place. Wide and majestic, powerful and frightening.

There it was: the river, the Tumen.

Like a beast writhing or an enemy sleeping, tempting you closer, daring you to touch, waiting until you were next to it and it could turn and swallow you whole. And far away, past it, over it, through it – China.

We crouched there, watching and listening in awe and in wonder. The moon was barely a crescent, its reflection broken and glistening on the surface of the water, tossing and dancing, leaping and jiving, and the damp air filling our lungs and wetting our faces.

So much water and so far across.

My hands and my arms instinctively drew round my baby, and I peered down at his tiny face and his blinking eyes.

Is this the right thing to do? I wanted to ask him. The water looked so deep, so cold, so dangerous.

Sook tapped me on the arm, pointing to a cluster of trees just visible on the riverbank. I nodded and we edged slowly and carefully down the hill.

"I thought it would be frozen," he whispered. "I thought we'd be able to walk across on the ice."

"I can't swim," I blurted as we reached the bottom.

"Me neither," he replied and the shadow of him turned to me, his teeth clicking together through cold or nerves. "I don't think it's very deep. I think we'll be able to walk it."

"It's going to be cold, isn't it?"

We both stared around at the countryside, all its colours muted to nothing more than shades of grey and edges of black and highlights of white. Above us, the sky was pinpricked with diamonds of glistening stars, yet empty of clouds that could've kept out the frost. Underneath us the ground was frozen solid and charcoal in colour, but tipped with ice that crunched underfoot, and behind us barren trees stuck up like bones from a dead earth, brittle and bleached nearly white.

And in front of us? In front of us stretched a mass of blackness, of darkness, of emptiness over the river, with no edges or highlights or detail. A nothing, an unknown, a void, hiding our route and our fate from us.

"Freezing," he replied. "But over there," he said, pointing across the river, "we'll be warmer again. Just think of that."

We had only a few possession between us: some spare underwear, a cup and a plate, a knife and a fork, a few spare clothes and some rags we'd collected for the baby, all stuffed inside a bag slung over Sook's shoulder, but he swung it round and pulled three plastic bags from it, passing one to me.

"Take your clothes off, Yoora, down to your underwear, tie them into the bag and we can keep them dry. Then when we get to the other side you can put them back on and you'll be warm."

I stared at him for a second, hesitating, feeling embarrassed even though the night-time hid me. Slowly I pulled off my jacket, my jumper underneath, down through more and more layers to where my baby snuggled his head into me. Cautiously I unfastened my trousers, let them fall down my thin legs into a pile on the ground, and I peeled off my shoes and shook off my socks, rolling and piling everything into the bag.

I kept my eyes away from Sook, curious yet embarrassed by his undressing and his nakedness. And I tried not to look at his body that I remembered being stronger and fitter and healthier, and instead looked at his face or his head or into his eyes.

Still tied around me, in his makeshift sling, was the baby, his eyes scrunched up tight, and his face contorted and angry, his mouth splitting open as his whispered cry complained to me.

I lifted him to my face, hoping my breath would warm his skin, kissing him on his cheek.

"Let me take him," Sook whispered, an arm outstretched to me, a plastic bag dangling from his fingers.

"Why?" I felt astonished.

"I'm taller than you. I can keep him out of the water."

I looked down at this tiny face, whose life I was responsible for, whose trust was solely in me.

"What about the bag?"

He sighed and shook his head. "I'm going to wrap it round his body, over his blankets and rags, in case he gets splashed. Or if I slip."

Trusting him was still a lump in my throat, and this was the most trust I could give anyone. This was my baby's life. I paused. Thinking. Waiting. For what? I didn't know.

"Yoora..."

"I know, I know." I sucked in a deep breath and passed my baby to him with guilt already pulling at me, and grief and anger standing by ready to assail me. I watched Sook take the baby from his sling, rewrap his blankets and old clothes so they cushioned his head, and wrap the plastic bag round his tiny body. I watched him place the baby back in his sling, and helped tie it round his back, hoisting the baby as high as possible, up on his chest, tucked under his chin.

And together we stepped out from the protection of the trees and with everything we possessed tied round us, took the few steps to the water's edge.

Chapter Fifty-four

My skin didn't just prickle with the cold, it screamed with it. Every muscle tensed and every nerve ached. My body shook and my breath came stuttering and painful in my lungs. I followed behind Sook as he stepped over the frozen earth, hard and painful underfoot, jabbing into my toes or my heels, sucking the heat from them with every step.

At the river's edge the mud gave way to stones, pressing and cutting into my skin, and I took every step on tiptoe with my body tense and my arms in the air to keep my balance. My eyes flitted up and down the riverbank, this side and that, searching and checking as much as I could, scared, so scared, of guards waiting for us, watching us with guns raised, eyes peering down sights and fingers on triggers.

And smiles on their faces.

The darkness, the hint of light from the moon, the shadows, all played tricks on me, shapes hidden, moving, closing in. And the sound of the water was closer now, clearer, louder. The slosh and flap of it as it sucked over the stones near my feet. And I heard Sook's breathing, going from steady, slow and heavy to a sudden stop, to small gasps tightly drawn.

I lifted a foot and placed it down, and the shock made me gasp, made me hold my hand over my mouth to stop myself from crying out. It was so cold. So incredibly cold.

It was a thousand needles in my skin, a million blades in my toes, it was pain like shard after shard after shard of pointed ice, pressing and spearing and driving into me.

And my other foot went down into it. Yes, it hurt. Yes, it was cold, more than cold. But no, I wasn't going to give up.

I watched Sook's back, his shoulders tense, the lumps of his spine straining against his skin, and he turned his head to me with a question in his eyes, and I nodded, and he carried on.

With each step, the water reached further up me. My

ankles, calves, knees, thighs. When it hit my stomach I gasped in pain and shock, holding my breath, then let it out quickly, breathing in and out in short bursts, too painful to suck right into my lungs. My head began to spin, and I felt panic tearing through me, thoughts and images flashing by of Sook falling, my baby drowning, of a gunshot hitting me, my body floating downstream.

Stop it, I told myself. *Stop it, stop it.*

I thought again of my grandfather and imagined him at my side, mimicked his steady breathing and his calm, and I took one careful breath after another, remembering his words – *One step at a time, one foot in front of the other.*

The water crept up to my chest, but I thought only of my breathing, and of one foot lifting, moving, stepping down, and the next lifting, moving, stepping down. I watched clouds of warm air form in front of me as I breathed, then disappear away on the cold breeze.

How much further? How much deeper? No, don't think that. What about the baby? No, enough, I told myself.

The cold was bitter, painful, aching, hurting. My body was heavy and my legs were numb. The riverbed turned from stones to mud, and I felt my feet slip and slide as I struggled for every single step. Still the water became deeper. Blood pounded in my ears, something floated by me, touching my leg, grass or weeds. I looked up at the sky so dark, the stars shining bright. And across to the other side, a black void.

Closer now, I thought. *I must be.*

Sook turned again, his face awkward and pained, his skin ghostly, and I could just see my baby. Sook turned back again, and as he did, the crescent moon moved behind clouds and everything disappeared.

How much deeper? I thought.

I walked forward still, a slosh, a splash, the current licking against me. Forward. In blackness. In emptiness. The water on my neck, my chin tilted upwards.

How much deeper?

Still dark.

They can't see us, I thought. *Even if they are there. They can't see us in this dark.*

I breathed deep and calm. Heard the quietest murmur from the baby, a gentle *shhh* from Sook, and the water was still at my neck.

Forward. Forward, I told myself. I counted. To five, and the water was on my shoulders. To ten, and I thought maybe, just maybe it was a little lower. To twenty and it was on my chest. And the sounds changed, almost imperceptibly, the glide of my arms on the surface, the slap of waves on the banks.

I sighed. Heard Sook some distance ahead of me, his legs splashing, it seemed, out of deep water, shallower, longer strides. And I felt a smile of relief dare to stretch on to my face.

Another step forward. But the ground slipped and disappeared from under my feet, a drop suddenly in front of me, my footing lost, the water suddenly deeper, tricking me. I fell backwards, my arms flailing through nothing, my feet with no ground to rest on. My body slipped under and my head was below the water and the cold squeezed at my lungs and stole away my breath.

I could see nothing, feel nothing but cold, icy, sharp daggers all over me. Sound was muted and confused. Fear and panic gripped me and pulled me down. I felt my head break the surface, sucked air into my lungs. Tried to shout out, but was under again. My legs kicked out, my arms thrashed. Again my head was clear. "Sook!" I shouted, but again was down.

I felt so weak. I couldn't fight. I couldn't breathe. I couldn't find the ground beneath me or the air above me. My head pounded and my lungs screamed and burned. A moment of calm fell over me. Pinpricks of light danced in front of my eyes. My legs stopped kicking, my arms hung by me, my body drifted with the current.

This is it, I thought. *This is as far as I go.*

Chapter Fifty-five

In those seconds, I believed it.

I had done so much, achieved so much, fought so much, but that was enough now. That was me done.

I'm sorry, Grandfather, I thought as the water foamed and bubbled around me, *but there are no more steps to take.*

I'm sorry, Grandmother, for making you angry.

I'm sorry, Father, for not believing you.

I'm sorry, Mother, for not arriving sooner.

And I'm sorry, my little baby boy, that you'll never know me.

I had made it so close to freedom.

But hands grabbed me and the air woke me. Then his face was in front of me, staring and gasping, his body shaking, water dripping from his hair, down his face and mixing with his tears as he held me upright with more strength than I thought possible.

Sook.

I sucked air deep into my lungs, my head and everything around me spinning and turning and tilting. My legs weak under me, my body shaking so much I couldn't keep still. His arms wrapped round me and his hands holding mine guided me to the shore, barely ten more paces away, and gently he lowered me to the ground next to where he had placed my baby.

I was alive.

I looked at them both.

We were alive.

*

With dry clothes on, we stood together on the riverbank looking across the expanse of water to our old country, hiding in darkness a few hundred metres away. All those secrets, all those people, all those lies, all believed true. Would things change now they had a new leader? Would we ever know?

I sucked in a breath of air fresh and clean. Air of freedom. Air of my future. And I turned and smiled at the boy, no, the man, standing next to me, who was the beginning of this journey so far back in time and in memory, so far away in that village.

I was lucky. So lucky. And that I would never forget.

In my arms, the baby cried. We moved away from the bank and up a slope, hiding in the undergrowth while I fed him, worried still that we might be seen, might be found. Maybe there weren't any soldiers or guards that night on that stretch of river, maybe they just didn't see us, maybe they were grieving too much for their Dear Leader to be able to see through their tears. It didn't matter.

I listened to the quiet sounds around me: the rush of water, the rustle of leaves, the snuffle of the baby as he fed, the breathing of the man I loved next to me and I felt calm.

"You should call him Hyun-Su," Sook whispered. "After your grandfather."

Of course, I thought.

I looked out over the river, remembering the different life that I'd left behind over there, along with all those I had loved so much: my mother and father, my grandmother and, of course, my grandfather. The bravest man I had known, a man I knew I would never see again, who blamed himself for everything that befell us, just as I felt the blame lay with me. Who had saved me with his actions, but even more so with his words.

The sky began to lighten as the sun reached out for

a new day, a new life for us. Orange and yellow and red bleeding across the blue, so bright that it hurt my eyes and obscured everything else from view.

Above me I heard a noise and lifted my head to the sky and saw the most beautiful sight: a formation of geese, a V shape, their long necks stretching forward and their wings easing through the air.

It's late for them to be migrating, I thought. *But at least they're going.*

Still in my pocket was that postcard – the city of my dreams, the city of lights. I would keep it, for if things became hard, for if I started to doubt whether or not we would make it. And I would remember those windows lit orange or yellow or white, the red jostling with green on street signs and the pink with blue on shops flashing neon letters and symbols, and the smells of food drifting from restaurants and takeaways, and the rhythms of the music.

I would remember that it was real. And that one day I wouldn't need the postcard any more because I would be there, I hoped, and it would be all around me. And on that day, I would rip that postcard in half, and in half again and again, and I would release the pieces on the wind like dry leaves dancing on the breeze.

I stood up and took a deep breath in, and with Hyun-Su in my arms and Sook at my side, my new family now, I smiled and turned away from the river.

How many miles I had travelled, I had no idea. How many more were ahead of me, I didn't know either. But I wasn't worried any more and I wasn't scared.

Remember Grandfather, I told myself, *remember his words*. And I took one step.

Acknowledgements

Huge thanks are long overdue to my wonderful agent, Carolyn Whitaker, and my brilliant editor, Nick Lake, for all their support, encouragement, understanding and patience and... well, everything really. Thanks also to my friend Rebecca Mascull, for the long chats over the piano or in the hallway, for really understanding and for that shared realisation that 'hey, we're not like those deluded contestants after all' – you know what I mean! Thanks to my friend (and ex-nurse) Jackie Hall, for all the advice, information and chats about nutrition and pregnancy while we skated, or ran, or cycled, and to my Auntie Janet, for helping me with those darn worms and insects! Of course, thanks must go to my long suffering husband, Russ, who never seems to tire of having pieces of paper thrust into his hands, with the accompanying words – 'just read this and tell me what you think' – and to my children, Jess, Dan and Bowen for putting up with me being slightly grumpy sometimes, and often distracted.

Author's Note

Researching North Korea (or Democratic Peoples' Republic of Korea, as it's also known) was both inspiring and heartbreaking.

A closed country, it has strict controls on media, visitors and journalists, and so while there was information to be found, some specifics were difficult to prove. For this reason, rather than base the town where Yoora finds her mother on one in particular, I decided to base it on a few northern towns mixed together, hence the name *Chongyong* is a prefix from one town and a suffix from another. I believe also that the traffic wardens mentioned here may only be found in the capital, Pyongyang, but decided against excluding them as the absurdity of the image was so powerful.

While Yoora's story is fiction, it has its basis in fact and in research. The scene of her father's execution was based on a video clip smuggled out of the country, as was the description of the market in the northern town, and parts of her journey on top of the train.

There are somewhere between twenty-one and twenty-six prison camps in North Korea. Yoora's shares most with Camp 22, located in the north. It is roughly the size of Los Angeles and holds approximately 50,000 prisoners of every age. I'd like to say that the story of what happens to babies in these camps is made up, but unfortunately it isn't.

Researching and writing this has taught me a lot about the strength of the human spirit, and how we are capable of far more than we often think. I've been saddened by people's stories yet inspired by their determination. As such, I'd like to acknowledge the bravery of those who have managed to escape the prisons or the country, I hope I've done you justice, and thank those who have taken photos, or videos, or written accounts and enabled myself, and hopefully you the reader, to understand this country and its people a bit more.

Also by Kerry Drewery

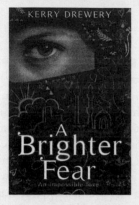

"What do I want for my future?
Is it survival?
No. I don't want to survive.
I want to live..."

A Brighter Fear is the story of Lina,
a teenage girl growing up in Baghdad.
It starts in 2003, as bombs begin to fall on the city.

It is many things:
It is a love story, for a country and for a person. It is
the coming-of-age story of an amazing girl, growing up in
the worst circumstances imaginable. It contains a necklace,
that was lost but might still be found, and it will break
your heart, only to put it back together again...